Anne grabbed the hilt of the sword. It came free of the scabbard with a satisfying hiss of metal.

She spun around. Simon had started to move towards her but he was too late. As he took the final step she brought the tip of the blade up to rest against his throat like a lover's caress. Simon stopped abruptly. The smile in his eyes deepened to something like admiration.

'I cannot believe,' he said, 'that I was so careless.'

LORD GREVILLE'S CAPTIVE

Nicola Cornick

All the characters in this book have no existence outside the imagination of the author, and have no relation whatsoever to anyone bearing the same name or names. They are not even distantly inspired by any individual known or unknown to the author, and all the incidents are pure invention.

First published in Great Britain 2006
Harlequin Mills & Boon Limited,
Eton House, 18-24 Paradise Road, Richmond, Surrey TW9 1SR

© Nicola Cornick 2006

ISBN 0 263 84660 1

Set in Times Roman 10¾ on 14 pt.
04-0706-79977

Printed and bound in Spain
by Litografia Rosés S.A., Barcelona

Nicola Cornick became fascinated by history when she was a child, and spent hours poring over historical novels and watching costume drama. She still does! She has worked in a variety of jobs, from serving refreshments on a steam train to arranging university graduation ceremonies. When she is not writing she enjoys walking in the English countryside, taking her husband, dog and even her cats with her. Nicola loves to hear from readers and can be contacted by e-mail at ncornick@madasafish.com and via her website at www.nicolacornick.co.uk.

Recent novels by the same author:

THE EARL'S PRIZE
THE CHAPERON BRIDE
WAYWARD WIDOW
THE PENNILESS BRIDE
THE NOTORIOUS LORD*
ONE NIGHT OF SCANDAL*
THE RAKE'S MISTRESS*
THE FORTUNE HUNTER in *A Regency Invitation to the House Party of the Season*

Bluestocking Brides series

Prologue

❦❦❦

Grafton, Oxfordshire, England
Summer 1641

It was high summer and the village of Grafton was garlanded for a feast to celebrate the betrothal of the Earl of Grafton's only daughter to the eldest son of Fulwar Greville, the Earl of Harington. This dynastic match was no surprise, for the two Earls were old friends, one-time comrades in arms and godfather to each other's children. It was a day of great rejoicing.

In her chamber in the west wing of the old manor house, Lady Anne Grafton's women were helping her dress for the banquet.

'Do you like Lord Greville, Nan?' Anne's young cousin Muna asked, as she slid the petticoats over Anne's head in a ruffle of white. 'He seems to me quite stern and cold.'

'Like his sire,' commented Edwina, Anne's former nurse, with a shiver. She pulled Anne's laces tight. 'They do not call him the Iron Earl for naught.'

Anne laughed, stopping abruptly as the pull of the laces stole her breath. 'Oof! Edwina, you are smothering me!' She slipped obediently into the red velvet gown that her nurse was holding for her. 'Uncle Fulwar is the kindest man in the world,' she said, muffled. 'As for Lord Greville—' She stopped. The truth was that she did not know Simon Greville well, for all that their fathers had served together in the wars on the continent. Simon was eight years older than she and already a battle-hardened commander who had been commended for his bravery. Muna was right—there was something distant and a little stern in his demeanour, as though all that he had seen and done in his life had already made him older than she by far more than years.

In the week that the Earl of Harington and his son had been at Grafton, Anne had not spent any time alone with Simon. It was not expected. It might be her hand in marriage that he had come to sue for, but it was her father's permission he needed, not hers.

And yet, there had been a moment that had taken Anne quite by surprise. Simon had ridden in late one evening when the full moon was rising high over the tall crops in the fields. Anne had, naturally, been curious to see him; although she understood that it was her duty to marry this man, there was a part of her that hoped that she might find him personable as well. Thus it was that she had been leaning out of the mullioned window, in a most hoydenish fashion, when the horses had clattered over the drawbridge and into the courtyard.

She had known that she should draw back in all modesty, but something had held her still, watching. The air had been warm from the heat of the day and full of the scent of honeysuckle. There had been no sound except the flutter of the doves settling in the cote.

Simon Greville had swung down from the saddle and then he had looked up, directly at Anne's window. Instinct had prompted her to draw back. Curiosity had held her still. He had a hard, handsome face tanned deep by the sun, and he had raised his plumed hat and brought it sweeping down in a low bow. His hair was thick and dark, and a wicked smile had lit his eyes as he looked upon her. To her astonishment Anne had felt a shiver run all the way down her spine. All thoughts of duty flew straight out of the window. She had a suspicion that it might be an absolute pleasure to marry Simon Greville.

'Look at my lady's face!' Edwina said now, her own beaming. 'You like him well enough, do you not, my pet, and quite right too! I'll wager Lord Greville is a lusty man who will make you happy.'

One of the maids giggled.

'Edwina!' Anne pressed her hands to her hot cheeks. She was seventeen, old to be unwed and painfully aware that her father's protectiveness and his negligence in arranging her marriage meant that she knew little of these mysterious matters. There were girls far younger than she who were already mothers.

'Peace, I beg you,' she said. 'I marry Lord Greville because it is Papa's will.'

Edwina smiled. 'That is all very well and good, pet, and indeed as it should be.' She bustled around Anne's head, fixing a circlet of silver in place. 'But I have been thinking about the wedding night.'

Anne looked up. She remembered Simon Greville's dark gaze upon her and gave a little shiver.

'I have been thinking,' Edwina continued, 'that as you have no mama to speak to you, I should take that role.' She gestured to Muna. 'Come closer, pet. You must listen too, for no doubt you will soon be wed as well.'

Anne sighed. 'Must we endure this, Edwina? I have a feeling that Muna and I shall be monstrously embarrassed at what you have to tell.'

Muna giggled. 'Madam Elizabeth from the village told me that, as long as I kept quite still and closed my eyes and did not move, no matter what my husband did to me, I should prove a very satisfactory wife.'

'Lord have mercy,' Anne said drily. 'I do not think that sounds very satisfactory at all, Muna.'

Edwina put her hands on her hips and huffed. ''Tis not a matter for jest, my lady. The demands of a husband can come as a shock to a gentlewoman. Why, my own husband kept me busy nigh on five times a night.'

Muna clapped her hands to her mouth. 'Five times! Every night?'

'I heard tell that he was a very lusty fellow,' Anne said, smiling. 'I am not sure whether you are to be congratulated or commiserated with, Edwina. Did you ever get any sleep?'

'You are not taking this seriously,' the maid grumbled. 'Well, do not come complaining to me when you receive a shock on your wedding night!'

'I promise I shall not complain,' Anne said. 'And,' she added firmly, 'I should like a little time alone, if you please, before the feasting starts.'

They went grumbling, Edwina herding Muna and the younger maids before her, closing the door on their chatter. Anne sank down on the window seat with a heartfelt sigh. She had so little quiet. The burden of managing the household had fallen on her shoulders since her mother had died. Always there was someone or something demanding her attention, from the maids who fussed and fluttered around her to the villagers who brought her their problems and requests, knowing that she would present their petitions to her father with soft and persuasive words. She loved the people of Grafton and she knew they loved her. Her entire life had been lived out in this land. And now through this betrothal she knew that the Earl of Grafton was seeking to ensure her a safe future, knowing that his health was starting to fail and that Grafton and its lady needed a strong lord to defend them.

Anne felt the prickle of tears in her throat. She swallowed hard, and deliberately turned her thoughts aside from her father's ill health. The room was hot, its walls confining. Suddenly she did not wish to sit waiting here for the summons to the betrothal feast. The air would be fresher in the garden.

So it proved. She skirted the kitchens, where the cook was bellowing at the scullions and sweating to provide the finest banquet that Grafton had ever seen. The villagers were already flocking to fill the ancient tithe barn and share in the feast. But no one saw Anne as she slipped through the doorway into the walled garden and walked slowly through the parterre to the sundial at the centre. The shadows were lengthening and the smell of the lavender was still in the air. She ran her fingers over the sundial's smooth surface. Sometimes it felt as though time stood still at Grafton. In her memories there was always the sun.

'Lady Anne.'

Anne jumped, a small cry escaping her lips. She had not seen the man who was standing in the shadow of the doorway, but now he came forward, his footsteps crunching on the gravel, until he was standing before her.

'I beg your pardon,' Simon Greville said. 'I did not intend to startle you. Your father is looking for you, Lady Anne. We are ready for the feast.'

Anne nodded. Her heart was beating swiftly, not only from the shock of his sudden appearance but also from the knowledge that they were alone for the first time. During the previous week they had ridden out together, danced under the indulgent gaze of the household and conversed on generalities. But suddenly it seemed precious little upon which to build a marriage; even as Anne reminded herself of her duty, the fear clutched at her heart.

'Of course,' she said. 'Excuse me, Lord Greville.'

Simon did not move. He put out a hand and caught her arm. 'A moment, Lady Anne.'

Anne looked up. The evening sun was in her eyes and she could not see his expression. She waited, her heart racing.

Simon slid his hand down her sleeve to capture her fingers in his. His hand was warm, the shock of his touch sufficient to send a shiver through Anne's entire body.

'I have your father's permission to wed you, Lady Anne,' he said, 'but I do not yet have yours.'

Anne stared. 'You do not need mine, my lord.'

Simon smiled into her eyes. 'Yes, I do. I will not force an unwilling maid. So speak now, Anne of Grafton, if you do not wish to take me as your husband, for soon we shall be troth-plight.'

His hands tightened on hers as he waited for her answer. Anne searched his face, so dark, so stern. She felt a little quiver of apprehension.

'I will do my duty—' she began.

'I do not want your duty.' Simon sounded angry now. 'I want you.' He moderated his tone. 'And I had thought—forgive me—that you might in some small way feel the same…'

Anne remembered the moment in the courtyard when she had first set eyes upon him. Then she remembered Edwina's words about the wedding night. An involuntary smile curved her lips.

'Well, I—'

She got no further, for Simon leaned down and kissed her, his hands suddenly mercilessly hard on her slender frame, his mouth hungry. Anne's exclamation of shock was smothered beneath the relentless demand of his lips. Her head spun and the blood pounded in her veins.

He released her gently and she steadied herself with one hand against the mossy stone of the sundial. She was trembling down to the tips of her toes. She pressed her fingers against her lips in confusion and the beginnings of desire.

'So is that a yes?' Simon demanded. His eyes were bright

and hard with passion. Anne saw it; for the first time in her life, she understood the truly awesome strength of her own power and felt the excitement flood her body. To be able to do this to such a man… She could bring him to his knees. She felt dizzy at the thought.

'I am considering it,' she said demurely. ''Tis true, my lord, that you are very pleasant to look upon…'

His lips twitched in response, but she could feel the impatient desire in him, barely held under control. 'Thank you,' he murmured. 'And?'

'And I have…enjoyed…the time that we have spent in each other's company…'

'And?'

'And indeed I think you must kiss very nicely, my lord, although I have no means of comparison.'

Simon made a movement towards her, but she evaded him, dancing away down the path. She was laughing now, the exhilaration burning in her veins.

'So having given consideration to your offer…'

She paused, looked at him. He caught her wrist, pulled her close and held her still.

'Yes?' he said.

'I will marry you,' she whispered, as their lips met again. 'With all my heart.'

Chapter One

Grafton, Oxfordshire, England
February 1645

The snow had been falling all day. It hung like a shroud between the besieged manor house of Grafton and the army that encircled it a bare half mile away. Now, as the church bell tolled midnight, the darkness had an unearthly glow that struck a chill into the men's hearts. In the morning they were to do battle, but for tonight they huddled in the byres and barns of the village, around the fitful fires. They drank the last of their ale, talked in low voices and tried not to think of the morrow.

When the knock came at the door, Simon Greville thought at first that he had imagined it. He had already met with his captains, they had talked of their strategy for the morning and had retired to wait for dawn and get what little sleep they could. He had given specific orders that he should not be disturbed further that night. Yet the knock came once again, soft but insistent, on the barn door. Simon was not angered to have his instructions gainsaid, but he was curious. His authority was such that only in the direst emergency would his men disobey his direct command.

He strode across the room and flung wide the door. It shook on its hinges and a flurry of wind swept in, bringing with it night chill and a scattering of snowflakes. The candles guttered and the smell of tallow stung the air.

'What is it?' He knew that he sounded brusque. Even he, renowned for his steady nerve, could be forgiven a certain shortness of temper the night before a battle.

It was the youngest of his captains who stood there, a youth barely out of his teens called Guy Standish. He was looking terrified.

'Your pardon, my lord. There is a messenger from Grafton Manor.'

Simon turned away. He might have known that the Royalist garrison in the house would try this last-ditch attempt to beg a surrender and avoid bloodshed. He had been waiting all day for them to try to negotiate a truce. And now it had happened. It was typical of the cowardice of the King's general, Gerard Malvoisier, to try to bargain for his miserable life.

Two weeks before, Malvoisier had murdered Simon's younger brother, who had gone to the Manor under the Parliamentarians' flag of truce. Malvoisier had sent Henry back in pieces, no quarter given, but now he evidently expected Simon to spare his worthless life. Once again Simon felt the ripping tide of fury that had swamped him when he had learned of Henry's death. A fortnight had allowed no time for that grief to start to heal. He had had the anguished task of writing to their father with the news as well. Fulwar Greville, Earl of Harington, supported the King whilst his sons were loyal to the Parliamentarian cause. And now Simon had written to tell their father that one of those sons was dead, fighting for a cause that betrayed their father's fealty.

Simon knew that his and Henry's defection had broken their father's heart. He had the deepest of respect for the Earl, despite their political differences. And now he felt a huge guilt for allowing Henry to die. All he could do was to turn that anger and hatred on to Gerard Malvoisier, stationed at Grafton. There would be no mercy for the besieged army in the Manor house, not now, not ever. It made no odds that Grafton—and its mistress—had once been promised to him. The Civil War had ripped such alliances apart.

Standish was waiting.

'I will not see the messenger,' Simon said. 'There is nothing to discuss. The time for parley is long past. We attack on the morrow and nothing can prevent it.'

His tone was colder than the snow-swept night and it should have been enough, but still Standish lingered, his face tight with strain.

'My lord…'

Simon spun around with repressed rage. 'What?'

'It is the Lady Anne Grafton who is here, my lord,' the boy stammered. 'We thought… That is, knowing that it was the lady herself…'

Simon swore under his breath. It was clever of Malvoi-

sier to send Lady Anne, he thought, knowing that she was
the one messenger he would find difficult to turn away in all
courtesy. They were on opposing sides now, but it went
against the grain with him to show a lady anything less than
respect, Royalist or not. Besides, he had been Anne Grafton's suitor four years before, in a more peaceful time before
the bloody Civil War had come between them. There were
memories there, promises made, that even now he found difficult to ignore.

But this *was* war and he had no time for chivalry. His
brother's brutal death at Malvoisier's hands had seen to that.

'I will not see her,' he said. 'Send her away.'

Standish looked agonised. Despite the cold there was
sweat on his brow. 'But, sir—'

'I said *send her away.*'

There was a clash of arms from further down the street
and then the sound of raised voices and hurrying footsteps,
muffled in the snow.

'Madam!' It was the anguished cry of one of the guards.
'You cannot go in there!'

But it was already too late. The barn door crashed back on
its hinges and Lady Anne Grafton swept past Guy Standish
and into the room. The snow swirled in and the fire hissed.

Lady Anne flung back the hood of her cloak and con-
fronted Simon. She was wearing a deep blue gown beneath
a fur-trimmed mantle and looked every inch the noble-born
lady she was. Her face was pale, her hair inky black about
her shoulders. She looked like a creature of ice and fire from
a fairy tale.

Simon felt his heart lurch, as though all the air had been punched from his lungs. He had not seen Anne Grafton in four years, for their betrothal had been broken almost as soon as it had been made. He heard Standish gasp as though he, too, was having difficulty remembering to breathe properly. Every man who besieged Grafton had heard the tales of the legendary beauty of the lady of the manor, but even so the impact of her appearance was quite literally enough to take a man's breath away.

It was not a comfortable beauty. Anne Grafton was small and slender, but for all that she had an aristocratic presence that could command a room. Her face was heart-shaped, with high cheekbones and winged black brows. There was no softness in it at all. Her eyes were very dark, only a couple of shades lighter than the ebony hair that spilled over the edge of her hood, and in them there was a fierce light that reminded Simon of a wild cat. This was no cosy armful to warm a winter's night.

At the beginning of the siege Simon had heard his soldiers joke about taming the wild beauty of the Lady of Grafton. They had said it softly, knowing he would stamp down hard on any ribaldry or licentiousness in the ranks and knowing too that the lady had once been promised to him. Now he watched those same boastful soldiers shift and shuffle, held spellbound by Anne's beauty but utterly unnerved by her defiant pride. Neither of the guards made any attempt to restrain her and Standish looked as though he would rather extract his own teeth than be obliged to confront her. Simon almost smiled. The Anne Grafton that he had known had been an unawakened girl of seventeen. This woman was a very different matter—and an enemy to respect.

And then he saw Anne press her gloved hands together to quell their shaking. He realised with a shock that she was trembling, and with nervousness, not with the cold. That flash of vulnerability in her made him hesitate a second too long. He had been about to turn her away without a word. Now it was too late.

'Madam.' He sketched a curt bow. 'I regret that my guards saw fit to let you pass. It was ill considered of you to venture here tonight.'

Anne looked at him. Her gaze was bright and appraising and beneath it Simon felt very aware of himself—and of her. No woman had ever looked at him like that before. They had looked on him with pleasure and with lust and with calculation, but never with this cool assessment, soldier to soldier. He could feel her weighing his valour. He drew himself up a little straighter and met her gaze directly.

Four years had changed her beyond measure; changed everything between them beyond recall. The Civil War had taken all that was sweet and precious and new between them and had destroyed it along with the lives and hopes of thousands of others. When he had gone to Grafton all those years ago, it had been at his father's bidding and to make a dynastic match. He had not expected to be attracted to his potential bride. At twenty-five he had fancied himself a man of experience and he had been downright disconcerted to find Anne Grafton so irresistibly alluring. He had desired her. He had been more than half in love with her. And then war had followed so swiftly. He had taken the Parliament's side and the King had summarily ordered the betrothal broken. And later, he had affianced Anne to Gerard Malvoisier.

It had been a long time ago, but it might only have been months, not years, so fresh it was in his mind. And now Anne Grafton was here and the unawakened fire he had sensed in her all those years ago when he had kissed her was blazing, powerful enough to burn a man down. He wondered what had awoken that spirit, then thought bitterly that during the intervening years of civil war, loss and sorrow had touched every man, woman and child in the kingdom. No one retained their innocence any longer in the face of such bitterness. Everyone had to fight and struggle to survive.

Anne came closer to him now and tilted her chin up so that she could meet his eyes. Her head only reached to his shoulder. He was over six foot tall. Yet it did not feel as though there was any disparity between them. She spoke to him as equal to equal.

'Good evening, Lord Greville,' she said. 'I am here because I want to speak with you.'

Her voice was soft, but it held an undertone of iron. She did not beg or even ask for his attention. She demanded it imperiously. And yet when Simon looked more closely at her face he could see the lines of fatigue and strain about her eyes. It was desperation that drove her on rather than defiance or anger. She was very close to breaking.

Simon hardened his heart to the treacherous sympathy he was feeling for her. He did not want to speak with her at all. He wished that they had never met before and that his thoughts were not shadowed by memories of the girl she had once been. It was far too late for that, too late for regrets, too late for compassion. They supported opposing sides now. He knew that she was going to beg for the lives of the innocent inhabitants of Grafton Manor and he could not afford to hear such stories. Within every siege there were the helpless victims, the servants, the people caught up in the struggle who had no choice. It was brutal, but war was indiscriminate. His reputation was built on fairness and justice, but he was also known as a ruthless soldier. And he was not about to compromise now.

He rubbed a hand across his forehead. He looked at the two guards, who had skidded to a halt inside the door, clearly unwilling to lay violent hands on a lady. Now they stood ill at ease, hesitating and awaiting his orders. Guy Standish hovered in the background, looking equally uncomfortable.

'I will not speak to you,' Simon said. He dragged his gaze from hers and turned to the guards. 'Layton, Carter, escort the Lady Anne out.'

No one moved. The soldiers looked agonised and scuffed at the cobbled floor with their boots. A faint smile touched Anne Grafton's lips.

'Your men know that the only way they can get rid of me is to pick me up bodily and throw me out,' she said drily. 'They seem strangely reluctant to do so.'

'Fortunately I suffer from no such scruples,' Simon said harshly. 'If you do not leave of your own free will, madam, I shall eject you personally. And believe me, I will have no difficulty in picking you up and throwing you out into the snow.'

He saw the flare of anger in her eyes at his bluntness.

'Such discourtesy,' she said sweetly. 'You have been too long a soldier, Lord Greville. You forget your manners.'

Simon inclined his head in ironic acknowledgement. 'This is a war, madam, and you are an enemy with whom I do not wish to have parley. Leave, before I show as little respect for the laws of truce as General Malvoisier did.'

He took a step closer to her so that he was within touching distance. At such close quarters he could see the pale sheen of her skin in the firelight and the telltale pulse that beat frantically in the hollow of her throat, betraying her nervousness. Her hair smelled of cold snow and the faint perfume of jasmine. Her eyes, very wide and dark, were fixed on his face. He put his hand out and took hold of her arm, intending to hustle her out of the door. And then he stopped.

It had been a mistake to move so near to her and even more of one actually to touch her. Simon's senses tightened and he was suddenly sharply aware of her. He remembered in exquisite detail exactly how it had felt to hold her in his arms all those years ago. He felt a powerful need to pull her to him and slake his misery and his exhaustion against the softness of her skin. He needed her sweetness to cleanse all the brutality and wretchedness of war. He needed to forget it all. He longed to. He ached to go back to the way they had once been, and lose himself in her embrace.

The overpowering intimacy of the feeling held him still, shocked, for a moment. He saw a tiny frown appear between Anne's brows and then her eyes searched his face and the need in him communicated itself to her. Her gaze widened and the colour swept up under her skin. Simon knew he was looking at her with a soldier's eyes and with the hungry desire of a man who had been on campaign too long. He had been without a woman for months and he wanted her. Yet there was something beyond mere lust here. The truly shocking thing was the deep feelings and memories that stirred when he touched her. They threatened to make him forget his purpose. She was a *Royalist*. She was his enemy.

He let go of her abruptly, furious with himself and with her.

'Go. Now.' His voice was rough. 'Captain Standish will escort you back to Grafton.'

He saw Guy Standish's reluctance to take the commission although the captain did not demur. He even stepped forward—slowly—to indicate his willingness to obey the order.

But Anne was shaking her head. She had moved a little away from him and Simon could sense that she wanted to be gone and that it was only sheer determination that kept her there. He was starting to feel frustrated as well as angry now. This was folly. Was Anne Grafton simple-minded, that she did not understand the risk she was running in coming alone to the enemy camp? His soldiers were not as rough as some—his discipline was too good for that—but there was such a thing as looking for trouble. He could not guarantee her safety. Damn it, he needed to protect her from himself as much as from his men.

He took a step towards her, intending to throw her out without further ado, but she spoke quickly, staying him.

'You do not understand,' she said. 'I have urgent news, my lord. I need to talk to you—'

Simon's temper snapped. 'There can be nothing so urgent that I wish to hear it,' he said. 'I know you are only here to beg for mercy for Grafton and I have no wish to hear your pleas.' He allowed his gaze to travel over her with insolent thoroughness. 'Take this reply back to Gerard Malvoisier, my lady. Tell him that I am not interested in talking terms with him, no matter how…temptingly…they are packaged, and if he sees fit to send you to parley with the enemy I cannot promise you will return with your virtue, let alone your life, intact.'

Anne's eyes narrowed with disdain at the insult. Her chin came up.

'I am not accustomed to being spoken to like a camp follower,' she said coldly, 'nor do I come from General Malvoisier. I wish to speak with you on a personal matter.' Her gaze lingered on Guy Standish and the guards. 'Alone, if you please, my lord.'

Simon strolled across to the table and poured himself a goblet of wine. He was shaking with a mixture of fury and frustration. He spoke with his back turned to her.

'Have you then come to plead for your own life rather than for your betrothed and the people of Grafton, Lady Anne?' he said. 'Your self-interest is enlightening.'

'I have not come to plead at all.' There was cold dislike in Anne's voice now. She took a deep, deliberate breath. 'I have come to strike a bargain with you. I am here to tell you of your brother, my lord.'

Simon heard Guy Standish gasp. The guards shifted, looking at him, their gazes flickering away swiftly as they saw the way his own expression had hardened into stone. His men had all been with him when Henry's body had been returned, bloody, beaten and unrecognisable, in defiance of all the laws of truce. They had seen his ungovernable rage and grief, and they were no doubt uncertain how he would react now that someone dared to raise the subject again.

'My brother is dead.' Simon's tone was unemotional, masking the images of death that still haunted his sleep. 'I imagine that you must know that, my lady. It was General Malvoisier who sent him back to me—in pieces.'

Anne met his shuttered gaze with a direct one. 'It is true that he sent a body back to you, my lord, but it was not that of your brother.'

This time, no one moved or spoke for what felt like an hour. It was as though none of them could believe what they had heard. Simon found he could only observe tiny details: the crackling of the fire, the snow melting from Lady Anne's cloak and forming a small puddle on the cobbled floor. He looked about him. The small barn was untidy. Despite all his attempts to make it more homely, it still looked what it was— no more than a glorified cowshed. There were maps and plans lying scattered across the wooden table where he and his captains had plotted the following day's attack earlier that evening. There was a carafe of red wine—bad wine that tasted of vinegar—staining the surface of the parchment. His trestle bed was tumbled and disordered in testament to the fact that he had been unable to sleep. It was no place for a lady. Yet this lady had forced her way into his company and dared to broach the one subject that drove his rage and his anguish.

'What are you saying?' His voice sounded strange even to his own ears. He cleared his throat. 'That my brother is alive? I regret that I cannot merely take your word for it, my lady.'

Lady Anne drew a step nearer to him. She put out a hand and touched his sleeve. He wondered whether she could read in his face the desperate fear and the spark of hope that he felt inside. Her voice was soft.

'Take this, my lord, as a pledge that I tell you the truth.'

Simon looked down. She was holding a ring of gold with the arms of his family cut deep in the metal. It was true that Henry had not been wearing the signet ring when his body was sent back, but Simon had assumed that Malvoisier had added looting the dead to his other sins. Now he was not so sure. Hope and dread warred within him. He found that his hand was shaking so much he dropped the ring on to the table, where it spun away in a glitter of gold, momentarily dazzling him. He heard the guards shuffle with superstitious discomfort. Standish was looking strained, incredulous.

'Forgive me, my lady, but it is easy to take a ring from a dead man.' His voice was rough. 'It proves nothing.'

The tension in the room tightened further.

'You do not trust me,' Anne said bluntly.

Their eyes met. 'No,' Simon said. 'I do not. I trust no one.' The anger seethed in him. He *wanted* to believe her; his heart ached to believe her, but that was the very weakness his enemies were trying to exploit. Suddenly his ungovernable rage swelled up. He swept the maps and plans from the table in one violent movement and turned on her.

'Does Malvoisier take me for a fool to send you here on

the night before battle to pretend that my brother is alive? He does it deliberately, in the hope that I will call off the attack! Dead or alive, he seeks to use my brother as a bargaining tool!'

'General Malvoisier knows nothing of this,' Anne said. She sounded calm, but she was very pale now. 'Only your brother and a handful of my most trusted servants were party to the plan. I have come to ask that you call off the assault on Grafton, my lord. Your brother is alive; if you attack the Manor, you will surely kill him in the process.'

Simon stared at her, as though by searching her face he could read whether she told the truth. Her gaze was steady and unflinching. She looked as candid and honest as she had when she had accepted his proposal that hot summer evening in the gardens at Grafton. But that had been a long time ago and looks could be terribly deceptive.

He made a slight gesture. 'Why come now? I thought my brother dead these two weeks past. Why wait so long?'

'It was impossible to arrange safe passage out of Grafton sooner,' Anne said. 'General Malvoisier—' She broke off, then added carefully, 'The Manor is closely guarded.'

Simon knew that was true. He had been studying Grafton's defences for all the months of the siege and knew there were few weaknesses. The Manor was small, but it was battlemented like a castle and ringed with a moat and low-lying marshy ground. There were snipers on the battlements and the house was garrisoned with a whole regiment of foot soldiers. He also knew that, despite Malvoisier's reputation for drunkenness, his men were well drilled, and frightened into obedience. No, escape from Grafton was well nigh impossible.

'Sir Henry said that you would not believe me, my lord,' Anne said. She quoted wryly, 'He said, "Tell that stiff-necked fool brother of mine that he must listen to you, Anne, for all our sakes."'

Simon heard one of the guards give a guffaw, quickly silenced. It did indeed sound like the sort of comment that Henry would make. He was irreverent and light-hearted even in the face of danger, but his flippancy hid a cool head and quick mind. On the other hand, Anne had known Henry when they were both young. She would remember enough about his brother to deceive him if she were so minded.

'If Henry has truly sent you,' Simon said, 'I will wager that he gave you some other proof to satisfy me.'

Anne's tone was dry. 'If you are minded not to trust me, my lord, then no proof on earth will persuade you, other than seeing your brother with your own eyes. And that I cannot arrange.' She paused. 'He did mention to me an anecdote that might convince you. It was not something that I had heard before, for all that we spent some of our childhood together.' She paused, as though the thought was a painful reminder of a past that could not be recaptured. Then she cleared her throat and resumed.

'Apparently there was an occasion on which you lost Henry in the woods when he was a child of eight. He told me that you preferred to dally with the milkmaid than act as nurse to your young brother that day...'

Simon froze. It was true, but he had long forgotten the

incident. He had been eighteen and had much preferred to take his pleasure with a willing maid that summer afternoon so long ago. He had left Henry to fend for himself in the woods for a little while and had been mortified on his return to find that his brother had completely vanished. Now that Anne had reminded him, he could recall the desperation of the hasty search, the fear that had gripped his heart before he had found his little brother hiding in a forester's hut. That fear had been a faint echo of the anguish he had felt when he had been told that Henry was dead. He had always tried to look after his brother.

He saw Guy Standish's face split into a broad, incredulous grin before the captain regained control of his expression. This story would be around the barracks before an hour had passed and there was nothing he could do to stop it. He laughed reluctantly and the tension in the room eased.

'Damn him,' he said. 'Henry swore he would never tell anyone about that. I made him promise on a dozen oaths.'

'Sir Henry swears that he has kept his word until now,' Anne said, 'but desperate times require desperate measures.'

'They do indeed.' Simon looked at her. 'Which is why you are here.' His tone hardened. 'You wish to bargain for Grafton's safety with my brother's life.'

Anne made a slight gesture with her hands. 'I would do anything to keep my people safe, Lord Greville.'

Simon nodded, though he did not answer at once. He had seen for himself just how much the people of Grafton loved their lady—and the devotion she had for them.

He turned back to his men. 'Layton, Carter, get back to

your posts. Guy—' Standish bowed, the smile still lurking about his mouth '—be so good as to fetch a flagon of wine for us. The good stuff…' Simon gestured towards the table '…not this poor excuse for a drink.' He turned to Anne. 'You will join me in a glass of wine, madam?'

Anne shook her head. 'I cannot tarry, my lord. I came only to give you the news that Sir Henry was still alive and to extract your promise that you will call off the attack on the house.'

Simon moved to bar her exit. His men had gone out into the snow, leaving them alone in the firelit shadows of the barn.

'You cannot run away now,' he said softly, his eyes on her face. 'You have told me but a quarter of the tale.'

He closed the door behind Standish and moved to set a chair for her. It was of the hard wooden variety, for there was not much pretence at comfort here in the barns and byres of the village of Grafton.

Simon had been shocked to find the village in ruins when his troops had arrived to lay siege to the Manor. He soon discovered that it had been Gerard Malvoisier's Royalist troops who had burned, looted and ravaged the area at will, taking whatever they wanted and destroying the rest for sport. Malvoisier's conduct had been all the more unforgivable since Grafton had always held for the King. Now the populace was scattered, the houses in ruins and the people sullen with resentment, though they still held fast to the Royalist allegiance of the old Earl.

Simon's troops had encircled the Manor, living alongside the remaining villagers for three months in an uneasy truce.

They had won a grudging respect from the people through sheer hard work, by treating the villagers courteously, sharing their food and helping with everything from the felling of timber to the rebuilding of cottages. Simon's men mingled with the people in the streets, but it was an uncomfortable co-existence with all the tension of occupation, and at any moment it could erupt.

To Simon's mind, sieges were the most wearing and dangerous form of warfare. Only time, starvation and ultimately brute force could break the garrison in the Manor, and during those long days a man could get bored or careless, and forget to watch his back and be picked off by a sniper or knifed by a Royalist agent in the dark alleys of the village. Simon had lost half a dozen men that way in three months and the constant vigilance was rubbing them raw. They were all desperate to see action on the morrow. But now this news, on the eve of battle…

Simon watched Anne as she reluctantly came closer to the fire, pulling her damp cloak closer about her like a shield. There was an uneasiness in her eyes as though she felt that she had already stayed too long. He thought of the haughty composure that she had assumed to get her past his men and into his presence. It could not be easy for a young woman in her situation to hold the people of Grafton together whilst her father lay dying, her home was overrun by Royalist troops and the threat of siege could end only in disaster and bloodshed. She was only one and twenty.

Once again the treacherous sympathy stirred in him and he pushed it violently away. He had a job of work to do and he did not trust Anne Grafton any more. He could not.

He moved to light another candle, keeping his eyes on her face. She looked so delicate and yet so determined. The line of her throat was pure and white above the collar of her blue velvet gown and the material clung to her figure with a seductive elegance that put all kinds of images in his head that were nothing to do with war at all. Then her hand stole to her pocket and he remembered his own safety with a flash of cold reason and all desire fled.

'You carry a dagger, do you not?' he said. 'Give it to me.'

Her head came up sharply and she bit her lip. Her hands stilled in the folds of her cloak and she straightened. 'I should feel safer to keep it,' she said.

'No doubt,' Simon said, 'but it is a condition of our parley that you are not armed.' He gestured to his sword belt, which lay across the back of one of the chairs. 'I ask nothing of you that I am not prepared to concede myself.'

Still Anne did not move and Simon knew she was thinking of her virtue rather than her life. Then she sighed and reluctantly placed the dagger on the table between them.

'Thank you,' Simon said. 'You are in no danger, I assure you.' He smiled a little. 'Tell me,' he added casually, returning to a thought that had struck him as soon as she had entered the room that night, 'are all men afraid of you?'

She looked at him. Her eyes were so dark and her face so shuttered that for a moment it was impossible to read her thoughts.

'No,' she said. 'A few are not.'

Simon laughed. 'Name them, then.'

'My father.' Her face went still, as though mention of the

ailing Earl of Grafton was almost too much for her to bear. 'And your brother, Sir Henry, treats me as though I were his elder sister.' She looked up again and met his gaze. 'And then there is you, my lord. I heard tell that you were afraid of nothing.'

'That is a convenient fiction to encourage my men.' Simon spoke shortly. He was surprised to feel himself disconcerted by her words. 'Only a fool is not afraid on the eve of battle.'

She nodded slowly. 'And surely you are not that. One of the youngest colonels in the Parliamentarian army, renowned for your cool strategy and your courage, a soldier that the King's men fear more than almost any other…'

They looked at one another for a long moment, then Simon moved away and settled the logs deeper in the grate with his booted foot. They broke apart with a hiss of flame and a spurt of light, spilling the scent of apple wood into the room. Inside it was shadowy and warm, giving a false impression of intimacy when outside the door the snow lay thick and an army of men prepared for battle.

'I was very sorry to hear of your father's illness,' Simon said. 'The Earl of Grafton is a fine man. We may not support the same cause, but I have always admired him.'

'Thank you.' Anne pushed the dark hair back from her face. It was drying in wisps now, shadowy and dark about her face. She looked pale and tired.

'Will he recover?'

Anne shook her head. 'He lives, my lord, but it would be as true to say he is dead. He neither moves nor speaks, and he takes little food. Nor does he recognise any of us any more. It is only a matter of time.'

Simon nodded. It was very much what he had already heard from the talk in the village. The Earl of Grafton had been ailing for years and it was no surprise that the King had recently sought to reinforce Grafton with troops from Oxford, under the control of General Gerard Malvoisier. Grafton was ideally placed to keep the route from the West Country to Oxford open for the King, and it had been strongly equipped with arms and men. The Parliamentarian generals also suspected that there was a quantity of treasure hidden at Grafton, sent by Royalists in the West Country to swell the King's coffers. Therefore General Fairfax had sent Simon, with a battalion of foot soldiers and a division of cavalry, to take Grafton from the Royalists once and for all.

It was King Charles himself who had ordered the betrothal between Gerard Malvoisier and Anne soon after war had been declared in 1642, and Simon therefore had all the more of a grudge against the Royalist commander. Grafton had been promised to him—and so too had its heiress, before the King had intervened. Simon had always despised Gerard Malvoisier, whom he considered nothing more than a thug who tried to conceal his brutality beneath a cloak of soldiering. When he had thought Malvoisier had murdered Henry, he had hated him even more. As for the idea of Anne's betrothal to him, it was repugnant. The thought of Malvoisier claiming Anne, taking that slender body to his bed, breaking her to his will with all the brutality of which he was capable made Simon feel physically sick.

Looking at her now, with her hair drying in the warmth of the fire and the candlelight casting its shadow across the fine line of her cheekbone and jaw, he felt something snap deep within him. Malvoisier would never have her. Unless… Simon paused. Perhaps it was already too late. Rumour said that Gerard Malvoisier had made sure of Anne by following up their betrothal with a bedding immediately after. She was in all likelihood already his mistress.

There was a knock at the door and Standish stuck his head around.

'The wine, my lord.' He withdrew silently and the door closed with a quiet click.

Simon poured for them both and passed Anne a glass. His hand touched hers; her fingers were cold. A strange feeling, part-anger, part-protectiveness, took him then, once again piercing the chill that had encased him since Henry's death.

'Come closer to the fire,' he said abruptly. 'You are frozen. It is a bad night to be out.'

She shot him a quick look, but drew her chair obediently closer to the flames. Now that they were alone with no further interruption, she seemed to have withdrawn into her own thoughts. The vivid spirit that had burned before was banked down, invisible, leaving nothing but the outward show of beauty. Simon took the chair opposite and studied her for a moment, until she lifted her gaze to his.

'What can we make the toast,' he said, 'given that we support different causes now?'

'All men's loyalties are tangled and confused by this conflict,' Anne said. 'It spirals out of our control. I know not where it will end.' She hesitated. 'I had heard that you were estranged from your father because of your allegiance—' She broke off, colouring slightly.

'You heard correctly,' Simon said abruptly.

Anne looked away. 'I am sorry,' she whispered.

Simon felt her grief touch his own heart. His estrangement from his father was never far from his mind. Less than five years before he had sat beside Fulwar Greville in Parliament. Looking back, it seemed that the country had slipped almost insensibly into civil war. Fulwar had not approved of the King's arrogance towards his subjects, but he had served the crown for forty years, had broken bread with his sovereign and could not forsake his allegiance now. Simon, on the other hand, had seen only a monarch who had gathered an army to fight his own countrymen and whose power had to be curtailed. When he had signed the militia oath to protect the Parliament he had seen his father's face grow old before his eyes. They both knew what it meant. Did he honour his father or his country? His loyalty was torn for ever.

'Perhaps the only true toast can be to loyalty itself,' Simon said, 'though it may mean different things to different men.' He touched his glass to Anne's and a moment later she smiled and raised her glass in silent tribute, taking a small sip of the wine.

'Loyalty,' she said. 'I can make that my pledge.'

A flush crept along her cheek, rose pink from the fire and the warming effects of the drink. It made her look very young.

Simon sat back. There was no sound, but for the brush of the snow against the roof and the crackle of the fire in the grate. For a moment the room was as close to peace as it could come.

Then Anne broke the silence. 'So,' she said, 'will you stand down your troops, Lord Greville? Do we have an agreement?'

'No,' Simon said. 'Not yet.'

Anne started to get to her feet. Her hand moved to take the dagger from the table, but Simon was too fast for her. He caught her wrist in a bruising grip.

'You are too hasty.' His tone was smooth, belying the fierceness of his clasp. 'There are questions I wish answered before we strike a bargain. Stay a little.'

He released her and Anne sat back, rubbing her wrist. Simon picked up the knife and turned it over in his hands. The firelight sparkled on the diamonds in the hilt.

'This is a fine piece of work,' he said.

'My father gave it to me.'

'And no doubt he taught you to use it too.' Simon pocketed the knife. 'You will forgive me if I keep it for now. I have no wish to feel it between my shoulder blades.'

Anne shrugged. Her gaze was stormy. He knew she was angered by his blunt refusal to agree terms, but she was unwilling to let it show.

'I have little choice, it seems,' she said. She looked at him. 'You said that you had questions, my lord. Ask them, then.'

Simon nodded slowly. 'Very well.' He paused. 'Is it true that General Malvoisier does not know that you are here and is not party to your decision to tell me about Henry or to bargain for the safety of the manor?'

Her gaze flickered at his use of Malvoisier's name, but it was too quick for Simon to read her expression. 'It is perfectly true,' she said. 'Malvoisier does not care for the welfare of the people of Grafton as I do. He would not have agreed to try to come to terms with you.'

'So you have betrayed your ally?'

The look she gave him would have flayed a lesser man alive. 'I am the ally of the King. I have not betrayed my Royalist cause and never would I do so!'

Simon inclined his head. She was not going to give an inch and would certainly do nothing to compromise her loyalty. He could feel the conflict in her; she wanted to tell him to go to hell, but too much was at stake. He could also sense her desperation. She cared passionately about the fate of Grafton. It had to mean that she was telling him the truth about Henry. Either that, or she was a damnably good actress.

'So you maintain that it is true that Henry is alive and well, and that Malvoisier lied to me about his death,' he pursued.

Again he saw that flicker of feeling in her eyes. 'It is quite true,' she said. Her gaze dropped. 'That is, Sir Henry is alive, but he has suffered some hurt.'

Simon felt a violent rush of anger and hatred. 'At Malvoisier's hands?' He brought his fist down hard on the table. 'I might have known it. Damn him to hell and back for what he has done!'

'Sir Henry will recover,' Anne said. He saw her put her hand out towards him briefly, but then she let it fall. 'Your brother is young and strong, my lord, and given time…' She stopped and the silence hung heavily between them. Simon knew what that silence meant. Henry would recover if he survived the assault on the Manor the next day. He would recover if Gerard Malvoisier did not use him as a hostage, or make an example of him by hanging him from the battlements.

He got to his feet in a surge of restlessness. He was torn. When he had thought Henry dead there was nothing to lose with an all-out attack on Grafton. But to attack now, knowing that his brother was a prisoner within… It was dangerous— perhaps even reckless—but he was not going to let a man like Malvoisier hold him to ransom.

He strode across the room, unable to keep still and contain the rage within him. 'He sent me a body,' he said, through shut teeth. 'If Henry is alive, how is that possible?'

Anne's very stillness seemed a counterpoint to his fury. She did not even turn her head to answer him, but he saw her clench her hands together in her lap and realised that she was nowhere near as calm as she pretended.

'The dead man was one of Malvoisier's own troops,' she said. 'He died of a fever.'

Simon felt revolted. He spun around to look at her. 'Malvoisier denied one of his soldiers a true burial? His body was defaced to make me believe that it genuinely was Henry?'

Anne's expression was sombre. 'They were the same height and build, my lord. All Malvoisier had to do was to dress the body in your brother's clothes.'

Simon's fingers tightened about his wineglass so that the crystal shivered. He had never questioned that the dead man had been Henry. The body had been so mutilated that it had been impossible to recognise, and, drowned in his misery and regret, he had never once imagined that Malvoisier had deliberately played him false. He had buried his brother with all honour, had written to their father apprising him of his younger son's death in action, and had laid his own plans for a cold and brutal revenge. No matter that to attempt an assault on the garrison of Grafton was a foolhardy undertaking. He cared nothing for that. All he wanted was to wipe out the stain on the family honour and grind Gerard Malvoisier into the dust.

'Why did he do it?' he asked softly. 'Why make me believe my brother was dead?'

'You are the strategist, my lord,' Anne said. 'Why do you think he did it?'

Simon considered. 'He wanted me to believe Henry dead in order to provoke me,' he said slowly. 'He wanted to end the siege, to drive me out into the open so that he had a better chance to defeat me.'

'Exactly so.'

'So now he has two advantages.' Simon was thinking aloud. 'He has forced me into a rash course of action and he still holds my brother.' He nodded slowly. 'It is very cunning. I might almost admire his tactics.' He came across to Anne's seat and leaned on the table beside her, so close that his breath stirred her hair. 'That is—if it is true, Lady Anne. Almost I believe you.'

He knew that to trust her was madness. Even now she might be lying to him, tempting him to withdraw his troops, tricking him to defeat. Every instinct in his body protested that she was honest, but he could not afford the weakness of allowing himself to feel sympathy for her. He was tired. His mind was clouded with fatigue and the prospect of the killing to come and he knew it could be fatal to his judgement.

Anne turned her head abruptly. Her dark glare pinned him down like the dagger's point. She tried to rise, but Simon caught her arm and held her still. They were so close now. A mere hair's breadth separated them.

'I do not lie,' Anne said disdainfully. 'If I were a man, you would answer for such an insult.'

Simon pulled her to her feet so abruptly that her chair rocked back and almost fell. She felt taut beneath his hands, shaking with anger and resentment.

'Fine words, my lady,' he said. 'Yet you must have lied to one of us, to Malvoisier or to me. And he is your ally now.'

Anne wrenched her arm from his grip, suddenly furious. 'Do not dare to accuse me of disloyalty to my cause,' she said. Her voice shook. 'I serve the King and until and unless he releases me of that charge my loyalty is absolute. Malvoisier—' She stopped, and there was an odd silence.

'Aye?' Simon's voice was harsh as he prompted her. He was breathing fast. 'What of him?'

Anne paused. 'Malvoisier and I share the Royalist cause, but our other loyalties are different,' she said slowly. 'My first loyalty is to the King, but my next is to my people. I have to protect Grafton. So…' She spread her hands. 'I came here of my own accord this night to beg a truce, my lord. If you attack the Manor, you will almost certainly kill your brother along with half the population of the castle. You have cannon—we cannot survive such an onslaught! Call it off and spare Sir Henry's life and that of my people!'

The silence spun out between them, taut with tension. It was, Simon knew, the closest that Anne of Grafton would ever come to begging. She had so much pride and she had humbled it to come here tonight to ask him to spare the lives of the people she cared for. And now he had to deny her. He shook his head slowly.

'No. I will not call off the assault.'

He saw the shock and horror on her face and realised that she had been certain, convinced, that he would do as she asked. She straightened up, her eyes riveted on his face.

'Do you not understand, my lord?' she demanded. 'Sir Henry is too weak to move—too weak to fight! When you attack he will be killed in the battle or, worse, Malvoisier will take him and string him up from the battlements! He is a hostage and Malvoisier will use him to barter for his freedom—or to buy yours! Whichever way you look at it your brother is a dead man!'

'And do you care about that?' Simon asked harshly.

'Of course I care!' Anne snapped. 'Your father is my godfather, Lord Greville. Henry is as dear to me as—' She broke off and finished quietly, 'as dear to me as a brother.'

'And yet you thought to use him to buy the safety of Grafton,' Simon said bitterly, 'and I cannot surrender to such blackmail.'

Anne stared at him, her eyes full of anger and disbelief. 'What, you will do nothing to help him?' she challenged. 'I do believe you have run mad. You would sacrifice your brother for nothing!' Her voice warmed into fury. 'Why not tell me the truth, my lord? You will not withdraw your troops because you have committed to make the attack on Grafton and you cannot be seen to weaken. Henry counts for nothing! It is all about your reputation in front of your men. That is all that *you* care for!'

They stared at one another for a long moment, dark eyes locked with dark.

'Even if I called off the attack, I could not free Henry,' Simon said. He tried to ignore her taunts and the anger they stirred in him. 'You are correct—he is Malvoisier's hostage. The only way I can save him is through taking the Manor.'

Anne grabbed her cloak. 'Then I am wasting my time here. Henry said you would listen to reason. Clearly he over-estimates you.'

Simon reached the door in two strides and blocked her path. He leaned his shoulders against the panels and folded his arms. Anne had come to a halt before him and was waiting impatiently for him to let her pass. He did not move.

'Of course it is the case that you have given me the means to counteract General Malvoisier's plan,' he said quietly.

Anne looked up at him and he saw the bewilderment in her eyes.

'What do you mean?' she said.

Simon gestured about the room. 'It is true that Malvoisier holds Henry, but you are here now, in my power. A hostage for a hostage, a life for a life.' He held her gaze. 'I will use *you* to free Henry, Lady Anne. You are my prisoner now.'

Chapter Two

The disbelief and disillusionment hit Anne with a shattering joint blow. For a moment all she could do was remember Henry Greville's words:

'My brother is an honourable man. He will thank you for your intervention. He will treat you with all respect...'

And she had believed him. She had remembered the Simon Greville that she had known all those years ago and she had believed without question. How unutterably foolish she had been. In her desire to do the right thing, to tell Simon Greville the truth about his brother and save both Henry and her own people, she had walked directly into peril and into the hands of a man at least as dangerous and ruthless as Gerard Malvoisier himself. She had risked all for justice and this was how Simon Greville, her former suitor, had repaid her.

She spun around so quickly that, on the table beside her, the wine cup trembled and almost fell.

'You will not do it!' Her voice broke, betraying her desperation. 'I trusted you! I came here in good faith to negotiate a truce.'

She saw Simon's expression harden. 'As I said before, it is best to trust no one.'

There was silence for a brief second. Anne looked at him. Clearly, the memories she cherished of their previous acquaintance had been misleading. In her mind's eyes she could still recall that long, hot summer at Grafton four years ago when Simon Greville had courted her—and kissed her with such passion and tenderness that she had tumbled into love with him. In all the time that had followed she had never met another man who had measured up to her memory of him. Consciously or unconsciously she had judged all men by his standard—and found them wanting. And now it seemed that it was her judgement that had been lacking. Simon Greville had no honour and no integrity and would use her for his own ends.

Physically he looked much the same. He had filled out over the intervening years so that now he was not only tall but broadly built as well. He was very dark, with the watchful gaze and the chiselled, patrician looks of a plaster church saint. Unlike his brother, he seldom smiled. But Henry Greville was little more than a charming boy. Simon was a man and altogether more formidable. He was powerful, cold, calculating—and merciless. She should have seen it. She should have run when she had the chance. Instead she had been lulled into a false sense of security by believing Henry and trusting her memories of his brother. She had put her safety in this man's hands. She felt betrayed. All her disgust, with herself as well as him, rose to the surface.

'I thought you a man of honour,' she said. 'It seems I was wrong.'

Simon was leaning against the door, arms folded, with a carelessness that she despised. It seemed so contemptuous. She could not see any evidence in his face that her accusation had stung him at all.

'Perhaps there is no room for honour in war,' he said. 'You have played into my hands by coming here, madam. It would be foolish of me not to take the advantages I am given.'

Anne made a sound of disgust. 'I thought you different.' She clenched her fists by her sides. 'Sir Henry *swore* that you were. It seems I made a mistake to trust him.'

Simon straightened up and faced her across the room. His presence was intimidating, but Anne was determined not to be afraid.

'You thought that I was different from whom?' he enquired softly. 'Malvoisier?'

'Perhaps. Different from most men—' Anne caught herself up on the betraying words, biting her lip. She was not going to pour out all her hatred of Malvoisier here and now to this man who had proved himself her enemy. She had detested Gerard Malvoisier from the first moment he had come to Grafton, with his bullying cruelty and his way of riding roughshod over people to get what he desired. Their political alliance had held together by the merest thread. She had rejected his proposal of marriage and had been incensed that he had put about the rumour that they were betrothed.

She looked at Simon, who was watching her with that dark, impassive gaze. He was not like Malvoisier—he did not bluster or shout or threaten—but he was twice as dangerous.

'I mistook you,' she finished starkly. 'You are just like all the rest.'

She saw something like anger flare in Simon's eyes, but when he spoke his tone was still even.

'I cannot afford to let such an advantage slip,' he said. 'Surely you understand? This way I may exchange you for Henry and no one is hurt.'

Anne felt the hope surge sharply within her. 'You mean that once the hostages are exchanged, you will call off the assault on the Manor?'

'No.' Simon shook his head. 'I will exchange your freedom for that of my brother, but Grafton must still fall to Parliament.'

Anne's heart plummeted into her shoes. 'So all you mean to do is buy your brother's life with mine and then attack my home and my people anyway!' She put her hands to her cheeks in a gesture of despair. 'Your callousness disgusts me, Lord Greville! You once promised my father to give your protection to this land!'

This time she heard the answering spurt of rage in Simon's voice. 'I regret that you see matters that way, madam,' he said. 'This is war—'

Anne's voice was contemptuous. 'Always you seek to justify your actions with that phrase!' She braced her hands on the back of one of the chairs. Simon's sword belt still rested there. She could feel the leather smooth beneath her fingers.

'Let us hope that Malvoisier thinks this bargain worth the making,' she said. 'I am not certain that he will.'

'Of course he will,' Simon said. 'You are the King's god-daughter.'

'Ah, yes,' Anne said, and she could not keep the bitterness from her tone. 'He will save me for that reason if no other.'

There was silence. The fire hissed. The room felt very hot now and heavy with the turbulent emotions between them. Anne suddenly flung her arms wide in fury, encompassing the table and its scattering of parchment. She was trying to keep her anger mute and under control, but it was difficult when she wanted to rail at him in her frustration and misery.

'Send to him, then!' she said. 'Why do you delay? Tell Malvoisier that you hold me hostage. My father is dying and I would rather be by his side than trapped here with you.'

Simon drained his second glass of wine and placed the goblet carefully on the table. His precision maddened Anne when she felt so close to losing control.

'I do not intend to negotiate with Malvoisier now,' he said. 'I will wait until the morning, when he drags Henry up on to the battlements to parley. Then I shall bring you out and strike a bargain with him.'

Anne whitened. 'Damn you! In that time my father may *die*, and you keep me from him.' She started to walk towards the door again. 'Well, if you wish to restrain me you must do so by force. I'll not go quietly with your plans!'

Simon moved between her and the door. He spoke quietly. 'Do not resist me, Lady Anne. If you make a scene before my men, it will end badly for you. They may have let you in here, but they will not let you out against my orders.'

Anne flashed him a look of challenge. 'Lay a hand on me, Lord Greville, and I shall bite you.'

'That would be a mistake.'

He moved before Anne could respond, grabbing her by the upper arms, dragging her against his body and holding her close with an arm about her waist. His grip was fierce and unrelenting. She tried to twist out of his arms, but he held her cruelly tight.

'Yield to me,' he said in her ear.

'Never!' Anne tried to kick him. 'You may go to the devil!'

Simon laughed. 'No doubt I shall do so in my own time. Now yield to me.'

In answer Anne turned her head and fastened her teeth on one of the hands that held her. She knew it pained him and felt a violent rush of satisfaction. Simon swore savagely under his breath and wound his hand into her silky black hair, ruthlessly pulling her head back. It did not hurt, but it rendered her incapable of further struggle without causing herself pain.

'Little wildcat!' he said. 'Surrender to me.'

Anne hesitated. She knew there was nothing she could do. She had to concede even though she hated to do it.

She relaxed a little and felt his grip ease in her hair. Her mind was whirling. She could not surrender to him. She surrendered to no one. There had to be another way…

'If I promise not to run,' she said, 'you must release me so that we may talk.'

Simon's fingers slid through the strands of her hair as he let her go. It made her feel strange, almost light-headed. His touch was feather-soft now, gentle, caressing. She found that she wanted to turn into his embrace now rather than escape it. She remembered the hardness of his body against hers and the breath of his lips against her ear with the oddest quiver of feeling.

His hands slid down her arms to hold her very lightly. He kept his gaze locked with hers.

'I agree,' he said. 'So promise me you will not try to flee.'

Anne hesitated. The touch of his hands and the steadiness of his gaze were confusing her. For a fleeting moment she remembered the desire she had seen in his eyes earlier in the evening. That had aroused a response in her that she had never expected to feel, did not want to feel. It reminded her too much of the pangs of first love she had felt when she was seventeen. Knowing that they had no future, she had tried to tell herself that her feelings for Simon Greville had been a childish infatuation. She had never quite succeeded in believing it.

'Well?' Simon prompted.

Anne inclined her head slightly, crushing down the treacherous ripple of feeling that coursed through her body.

'Very well. I promise not to run.'

She expected him to let her go at once, but Simon also hesitated, still holding her close to him even though his grip was gentle now. Anne could felt the warmth emanating from his hands and his body, and with it a sensation of reassurance and strength. She found that she wanted to press closer to him again and draw on his strength to comfort her. She started to tremble, both at the perfidiousness of her own body and the wayward nature of her thoughts. This was Simon Greville, her enemy, the man who held her hostage. She could show him no weakness.

But it was too late. The expression in his eyes changed and he pulled her to him, not hastily but slowly, inexorably, until her mouth was about an inch away from his. And then he stopped. She could see the stubble darkening his skin where he had not shaved and the shadow cast by his eyelashes against the line of his cheek.

Anne's throat dried. 'Release me,' she whispered. 'I do not trust you.'

'I know.' Simon's firm mouth curved into a smile. 'You are wise to trust no one.'

He let her go slowly and Anne stepped back. Her heart was pounding hard and her legs trembled. She caught the back of a chair to steady herself and prayed that Simon believed her weakness stemmed from fear rather than susceptibility to his touch. She raised her eyes to meet his mocking gaze.

'What would you like to talk about?' he asked. His gaze raked her, as it had done earlier. 'You know that you have nothing to negotiate with.' He paused. 'At the least, I assume you do not intend to try and bribe me with your body…'

Anne gave him a scornful look. Her fingers tightened on the chair back. There, beneath her hand was the sword belt. A plan was forming in her head. She prayed that she could carry it off. She had to keep him talking, distract him…

'You are contemptible,' she said.

'And you are helpless.' He looked rather amused.

Anne glared. 'That is not correct, of course,' she said. 'I have plenty of advantages. I know the lie of the land of Grafton, I know its weaknesses and I know Malvoisier's plans. I could even give you safe passage into the Manor were I minded to do so.'

Simon's gaze had narrowed on her face. 'But you would not do that,' he said. 'You would never betray your cause.'

'No,' Anne agreed bitterly. 'Everything I have done tonight has been to save Grafton. *I* do not sell my honour cheap.'

Simon smiled ironically. '*Touché*, my lady.' He made a slight gesture. 'But since you are not prepared to sell either your principles or yourself, you have nothing with which to barter.'

'I do not intend to barter,' Anne said. 'I intend to make you let me go.'

Simon folded his arms. He was smiling. It was all the extra incentive Anne needed.

'How will you achieve that?' he enquired.

In response Anne grabbed the hilt of the sword. It came free of the scabbard with a satisfying hiss of metal. She spun around. Simon had already started to move towards her, but he was too late. As he took the final step she brought the tip of the blade up to rest against his throat like a lover's caress. Simon stopped abruptly.

'Like this,' Anne said breathlessly.

The smile in Simon's eyes deepened into something like admiration.

'I cannot believe,' he said, 'that I was so careless.'

'Well,' Anne said. 'You were.'

'Please be careful,' Simon said. 'I sharpened the sword myself, this very night. It is very dangerous.'

'Good,' Anne said. She knew that he was using her own tactics now, keeping her talking to try and distract her. It was hideously dangerous to point a sword at a trained soldier, particularly one as experienced as Simon Greville. One second's loss of concentration and he would disarm her. He would be quick and ruthless. She kept her gaze fixed on the sword's point and did not look into his eyes.

'I have your life to barter with now, Lord Greville,' she said. 'Mine for yours. It is a fair exchange. Step away from the door. Slowly.'

Simon did as she ordered. Anne started to edge towards the door, still keeping the murderous weapon levelled at him. She did not want to have to kill him, but she did know exactly how to use it. The Earl of Grafton had never had a son, but he had certainly taught his daughter how to defend herself.

'Put up the blade,' Simon said. He raised his hands in a gesture of surrender. 'I will let you go.'

Anne laughed. 'You will let me go? You think that I believe you, after all that you have done? Nor do I need your permission to leave, my lord. I am the one holding the sword.'

Simon nodded. 'I acknowledge that. But you would not get five yards without my men capturing you. I demand parley. Put up the sword and declare a truce.'

Anne met his eyes briefly. It was a mistake. There was such a look of ruthless determination in them that she almost quailed. She dropped her gaze once more to the shining blade.

'Malvoisier did not respect the rules of parley,' she said. 'Why should you—or I?'

Simon did not move. 'You are not Malvoisier and neither am I, Lady Anne. Put up the sword and talk to me.'

There were rules of engagement. He knew it. She knew it. The fact that Gerard Malvoisier had no honour should not, Anne knew, bring her down to his level. She did not want to stay a moment longer and speak with Simon Greville. She did not trust him. But she had a code of honour and he had appealed to it.

'If I agree to parley and then you betray me,' she said, 'I will kill you.'

Simon nodded. He was not smiling now, but the respect was still in his eyes. 'That,' he said, 'is understood.'

Anne retreated until her back was against the door and then she lowered the sword until the tip was resting on the ground. She turned it thoughtfully in her hands, examining the balance of it. It had a long blade and a beautifully curved hilt.

'It is a fine weapon,' she said. 'A cavalryman's sword.'

'It was my father's.' Simon rubbed his brow. 'He gave me his sword and now I use it to fight for his enemy.'

Anne's heart contracted to hear the pain in his voice. It would be easy to accuse Simon Greville of having no integrity and selling out the Royalist cause of his father, yet she knew that countless men had had to make the decision to put their honour and principles before their family. They were fighting for what they believed to be right. The King had raised an army against his own Parliament and even she, for all her allegiance, could see that there were those who felt that Charles had betrayed his people.

'I am sorry,' she said softly.

Simon shifted slightly. 'It may be sentimental in me, but I would like to take that sword back from you, Lady Anne.'

Anne nodded. 'I imagine that you would.'

Simon's hand moved towards the pocket of his coat and Anne suddenly remembered that he had put her knife there. She raised the sword point to his chest and he stopped.

'Not so fast, Lord Greville.'

'I beg your pardon.' Simon said. 'I merely wanted to give you back your knife in case you hold it of similar worth.'

Anne felt the treacherous tears sting her eyes. She valued each and every thing that her father had ever given her, material or otherwise, and as he grew steadily weaker so the desperation in her grew steadily more acute. Soon he would be dead and she would have nothing of him left to hold on to but the example of his allegiance to the King and his loyalty to the people of Grafton. She had come to Simon's quarters that night because she knew it was what her father would have done. He would have put the welfare of his people first, before pride or military conquest.

She blinked back the weak tears. 'Put the knife on the table,' she said, a little huskily. 'Do it slowly. Do not come any closer.'

'I will not make that mistake,' Simon agreed.

Anne watched as he slipped a hand into his pocket and extracted the dagger, placing it carefully on the table between their two empty wine glasses. When he let his hands fall to his side and stepped back, she let out the breath she had been holding.

'Good. So…' She made her tone a match for his earlier. 'You asked for parley. What would you like to discuss?'

Simon rubbed his brow. 'There is nothing to discuss,' he said. 'I promised that I would not play you false. You are free to go.'

Once again the hope flared in Anne's heart, but this time she was more wary.

'What are you saying?' she whispered.

Simon gestured fiercely towards the door. 'I am telling you to leave. Go back to Grafton Manor. You came here to negotiate and I will not accept your terms. I have changed my mind about exchanging you for Henry. It will not serve. So there is nothing more to say.'

Anne did not move immediately. She felt bemused by this sudden change of heart. If Simon were to let her go now, what was to become of Henry? Malvoisier would still have him hostage and Simon would have nothing with which to bargain.

'But what of your brother?' she asked.

Simon laughed and there was a bitter edge to it. 'I am gambling, Lady Anne,' he said. 'I am risking my brother's life so that I can take Grafton Manor. The house must fall to Parliament. To negotiate with hostages now will only delay the inevitable battle.'

Anne shook her head, bewildered. 'But if Malvoisier should kill Henry…'

Simon shifted uncomfortably. 'Malvoisier will reason that a live hostage is worth more to him than a dead man,' he said. 'He will want to keep Henry safe in case he needs to barter to save his own miserable neck.' He turned away with a dismissive gesture, but not before Anne had seen the flash of genuine pain in his eyes and knew that he was not as indifferent as he claimed. He was merely hoping against hope that his words were true.

'This is not so easy for you as you pretend,' she accused. 'You know you are taking a desperate chance!'

Simon turned on her, his mouth twisted wryly. 'Aye, I know it! And if Henry dies because of it, I will have years of grief in which to regret my decision.'

Anne looked at him steadily. She sensed that his deliberate harshness was a defence to keep her at arm's length. He did not want her sympathy—or her thanks. He wanted nothing that threatened to bring them closer, threatened to make him feel.

'You care deeply for your brother,' she said. 'Aye, and for your father too. I believe that you are letting me go because you do not wish *my* father to die alone and uncomforted. You respect him. And you know what it is to be estranged from your family and to lose all that you hold dear.'

Simon's dark gaze was murderous now. There was so much repressed violence in him that she shivered to see it.

'Enough!' he said. He moderated his tone almost at once. 'You have said quite enough, madam. You may think that you know me, but you know nothing at all.' He straightened. 'You may disabuse yourself of the notion that I am letting you go through chivalry, or for pity, or generosity or any other virtuous reason.' There was a self-mocking tone to his voice now. 'I know nothing of such emotions now, if I ever did. The simple fact is that I do not need a hostage. I can take Grafton without.'

Anne's breath caught at the callousness of his words. 'You speak so easily of destroying my home,' she whispered. 'You are about to lay waste to my people's livelihood and I cannot stop you.'

For a moment she thought she saw something behind the unrelenting hardness of Simon's expression, some element of pity or sorrow or regret. She had already put out a hand to him in appeal when he spoke, and his tone was unyielding.

'No, you cannot stop me,' he said, 'but I admire you for trying to do so.' His tone hardened still further, cold as the winter night. 'Now go.'

Anne laid the sword down on the table, very gently, and started to gather up her cloak. Her throat was thick with tears. She did not believe his cruel words, but she knew that she could never make him admit to the truth. She knew he cared desperately for Henry. She had seen it in his face in the very first moments when she had told him his brother lived, when he could not repress the blaze of joy and relief and thankfulness. But there was too much at stake here for either of them to admit anything to the other. It was too dangerous to admit even to the slightest affinity in this conflict where one stood for the King and the other for the people.

And yet she could feel Simon watching her with those dark, dark eyes and his look made the awareness shiver along her skin. She could feel that look in every fibre of her being. It stripped away all her defences. Against all odds and against all sense there was still something between them, something shockingly powerful. There should not be. There *could* not be, for they were sworn enemies, and a part of her hated him whilst she was equally, frighteningly, as drawn to him as she had been four years before.

She slipped the cloak about her shoulders. Simon was standing by the door and she had to pass him to go out. She was desperate to be gone, yet when she got to the door she hesitated, and looked up into his face. Suddenly she did not know what to say to him.

Abruptly he caught her hands in his. The intensity of his gaze burned her. 'You are betrothed to my sworn enemy,' he said softly. 'I am about to lay waste to your home and your people's livelihood. If I say that I am sorry, you will only think me a liar, but believe that I will do what I may to lighten the blow that falls on Grafton.'

Anne trembled. She made an involuntary movement and his grip tightened.

'I understand,' she said. A faint, bitter smile touched her lips. 'As you have said before, this is war. In a war people will get hurt.'

'Be careful tomorrow,' Simon said. He looked down briefly at their joined hands, then up into her face again. 'Even if you do not trust me, take this advice. When the attack begins, take only those closest to you and lock yourself in the safest place in the house. I will send word to you as soon as I can.'

Anne stared up at him. 'You really do believe that you will win?' she whispered.

'Yes.'

Anne bit her lip. 'I fear for you,' she said.

The words were out before she had time to consider them and she heard his swift intake of breath. Standing there so close to him, feeling the warmth of his touch and the tension latent in his body, it was impossible to keep any secrets one from the other. Simon's dark eyes were brilliant with desire now and Anne knew that he wanted to drag her into his arms and kiss her until she was senseless. She wanted it too. Her whole body ached to meet his passion with her own, kindle fire with fire. She did not know why, she did not understand how this could happen when a part of her hated him for what he was about to do, but it was almost irresistible.

Simon took a harsh breath. 'If I should find Gerard Malvoisier before he finds me tomorrow,' he said roughly, 'do you want me to save his life for you?'

There was a pause, full of feeling, and then the hatred smashed through Anne in a wave of emotion. All evening she had managed to conceal from Simon her utter contempt for Gerard Malvoisier. A loyalty to the King's cause had been the only thing that had held her silent. Malvoisier was her ally, but now it was not possible to deceive Simon any longer. Nor did she want to.

'No,' she said, and her voice shook with feeling. 'I would not wish you to spare Gerard Malvoisier on my account, Lord Greville. He has taken everything that I care for and destroyed it or desecrated it beyond redemption.' She could feel herself trembling with hatred and passion, and knew Simon must be able to feel it too. 'He has taken my father's life, my home, the loyalty of my people…' She tilted her face up and met the intensity of Simon's gaze. 'If you wish to show your gratitude to me, Lord Greville, then you will take his life. Kill him for me.'

There was a moment when Simon stared down into her eyes and then he pulled her to him with one violent motion. His hand tangled in her hair and his mouth was hard on hers and Anne yielded to him with a tiny gasp and parted her lips beneath his. The fire in him woke her senses to life. Anne's head spun with sudden passion—and with recognition. The years fell away and she was seventeen again, and back in the walled garden at Grafton, feeling the sun beating down and the hardness of Simon's body against hers as he held her close.

But this was no youthful kiss now. It held all the fierce demand and desire of a man for a woman and it evoked an instinctive response in her. She yielded helplessly, conscious of nothing but the touch and the taste of him, the feel of his hands on her body, the scent of his skin so surprisingly and achingly familiar to her. Her knees weakened and Simon scooped her up with an arm about her waist and took two strides across to the truckle bed.

He laid her on the hard pallet and followed her down, taking her mouth with his again, fierce in his demand and his need. Anne responded with no reservations. All the anger and the fear and the desperation that she had felt that evening fused into one huge explosion of passion. She knew she ought to hate him, but she did not. She wanted the safety and promise their past had offered them. What she felt for him was dangerously akin to love.

She could feel Simon's hands shaking as he dealt with the hooks and bows and loosened her bodice. He bent to kiss the side of her neck as he slid his hand within her shift. A lock of his dark hair brushed her cheek and Anne trembled with need. In the mixture of fire and candlelight his expression was hard, concentrated, desire distilled.

He brushed her shift aside and bent to cup her breast, taking one rosy nipple in his mouth. Anne moaned and writhed beneath his touch, running her fingers into his hair and holding his head down against the hot damp skin of her breast. She was naked to the waist now, her bodice undone, her hair spilling across the pallet.

She felt Simon's hand on her thigh beneath the heavy weight of her skirts. The air was cold against her skin. Then he eased back for a moment. Anne felt the loss and reached blindly for him, her mind still a swirl of confusion and desire. He was not there. She felt cold and lonely.

She opened her eyes. Simon was sitting on the edge of the pallet bed, his hands braced beside him as though he was forcibly preventing himself from taking her in his arms again. He was breathing very fast and very harshly. And although his face was half- turned from her, Anne could see the same shock that she felt inside reflected in his expression.

The truth hit her then like a blast of winter air. Simon Greville had been about to take her, there in his quarters, like a soldier tumbling a camp whore in a ditch. And she had been about to let him do it. Simon Greville, her sworn enemy. It had happened so fast and so irresistibly. Now that sanity was returning to her she could not understand it at all.

The colour flooded her face; she made an inarticulate sound of shock and struggled to get to her feet, her hands shaking as she swiftly rearranged her bodice and dragged the fur-lined cloak about her. She held it wrapped tight to her like armour. She wanted to run away.

Simon had also got to his feet.

'Anne,' he said, calling her by her name only for the first time that night. His voice was husky with passion and she shivered to hear it. She thought that he looked as dazed as she, and she knew that in another second he would gather her up in his arms and carry her to the tumbled truckle bed and make love to her. He was as much deceived by the ghosts of the past as she.

She shook her head sharply. 'Do not. Do not say anything.' She huddled deeper within the cloak. She felt desperately cold and alone.

'I made a mistake,' she said. 'I thought we could go back, but we cannot.'

They looked at one another and Anne could see in his eyes that both of them were poignantly aware that they would never meet like this again. Perhaps they might never meet again at all, if Gerard Malvoisier won the day. Simon might die in the heat and pain of a bloody battle. Anne knew she could perish along with her people if the Manor was taken. This sudden and unexpected sweetness between the two of them, this dangerous temptation, was a moment out of time. She told herself fiercely that it was the product of memory only and the result of the heat and passion of the night before battle.

'Take care,' she said, 'on the morrow.'

She opened the door and the snow swirled in for a moment and she stepped outside. It was cold out in the night and she wanted to run back to the warmth and safety of that room, and, treacherously, into Simon's arms. But she knew that when they met again—*if* they met—she would be Anne of Grafton and Simon Greville would be the victor. Everything would be different. There would be bitter hostility between them. Once more he would be her enemy.

Chapter Three

'**M**adam!' Edwina met Anne as soon as she reached the top of the tower steps and was about to open the door of her chamber. In the torchlight the woman's face was strained. 'General Malvoisier is here,' she said meaningfully. 'He has been asking for you.'

Anne paused a moment as she felt the customary surge of aversion sweep through her body. Trust Malvoisier to have come looking for her on the one occasion when she had managed to slip away from his vigilance. Had he guessed that she had stolen out of the house and gone to visit his enemy? She shuddered at the thought and tried to calm herself. Closing her eyes briefly, she put her hand against the cold wood and pushed open the door of the chamber.

'Thank you, Edwina.'

There were so few seconds in which to prepare herself. Gerard Malvoisier was standing with his back to the fire, feet spread apart, hands clasped behind him. He was a large and fleshy man who commanded the room through his height and girth, and because he had the air of one who knows himself superior to other mortals. His bloodshot eyes were narrowed in his reddened face where the veins mottled the skin. Years of good living had stolen much of his youth and vigour, and now Anne could smell the alcohol on his breath, even across the room. She felt that probing gaze search her face and drew her cloak a little closer. Her lips still stung with Simon Greville's kisses and her skin was still alive to his touch. Would Malvoisier be able to read any of that in her face? Thank God she had paused inside the tower door to rearrange her hair and make sure her gown was secure. For a moment she allowed herself to remember Simon's hands on her body and his lips against hers, and she suppressed a shiver at the same time as she suppressed her wayward thoughts. Time enough to think on that when the current danger was past. Squaring her shoulders, she slipped off the cloak and turned to greet Malvoisier with every assumption of ease.

'Good evening, sir. In what way may I assist you?'

Anne was always formal with Sir Gerard Malvoisier. It was one of the many ways that she kept him at arm's length and held her fragile defences together against the threat of his presence. She saw him frown with displeasure as he took in her tone.

'You may tell me where you have been for a start, madam.' His voice was brusque. 'Your chamber women did not appear to know where you had gone.'

Over his shoulder, Anne saw Edwina make a slight shrug

of apology and spread her hands wide. The other occupants of the room, Anne's cousin Muna, a slender girl of eighteen, and her devoted servant John Causton, stood mute. Muna's head was bent and her eyes on the ground. Anne knew that her cousin hated Malvoisier as much as she did herself, but that she had the sense to hide it behind a show of dumb deference. As for John, every line of his body seethed with dislike. Malvoisier lashed out at him often, goading him until Anne knew not how John resisted retaliating. Somehow he kept quiet. When Malvoisier was about they all played their parts.

'I have been in the church,' she lied coolly, 'praying for a just outcome on the morrow.'

She could not be sure if Malvoisier believed her. There was an unconscionable amount of snow on her cloak to be accounted for on the short journey across the courtyard to the church. Malvoisier took a step towards her. It was clear that he was drunk and pugnacious, spoiling for a fight.

'And what would be a just outcome, Lady Anne?'

Anne opened her eyes innocently. 'Why, that is in God's hands, sir. I trust in him.'

Malvoisier made a noise of disgust. He had no time for divine intervention. 'We shall prevail tomorrow. After all, we hold Sir Henry Greville and will show that cur of a brother of his what he must do to get his flesh and blood back.'

Anne felt Muna make a slight move of protest, quickly stilled. The girl had been nursing Henry Greville herself and had fallen victim to his boyish charm very easily. It had been amusing to Anne to see how Muna's view of Henry had changed so swiftly. One minute her cousin had been speaking of a tiresome boy who had pulled her pigtails as a child, and the next she had a dreamy expression in her eyes and a light spring in her step. It would have been sweet were it not for the unavoidable fact that Henry, like his elder brother, was a Parliamentarian soldier.

Anne had warmed to Henry too, even knowing that he was her enemy. There was something about the vulnerability of an injured man that made it difficult to remember that he held a different allegiance. So she could hardly blame Muna, inexperienced and in the throes of a first love that was all too painfully familiar, for falling in love with a Greville.

Anne cast her cousin a swift, consoling look. Edwina had come forward to stand by her side, stoutly comforting. Muna looked dejected, knowing that in the morning Henry would be paraded from the battlements and either be dead or free within a few hours. Either way, she would never see him again.

'Sir Henry is too ill to be moved,' Anne said quickly, folding up her cloak and laying it on top of the Armada chest. 'I beg you to leave him to rest.'

Malvoisier snorted. 'Rest! He'll get precious little rest on the morrow. He'll be there as our shield against the enemy if I have to drag his unconscious body up on the roof. Save your concern for your father, girl. How does the old man?'

The careless disrespect in his voice made Anne's skin prickle with dislike, but she answered civilly enough.

'Lord Grafton is much the same, sir. I pray hourly for his recovery.'

She felt a small flash of triumph as she saw the flicker of

fear in Malvoisier's eyes. She knew that he could not quite disabuse himself of the superstitious belief that the Earl of Grafton would recover his health and strength, and demand from him an explanation of Malvoisier's stewardship of the Manor in the interim. Anne knew that it would never happen. Her father was dying and the tenacious desperation with which she wanted him to live could make no difference. But every day she used Malvoisier's anxieties against him, reminding him subtly of her father's presence, using the Earl as another line of defence. When Malvoisier had been drunken and enraged one night, and had come to her chamber intent upon rape, she had even resorted to invoking the name of King Charles. It had been enough to play upon the general's dread of reprisal and he had stumbled off down the stairs, raining curses on her head. Since then he had never attempted to touch her. Her resistance held, but she felt frighteningly imperilled and it was so exhausting that she was sure one day she would simply crumble. Not now though. Not tonight.

'We all pray for the master's recovery, madam,' John said loyally, and Malvoisier gave him a murderous look before he spun on his heel and made for the door.

'Have Greville ready in a few hours so that I may use him as my bargaining tool,' he said over his shoulder. 'As for the rest of you, you may rot in hell for all I care.'

The door thudded behind him and his angry footsteps clattered down the stone steps to the bottom of the tower. There was silence for a few seconds, then Edwina tip-toed across to the door and opened it a crack. The lantern light fell on the empty stairwell. 'John, some hot milk for my lady from the kitchens, if you please,' she said. She came over and took Anne's frozen hands in hers. 'You are chilled to the bone, pet, and too pale. Come closer to the fire.'

Anne let her draw her nearer the blaze, shivering a little as she remembered Simon Greville instructing her to do the same thing only an hour earlier. From the moment she had stepped into his room that night she had felt feverish, hot and cold as though she had an ague. In part her nerves had sprung from guilt; she had felt as though she was being disloyal in some way by going to him to try to strike a bargain for Grafton. Yet it had been the only thing that she could do to try to save everyone who depended upon her. Now she had to tell them she had failed. Anne wrapped her arms about herself for comfort as she thought of the devastation that might follow the battle.

Simon Greville… She had expected to be nervous to see him again. His reputation as a shrewd, cold strategist was sufficient to strike fear in the hearts of any man or woman he opposed. Cool, calculating, utterly ruthless, he was more than a match for the hot-blooded drunkenness of Gerard Malvoisier. What she had not expected that night, though, was that the attraction to him that she had experienced four years ago would return, all the more potent, all the more treacherous since Simon was now her sworn enemy…

Muna was touching her sleeve. 'Did you meet Lord Greville, Nan?' she whispered. A tiny, slender creature with huge dark eyes, Muna looked as though she would crumble at the first unkind breeze, but she was stronger than she looked. The illegitimate daughter of the Earl's younger brother, Muna had been taken into the Grafton household when her father had died and had been educated alongside Anne. Anne had never had any siblings and valued her cousin's friendship highly.

Now she smiled at her, a little sadly. 'I did meet him, Muna. I told him that his brother is alive.' She hesitated. 'He was mightily relieved to hear the news.'

Muna gave a small sigh. 'And what manner of man is he these days, Nan? Is he like Sir Henry?' She blushed a little as she spoke Henry's name and Edwina caught Anne's gaze and rolled her eyes indulgently. The sweet, passionless courtship of Muna and Henry Greville had consisted of nothing more than love poetry and hand holding, which, Anne maintained, was exactly as it should be. Edwina, a more earthy soul, snorted at the sonnets and laughed aloud at the bad poetry Henry penned. But Anne, with the memory of Simon Greville's caresses still in her mind, reflected it was a good job that his brother had been badly injured. If Henry's courtship was normally as direct as Simon's, then Muna's virtue would have been under dire threat.

Both Muna and Edwina were watching her with curiosity in their eyes. Anne sat down on the wooden settle with a heartfelt sigh.

'Lord Greville is very like Sir Henry, only more—' She stopped, aware of her audience's round-eyed interest. 'More forceful,' she finished carefully, anxious not to give too much of her feelings away.

'Lord have mercy!' Edwina said drily. 'Like Sir Henry,

but more forceful!' She looked closely at her former charge. 'You are very pink in the face, my lady. I seem to remember that you had a great regard for this Lord Greville when he came a-courting here at Grafton.'

There was the scrape of wood on stone as the door opened and John re-entered the chamber. Anne gratefully accepted the cup of warm milk that he pressed into her hands, wrapping her cold fingers about it and using the time it gave her to fend off Edwina's enquiries.

'It was many years ago that Simon Greville came here, Edwina,' she said. 'Have you forgotten that we are on different sides now?'

Edwina made a humphing sound. The loyalty of Anne's close servants was absolute, but they had a simpler view than she of allegiance to the King or the Parliament. To them such civil strife caused nothing but trouble, took food from the mouths of the poor, split brother from brother and took sons from their mothers. They supported the King mainly because the Earl was the King's man and they held fast to their fealty to him and to his daughter. And now Anne realized, with a sinking heart, that she had to tell them she had failed them.

'Lord Greville will not call off the assault on the Manor,' she said baldly. 'I asked him and he refused.'

She looked at them over the rim of the cup. There was a moment of stillness when she could see her own horror and misery etched clear on the faces of them all. They had thought that she would save them.

Then John cleared his throat.

'You did your best, milady,' he said gruffly. 'It was far

more than that miserable cur Malvoisier would do for us. Don't you go feeling bad about that.'

Muna gripped her hand hard. 'He would not even do it to save Sir Henry? Oh, Nan…'

Anne shook her head tiredly. 'I am sorry, Muna. I did my best. Truly I did. But Lord Greville believes that Sir Henry's best chance of safety is for him to take the Manor and so…' She let the sentence fade away.

'The King,' John said, his eyes lighting with hope. 'There is still time. Surely the King will come to save his treasure, madam?'

Anne shook her head. 'He cannot. It is too dangerous. If he were to attack and fail, the secret might be revealed. There is nothing we can do but keep silent.'

'So now we wait for the attack,' Edwina said, and though her tone was brisk her plump cheeks were pale. 'What will happen, madam? Will Lord Greville win?'

'I believe he may,' Anne said, so tired and heartsick that she could not bring herself to lie. 'He has cannon and Grafton cannot withstand a bombardment by artillery.'

She squeezed Muna's hand and got to her feet. 'John, Edwina, pray go to the kitchens and fetch bread, cheese and ale enough to feed us awhile. Bring the servants here with you for safety. We need kindling and water. I intend to secure this tower once the attack commences. Muna, go to Sir Henry. If he sleeps, pray do not wake him. I have no intention of handing him over to General Malvoisier if I may help it.'

Muna's face lightened a little and she scrambled up.

'Bless her,' Edwina said sadly as the girl hurried from the

room. 'She is naught but a child and fancies herself in love. Whatever happens this night will go badly for her, madam.'

'It will go badly for all of us,' Anne said bleakly. If Malvoisier won they would be free of the siege, but the village and surrounding countryside would once again be subject to his brutal regime. If Simon Greville took Grafton for the Parliament… Anne shivered. She would not permit herself to think of that. If Simon won, she would be all that stood between him and the King's treasure.

'I must go and see how my father fares,' she said.

She went out of her room, past the solar and along the little corridor to the Earl's bedchamber. When her father had first become ill, Anne had moved from her own quarters in the main part of the Manor and taken a set of rooms near her father so that she might tend to him more easily. The Tempest Tower was the oldest part of the building and as such had all the self-contained accommodation that she and her servants needed. It also had the inestimable benefit of being as far away as possible from the area where Malvoisier had quartered his men and established what she thought of as his court. Naturally he had objected to her independent household arrangements, but Anne had stood firm.

Her father's room was lit by one candle only, on a chest near the bed. In its faint light the room looked cold and shadowed, as though the still figure in the bed was slipping ever further into the darkness. And indeed Anne thought that her father did seem a little weaker. His breathing was shallower and when she touched his hand his skin felt cold and dry beneath her fingers. She sat down on the tapestry stool at his bedside and took his hand in her own. He did not stir. His face was serene now, at peace. He was already far away from her.

And yet, just when she thought that he would never stir again, the Earl moved. His eyelids flickered.

Anne leaned forward, straining to catch his words.

'Papa?'

'The King's treasure…' The Earl's words were a breath of a whisper. 'Safe?'

'Yes, Papa.' Anne's throat was suddenly rough with tears. 'Do not concern yourself. All is well.'

'And you?'

'I am well, too.' She found that she was gripping his hand too tightly and tried to ease her grasp. 'We all wish you to recover, Papa. Save your strength for that.'

The Earl's lips moved in a travesty of a smile. 'Nonsense. Don't give me false hope, child.'

'No, Papa.'

'I am dying.'

'Yes, Papa.' Anne gave him a watery smile. 'I wish it were not so.'

The Earl moved his head in a gentle gesture of denial. 'Malvoisier…' he said. He tried to moisten his lips and Anne lifted the cup of water to his mouth, spilling a little in her haste to help him.

'Never trust him,' the Earl said.

'No, Papa.'

'You need a strong man.'

'I shall be very well as I am.'

'Nonsense,' the Earl said again. He gripped her fingers hard, then relaxed his hand as though the meagre effort had taken the last of his strength. 'Take Greville when he offers. With my blessing.'

Anne frowned. Even through his fever and deteriorating health her father had been aware that Simon Greville was besieging Grafton, but why he should have taken it into his head that Simon would wish to wed her was a mystery, no doubt conjured by the confusion of his illness.

'You are misled, Papa,' she reminded gently. 'Lord Greville opposes us. It was a long time ago that he made an offer for my hand.'

'He will ask again.' A satisfied smile played about the Earl's lips. 'I know it. He is a sound man. Take him. It is my wish.'

Anne was silent. There was no point in upsetting Lord Grafton now. He wished to think her future secure, even if it meant her breaking her allegiance and marrying a Parliamentarian. It was the only thing that would bring him peace and she would not take that away from him now.

'Sleep now,' she said softly, and watched him turn his head against the pillow, close his eyes and sleep as obediently as a child.

Anne was unsure how long she sat at his bedside, but she felt stiff when she finally got to her feet and pressed a kiss softly against the worn cheek. It was a little rough against her lips and suddenly she wanted to cry. In her mind she knew that her father was gone from her, but whilst he had clung to life, she had clung to hope. And soon she would be alone.

Pressing one hand to her lips to steady herself, she made her way to the door. The tower was quiet. It was very late and suddenly she felt weary through to her very bones. She needed to sleep, but she knew that her mind would never rest with the prospect of battle in a mere few hours. The whole Manor was alive with the preparations for warding off the attack.

On impulse she went along the corridor to the chamber that had been her mother's. When Sir Henry Greville had been captured and wounded, Anne had countermanded Gerard Malvoisier's orders and had him taken to a room where she could oversee his nursing. Malvoisier had not dared to say her nay. He had ranted and raged about the Great Hall, smashing the crystal glasses in the grate and breaking the candlesticks for all the world like some rampaging giant, but Henry Greville had stayed in the Tempest Tower and he owed his life to Lady Anne Grafton.

Anne opened the door very quietly. As she had suspected, Muna was sitting by Henry's bed. She had evidently been reading to him from a set of psalters, but the book had slid from her lap when she fell asleep and now her head was resting against the back of the chair and her hand was clasping Henry's. The room had a deceptive air of peace about it.

Henry Greville looked sufficiently like his brother to make Anne's heart flutter once as she looked on his sleeping face, but even as she gazed on him her mind was slipping back to Simon. When he had looked at her she had seen the brilliant, calculating intelligence in the dark depths of his eyes and she had known that here was a dangerous enemy, a foe worthy of the name. She did not wish to have to cross wits with him.

Yet if she was to protect the King's treasure she would have to do just that. It was a thought that terrified her.

Memory was a strange thing, Anne thought, as she retrieved the psalter from the floor and placed it softly on the table so that she should not wake either Muna or Henry. She had not seen Simon Greville in four years and yet she had held fast to her girlhood remembrance of him, only to find that the man he had become was far more formidable and infinitely more attractive. She took one last look at Henry. Would Simon look like that when he was asleep and off his guard? A little longer with him in that room tonight and mayhap she would have found out. She would have tumbled into his bed, given herself to him with no regard for sense or modesty, all principles swept away by that wild tide of memory and emotion that had run between them. She had never experienced such passion. It had shaken her to the core.

She closed the door quietly behind her and stood in the darkened corridor, arms wrapped about her. Though the night was quiet there was expectation in the air, almost as though the very atmosphere trembled. The anticipation of battle, the threat of death, hovering like a shadow… Anne shivered convulsively. It had been the culmination of those fears that had driven her into Simon Greville's arms that night. She had wanted to stay with him and had ached to blot out the nightmare present with the strength and comfort of his arms. Yet such an idea was outrageous, borne of nothing but desperation. They were on opposing sides. They could never be anything other than enemies.

She went back down the stair and stood in a corner of the

courtyard watching the bustle as the soldiers prepared for battle. Malvoisier had placed no guard on the Tempest Tower. It was almost as though he cared nothing for the safety of the Earl or his daughter. Elsewhere, though, his troops were busy. Through the thick veil of snow Anne could see that they swarmed the battlements and manned the towers. There were soldiers with muskets to deter any attackers foolish enough to try to scale the walls. There were pike men with their bayonets and artillery men rolling out the huge barrels of gunpowder. The fires hissed and cracked, illuminating the grim scene. Anne knew that Grafton was well equipped with ordnance. It had been reinforced when Malvoisier had arrived. But that very pile of gunpowder and weaponry could go up in a fireball if once it caught alight. And then they would all be done for.

She shuddered and withdrew within the tower, slamming the heavy oaken door behind her and ramming the bolts into place. The torches hissed in their sconces as the wind whipped along the corridor and up the stone stair. Then there was silence. Anne reminded herself sternly that the Tempest Tower had withstood hundreds of years of warfare, but she was shivering and shivering as though she could not stop. She could hear the subdued tones of John, Edwina and the household women coming from the solar and before she pushed open the door she took a moment to compose herself. They were sitting tightly packed before the fire; when they saw her they turned their faces up to her with a hope that almost broke her heart. Many had husbands, fathers or sons fighting with the garrison.

'All's well, my lady,' Edwina said stoutly. 'Now we can only wait.'

Anne nodded and went back to her father's chamber and sat down again at his bedside. The candle had burned low now and there was the scent of tallow in the air. Lord Grafton's body made scarcely any impression under the pile of bed-clothes, so thin and frail had he become. His breathing seemed a little more tremulous than it had a half-hour before. A solitary tear slid down Anne's cheek and she brushed it away with an impatient hand. The physician had said that her father might recognise her voice, for all that he never showed any sign of knowing her. He had encouraged her to read to him, but tonight Anne had no heart for it. Instead she sat quietly, going over in her mind all that had happened since Gerard Malvoisier had come to Grafton, and she found herself praying fiercely for good to triumph. She felt so torn. She knew she should be praying for Gerard Malvoisier to win the day, but, if he did, then she knew that all hope of justice for Grafton was gone. The tears were drying on her cheeks when finally she slept.

'Madam! Madam!' Rough hands shook her awake. Anne's head ached. She appeared to have fallen asleep with her head resting on her father's linen sheet. His hand was beneath her cheek, parchment thin and cold, damp with her tears. She sat up slowly. Her entire body protested at the movement and she repressed a groan.

'What is it?' She could see the first grey hint of dawn edging the stone casement. 'What has happened? Has the attack begun?'

'Aye, my lady.' Edwina was almost incoherent with anxiety. She pulled on Anne's arm. 'Come, see!'

Anne stumbled across to the window. Her limbs felt stiff and cold. Before she reached the casement she heard the unmistakable boom of the cannon and the high-pitched splintering crack of the mortar striking stone.

'They are breaking down the walls!' Edwina said, her fingers digging into Anne's arm. 'The gate is already gone! Oh, madam…'

Anne leaned against the wall and stared out of the window. It was like a scene from hell. The snow had stopped, but the sky was a menacing pewter grey. The main gate of the Manor hung ragged on its hinges, a gaping hole in the wall beside it where the cannon ball had penetrated. The courtyard was littered with shards of stone. Men were fighting hand to hand with sword and pike, and the bodies of the dead were tumbled in the snow amongst the ashes of the fire.

Then, even as she watched, a cry went up. 'Fire!'

Anne looked down to the base of the tower. Gerard Malvoisier was there. For a moment he looked up and there was a smile on his lips as he struck the light and dropped it so very deliberately to the ground. The gunpowder caught and hissed, and Edwina gave a cry.

'He has fired the tower! He has condemned us to burn alive!'

The explosion shook the old walls and they staggered. The air in the chamber was cold, but it already carried the first hint of smoke. From outside in the courtyard came shouts and the hiss and crackle of flame. Anne spun around.

'We must get everyone out down the water stair. It is the only way!'

Edwina nodded. Her eyes were terrified.

'Madam, your father…'

Anne looked at the still figure on the bed. A cold finger of dread touched her heart. She knew he had already gone. He had died some time in the night and she had been asleep, too tired to notice. She felt beyond wretchedness.

'It is too late.' She spoke through chattering teeth. 'Come away.'

She propelled Edwina out into the corridor where the servants were already milling about like frightened animals. Babies were wailing, women crying. The air was starting to thicken with the smell of smoke and something more dangerous still. Anne recognised it. Brimstone. Malvoisier had used a poisonous mixture of straw and sulphur to burn the tower down.

'John!' She caught John Causton's arm. 'Take Muna and help Lord Henry down the stair. Edwina—' she gripped the nurse's hand '—keep the King's treasure close. Make sure all is safe.'

She herded them down the corridor to the tiny door that led to the water stair. The tower shuddered and groaned as the fire took a grip. Anne could hear it licking up the stairwell now as the tapestries caught alight. Her hand shook a little as she unlocked the door and opened it. A blast of cold air flooded in, fanning the flames.

'Quickly, everyone! Down to the moat!' She ran ahead of them down the stairs. The door at the bottom refused to open.

It had swelled with the damp and stayed obstinately shut until John gave it an almighty kick, and then they were through and standing on the small stone rampart above the water.

'I can't swim!' Edwina said, hanging back, grasping Muna's hand in one of hers and a small child in the other. The press of people behind her was almost sufficient to force her into the water. 'Oh, madam—'

The Parliamentarian soldiers had breached the outer defensive walls and were lined up on the other side of the moat in battle order, rank on rank of men in full armour. The Greville standard blew in the wind. Anne raised her voice to carry above the roar of the fire and crack of musket shot from the courtyard.

'Hold your fire! Help us! We have Sir Henry Greville!'

She saw the captain was Guy Standish and felt a rush of relief as he raised a hand and the musketeers lowered their weapons. Someone was running up with a rough pontoon bridge to lay across the moat. John grabbed the end and wedged it into place. And then the terrified servants were running across to safety, and John and Muna half-carried, half-supported Sir Henry, and the ranks of enemy soldiers fell back to allow through a man on horseback.

It was Simon Greville. His armour was pewter grey, lifted by the Greville colours of scarlet and black. He jumped down from his horse and Anne saw him catch Henry to him for a brief embrace and then he looked up and straight into her eyes. Anne felt her throat catch. The last of the servants had crossed the bridge now and Edwina, still holding fast to the little girl's hand, was beckoning her across. A cold, cold shiver ran down Anne's spine. She turned to look over her shoulder at the Tempest Tower. And then she turned on her heel and ran back up the stair.

The old tower was burning slowly. It was made of solid stone and held the damp of hundreds of years, but the gunpowder had fatally weakened it and now, as the fire took hold, it burned in its death throes.

Anne groped her way along the corridor to her father's chamber. The smoke was thick, catching in her lungs. She was not sure what she was doing, knowing only that she had to return to take a farewell. The desperate rush to help the servants out of the fire had given her no time. She wanted a moment of peace to say goodbye to him.

Anne dropped to her knees beside her father's bed and buried her face in the thick embroidered coverlet. An uncontrollable trembling seized her limbs. That he should have left her now, just at the moment when she needed him so much! She had seen him slip away day by day, his presence growing fainter until now the room was empty of it and she was truly alone. She had hoped against hope that he would regain his strength, even as she had known he would not, and now that hope was finally extinguished. She felt drained of everything but a weary misery.

The smoke was curling more thickly across the floor now. Anne struggled to her feet and bent to press one last kiss on her father's thin cheek. The door of the chamber crashed back on its hinges. Choking black smoke swirled in and filled her lungs, racking her with coughs. She could hear the sound of the fire closer now. Timber crashed in a flurry of flame. Suddenly she knew she had left it too late. She was about to perish with her father, as Malvoisier had intended.

Someone picked her up bodily and pulled her around to face him. Simon Greville. His face was dark and forbidding, streaked with soot, dust and sweat. There was a long sword slash on his arm below the rerebrace. Beneath his helmet his dark hair was plastered to his head. The expression in his eyes burned fiercely.

'What the devil do you think you are doing?' He held her cruelly hard and his voice was cold. 'If you do not come with me now, you will be following your father to the grave more swiftly than you think.'

Anne struggled against the arms that held her, twisting her head to gain one last look at the still figure lying on the bed. Simon swung her up in his arms with insulting ease and carried her towards the door, kicking it open so that it crashed completely from its hinges.

Tears streaked her face, mingling with the soot. The bed hangings were aflame now and in the livid light her father's face was grey. She gave a convulsive sob and turned her face into Simon's neck. Pride and grief warred in her.

'At the least let me go. I can walk!'

'You cannot walk through the flames.' Simon's voice was harsh. 'No, my lady. You and I go over the roof. It is the only way out now.'

He half-carried, half-dragged her through the doorway and into the inferno of the corridor outside. The tapestries were alight, the fire being driven by the fierce draught that sucked up the stone stair. Simon ducked through the flames, pulling her with him, giving her no time to resist. Her lungs were full of smoke and all about her was the roar of the fire. They were up the steps and out on to the roof, and then the icy morning air hit Anne in the face and made her cough all the more. The wind pulled on her hair, blinding her. Sparks flew like fire crackers before her eyes. Beneath her feet the roof was hot.

'Quickly!' Simon's tone was savage. His fierce grip on her arm did not waver. The slates slithered beneath her slippers. With a muttered curse Simon scooped her up into his arms again and picked his way across the sloping roof with the sure-footed skill of a cat. Anne tried not to breathe; she tried to be as light as possible, so afraid was she that the slightest shift in her weight would send them both tumbling over the edge of the curtain wall and into the moat below. They gained the shelter of the far turret and then he was placing her gently on her feet on the outside stair, steadying her with an arm about her waist. He did not seem out of breath or even disturbed, though Anne found shamingly that when she tried to go down the stair into the courtyard, her legs were so weak that she stumbled and almost fell. Immediately Simon's arms were hard about her again as he carried her down the final few steps to the ground below.

There was a massive crack, like the earth splitting apart, and the top of the tower crumbled inwards, taking with it all the floors below to settle in a crushing pile of mortar and rubble and flame. The fire hissed as it hit the snow, black ash settling on the white, and Anne turned her face away from the wreckage. She could hear John's voice and Edwina's as they ran towards her across the snow. Just for now she was too tired and too lonely and too miserable to insist that Simon let her stand on her own feet. Just for now she needed the strength of his arms and the illusory comfort that they offered. She rested her head against his armoured chest, closed her eyes and allowed herself to feel, for a little while at least, safe and protected, and not to think at all.

Simon Greville stood on the battlements of Grafton Manor and surveyed the wreckage of the courtyard below. He felt a savage satisfaction, all the more powerful for the fact that he had taken Grafton from Malvoisier, his hated enemy, with so little loss of life. His men had already removed the bodies of the dead Royalist soldiers. Simon would ensure that they had a proper burial the very next day. Unlike Malvoisier, he did not desecrate the bodies of his enemies, let alone his own men.

He leaned his hands on the stone parapet and took a deep breath of the cleansing night air. Grafton had fallen just as he had predicted, but Malvoisier had escaped. In the end his cowardice had proved such that he had not even had the mettle to stand and fight.

Standish had come to Simon early on to tell him that Malvoisier had fired the tower. At first Simon had thought it merely part of the defensive strategy, knowing that retreating troops would burn a manor down rather than let it fall into the hands of their enemies. Then Standish had said that captured Royalist troops had reported the tower occupied by

Anne and her servants. A blinding fury had seized Simon as he had realised the extent of Malvoisier's malice and duplicity. To fire the Manor, knowing that he would kill innocent Royalist supporters in the process, was beyond condemnation. The man was an outlaw now.

Simon's relief on seeing Anne across the moat had swiftly been superseded by anger and dismay when she turned back into the burning tower. Ignoring Standish's observation that the tower was unsafe, Simon had followed her in. He knew he had to do it. Something deeper than respect, deeper than honour, had prompted him to save her.

Nevertheless, he was furious when he had found her, so furious that he wanted to shake her to within an inch of her life. When he picked her up and felt how slight she was in his arms, the mixture of relief, desire and anger in him had threatened to overwhelm him completely. He had thought of nothing but Anne since the previous night. He had wanted her then with a strength of feeling he had never felt for anything in his life before and he wanted her still.

His body ached in response to the thought. It was no mere lust of a soldier for a woman, any woman. It was a deep need for Anne alone, and it disturbed him greatly. The only way that he could have Anne Grafton with honour would be to marry her. But she was his enemy and would never change her allegiance.

He straightened up. Grafton had fallen to him and its mistress would do the same. Once before he had been promised both. Now it was time to claim them.

Chapter Four

⸙⸙⸙⸙⸙

Lost in a grief that knew neither time nor place, Anne slept through the following day and night, and awoke only in the new dawn, aware that her heart had shattered but that there was also work to be done and her people's future to safeguard. She dragged herself from her bed, listlessly submitted to Edwina's fussing and thin gruel and demanded to know what had happened since the Manor had been taken. There was a purposeful bustle about the place that she could feel even from within her chamber, a vigour that reminded her of a time when her father had been hale and well.

'Lord Greville has already set his men to cleaning and re-pairing the Manor,' Edwina said comfortably, as she brushed Anne's hair. 'They are clearing the granaries and food is being brought in. Fresh bread and meat, madam! No more pickled venison or doused fish! We shall soon have you looking well again.'

Anne stared at her reflection in the burnished mirror. She looked tired and drawn. Black could be such a disfiguring colour. Sometimes it drained the remaining life out of those who wore it.

'My father,' she said, feeling a fresh wave of grief. 'Did they find his body?'

Edwina's brushing stilled and her face turned glum. 'No, my lady. There is nothing left of the Tower. All was burned to the ground.'

'A funeral pyre,' Anne said. She shivered, wrapping her arms about herself. 'And General Malvoisier? Has he been captured?'

'No, my lady,' Edwina said again. Her expression was troubled. 'He ran away and deserted his troops. No one knows where he went.'

Anne stared. 'He ran away? Of all the treacherous, cowardly actions—'

'Aye, my lady.' Edwina's mouth set in a line of powerful disapproval. 'Lord Greville is hunting him. Some of the General's regiment escaped, but most have been taken prisoner and sent to General Cromwell.' She paused. 'He is a good man, is Lord Greville. He could have had them shot, but he spared their lives.'

Anne looked up, her face horrified. 'Shot? I had not even thought of it!' She gasped. 'I should have done something to help them—'

Edwina patted her shoulder. 'You did plenty, madam. You saved us all when General Malvoisier sought to burn us alive! And there was nothing you could have done to help his troops. Whatever one thinks of Lord Greville he is fair and just, and showed clemency to our men.'

Anne smoothed her hands against the material of her black skirts. She knew Edwina was right. Simon could have slaughtered them all and no one could have gainsaid him. He had kept his word to deal fairly with his enemy. All except Malvoisier, who by his actions had put himself outside the law. Anne wondered where he had run. Perhaps he had hurried back to the court at Oxford, to be the first to tell King Charles of the fall of Grafton. That way he could put his own gloss on the story, paint himself in a different role from the coward and traitor that he really was.

'How many Grafton men did we lose?' Anne asked suddenly, twisting around on her seat. 'And Lord Greville— were any of his troops injured? I had not thought you might need me to help nurse them.'

Edwina sighed. 'None of the Grafton men were harmed. There were a few scratches here and there, but nothing that could not be treated. Malvoisier lost fifty or more men, but Lord Greville's casualties were no more than a half-dozen.' Her face puckered. 'I think he feels their loss sharply, though.'

Anne felt a pang of misery to think of the families of those soldiers who had lost their lives. 'And Sir Henry?' she asked. 'I hope his health has not suffered too greatly?'

Edwina smiled and wiped away a surreptitious tear. 'He is like a new man now that he is reunited with his brother. I swear that, for all Lord Greville's stern demeanour, he was moved to the soul to see his brother truly lived.'

'I imagine that he would be,' Anne said. She remembered

the grief and anger she had witnessed in Simon when he had still thought Henry dead. The bond between the brothers was unshakeable.

'Lord Greville has been asking after you, madam,' Edwina said. 'Several times a day he calls to hear of your progress.' She paused. 'He comes himself, madam, rather than send a messenger. He asked that we should tell him immediately you awoke.'

'And did you?' Anne asked. It would be an interesting test of her servants' allegiance, she thought, to see if they had instinctively obeyed Simon's instruction before consulting her.

Edwina looked at her out of the corner of her eye. 'Aye, my lady. I sent a message to him when you awoke this morning. Lord Greville is not a man whose orders one disobeys lightly, for where he asks he might simply take.'

'Yes,' Anne said with feeling.

'He asks that as soon as you are well enough you should call him and he will wait upon you,' Edwina continued. She stood back. 'Shall I call him now, madam?'

'I suppose I must see him,' Anne said. Simon Greville ran Grafton now. He could have summoned her to his presence with the arrogance of a conqueror, but he had not done so. He had offered to wait upon her instead. That had been diplomatic of him, but Anne thought that it meant nothing other than that Simon was treading carefully for the time being. He did not wish to antagonise her. Not yet.

'You know that we are all loyal to you, madam,' Edwina said suddenly, her words tumbling out in a rush. She put the brush down on the table and wrung her hands together. Her face crumpled as though she were about to cry. 'We love you. But with your lord father gone and Grafton fallen to Parliament, we do not know what will happen.' She sniffed. 'All we want is food on the table and peace in your father's hall. We know Lord Greville is your enemy, madam, but we just want peace for Grafton.'

Anne's heart sank. She understood what Edwina was saying. Although they would always give her their love and loyalty, her people wanted no more war. They had suffered dreadfully under Malvoisier's stewardship and the careless cruelty of his soldiers. Simon's arrival promised peace to live and to trade safely, to rebuild their homes and live out their lives without threat of rape and pillage. More appealing still, he would give them protection in a time of uncertainty. But the price was that they would compromise their loyalty to the Royalist cause and now they were torn, loving her, wanting to support her, yet desperately wishing for peace.

She reached out and touched the servant's arm. 'I know, Edwina,' she said. 'I understand. We all want peace at Grafton. We are all very tired of fighting. But I cannot—I will not—abandon my allegiance to the King.'

Edwina straightened her spine. 'No, madam. Of course not. And I won't give the King's treasure away, madam. I swear it! Although I want Lord Greville to bring peace here, I shall not say a word. Not even if they try to torture it out of me!'

'Mercy,' Anne said drily. 'Let us hope it does not come to that.' She sighed. 'I hope we may reunite the King with his treasure soon, without Lord Greville's knowledge.'

'Aye, madam,' Edwina said fervently.

Anne smoothed her skirts. 'You had best go and tell Lord Greville that I will see him now.'

After Edwina went out, she stared dispiritedly at her mirror one last time, then gave a sigh and pushed herself up from the chair. She could hide away for any length of time if she chose, using her bereavement as the excuse. But that was not her way. She could not simply sit here and let Simon Greville take her inheritance, which was what she suspected would happen if she did not make a stand.

She walked slowly along the stone-flagged corridor and through to the solar. Now that the Tempest Tower had been destroyed, she had taken back her old childhood rooms in the main house. There was something about their familiarity that comforted her. Here she had played chequers and draughts with Muna on rainy days, here they had gossiped and read and sewed their needlework, extremely badly in Anne's case. Here they had taken their lessons and studied astronomy and Greek and mathematics until their tutor had given them their freedom and they had run out into the green paddocks to play. Lord Grafton's attempts to give his daughter a boy's education had not always been successful. She had hated mathematics and the law, but she had loved languages and history. And she could fight with a sword and shoot straighter than many men.

The window of the solar looked out across the courtyard over the battlements and now she pressed one hand against the diamond pane and looked out at the green hollows and hills of Oxfordshire beyond. She ached to be out in the fresh air, to gallop over the springy turf, to be free once again. After three months of siege she was restless.

But that was not the only reason that she was pacing the floor. She knew that in a moment she would be face to face with Simon Greville again and the thought made her breath catch and her heart race.

It was impossible to think of him without a shiver along her nerves as she remembered the heat and bliss of being in his arms that night before the battle. It had been madness, but it had been a sweet madness and the memory of it stirred the sensuality in her blood. The feelings still shocked her. She was profoundly afraid now that his presence and his touch would undermine her resolve to fight for Grafton and for the King's cause. That she could never allow.

There was a brisk step in the doorway and then Simon was bowing before her. He was in uniform, the black and scarlet jacket and grey breeches of his own regiment of cavalry. Anne straightened. He looked powerful and far too dangerous. It was a reminder of his status at Grafton as the representative of the victorious Parliamentary forces. Remembering the battle-stained man who had rescued her from her father's chamber, Anne felt her pulse give a little treacherous flip before it steadied again. Their eyes met and she tore her gaze away. Her deceitful body and stubborn heart were telling her she had some kindred feeling for this man, but she had to dismiss such notions now. The future of Grafton was at stake, the very future of the King's cause was at stake, and she could not permit herself to become distracted by the sheer power of Simon's physical presence. He was the conqueror of Grafton and she was going to have to be on her guard to defend herself and her patrimony—and the King's treasure.

'Lady Anne.' Simon's tone was very formal. 'Please permit me to offer my condolences on the loss of your father.'

Anne inclined her head, equally formal. 'Thank you, Lord Greville.'

Edwina, obeying the order implicit in Simon Greville's glance at her, dropped a curtsy and withdrew. As soon as the door was closed, Simon came across to Anne and took her hand in his, drawing her towards the settle. She felt a rush of sensation skitter along her skin and tried to draw back. Her feelings for him were already too complicated. She was too vulnerable. She needed to keep a distance as a protection.

'You look tired, my lady,' Simon said. His dark eyes searched her face. 'You are quite well? I would not wish to add to your distress by discussing matters of business that could wait for a better hour.'

Anne raised her head and looked him straight in the eye. 'Are you then to cause me distress, Lord Greville?' she asked. 'I am sorry to hear it.'

She withdrew her hand firmly from his and moved as far away from him as was possible on the settle. It did not seem far enough, but she resisted the urge to get up and move to the armchair. She folded her hands in her lap.

Simon was looking at her. She found his stillness disturbing. 'It seems inevitable,' he said, 'that discussions about the future of Grafton will not be to your liking, my lady.'

He spoke courteously, but Anne was not deceived. Simon Greville was a hard man and he had a job to do at Grafton. She understood that. The battle for the estate was over, but the battle between them started right here, right now.

She smoothed her skirt with a quick, nervous gesture. 'I see,' she said. 'Then before we quarrel irrevocably, my lord, there is something I must say to you.'

Simon raised his brows. His dark gaze was unnervingly direct. Anne swallowed and looked away.

'I owe you my life,' she said, in a rush. 'I am sorry that I did not make it easy for you to save me.'

Simon smiled, a proper smile that reached his eyes, and made Anne feel very warm all over. 'You did not wish to leave your father,' he said. 'I understand that.'

Anne pressed her hands together hard. 'I hear that his body is unlikely to be found.'

'I believe so. I am very sorry.'

'Then I have a request to make of you, my lord.' Anne knew she sounded grudging. It went against the grain to have to ask him for anything at all. It seemed only to emphasise the fact that he was master of Grafton now—and she was in his power.

'It concerns my father,' she said. 'Despite the fact that I may not bury him, I wish to honour his passing. I am sure that the people of Grafton would wish to pay their respects and therefore I wondered if we might hold a wake for him?'

Simon nodded. 'Of course. I shall arrange it.'

Anne nodded. 'Thank you, Lord Greville. It is more than I might have expected—from an enemy.'

Simon bowed ironically. 'Which brings us neatly to speaking of the future of Grafton, Lady Anne.'

'The future of Grafton lies with me now,' Anne said. A restlessness possessed her. She jumped to her feet, taking a few short, sharp steps away before turning back towards him.

'And to that end, my lord,' she said, 'I need to know your plans. Grafton is my inheritance and I want to know when you will leave here. I understand that General Malvoisier is gone now and his troops dispersed. You have taken control of the armoury. Grafton is no longer a Royalist garrison and as such it can be no military threat to you.'

She stopped, for she could already read her answer in his face. The solicitude was gone now and he was looking hard and unyielding. For a moment there was a silence between them.

'I regret that it is not as simple as that,' Simon said slowly.

Anne stared at him. She had dreaded this. Her only hope had been that with the siege lifted and Malvoisier beaten, Simon's troops would move on from Grafton, leaving her to restore her lands to their former prosperity. Yet even as she had hoped for it with all her heart, her common sense had told her that the Parliamentarians would never let Grafton go now that it had fallen to them. It was too rich a prize.

Simon stood up too and moved across to the fireplace so that he faced her across the room.

'Lady Anne, you must understand,' he said. 'There are several reasons why I cannot leave Grafton Manor.'

'I understand nothing,' Anne said stonily, 'other than that Grafton is mine by right of inheritance and you have already outstayed your welcome here, sir.'

Simon made a slight movement. She could not tell whether he was angry at her outburst or utterly unmoved, for his face was as hard as granite.

'I require,' he said, 'that you agree to sign a document of military submission for Grafton on behalf of the Royalist cause, Lady Anne. After that we may talk of what is to happen next.'

The air between them suddenly crackled with emotion, like a summer storm. Anne clenched her fists at her sides.

'And if I refuse?'

Simon shrugged. 'Rebel commanders are hanged or shot or imprisoned,' he said, 'depending on the clemency or otherwise of the victor.'

'I am no rebel!' Anne spat. 'You are the one who has taken up arms against your anointed King!'

Simon's expression was impassive, but his tone flayed. 'Ah, yes,' he said. 'I forgot. You would rather ally yourself to a man like Gerard Malvoisier who was a Royalist, but held Grafton in an iron grip, and stripped from it all that was good and valuable, who sucked the very life from the place and ground your people beneath his heel. *That* is where your loyalty lies!'

Anne turned away from him in a blind fury. Once again she rested her hand against the cold glass of the casement window, uncurling her fingers against the pane as she tried to keep calm. She looked out across her lands. Although the fire in the Tempest Tower had burned out, the air was still thick with ash and smoke. She could smell it from here. It hung on the cold edge of the wind and mingled with the sprinkling of fresh snow. Simon's men were even now sifting the rubble and Anne shuddered as she watched their figures moving methodically about their work. She knew what they searched for and she prayed wholeheartedly that the fire had been sufficient to consume all the mortal remains of the late Earl of Grafton. She did not want there to be anything left to find.

In some ways the fire that had so brutally destroyed part of her home and her life had left her swept clean too. Her feelings were as empty and hollow as the shell of the house. She could not grieve properly. Instead, she could feel anger.

'You know that I hated Malvoisier,' she said bitterly. 'I admit it freely. He was venal and corrupt and cruel, and I hated the manner in which he was destroying Grafton. All we had to bind us together was the same cause.' She swung round, her face bright with emotion. 'But I am my father's sole heiress, Lord Greville. This may be a civil war, but the Grafton estate is legally mine by right of inheritance, and if you take it from me you will be breaking the law.'

Simon squared his shoulders. 'I have already taken it,' he said. 'Grafton was a military garrison. Therefore it is now mine by right of conquest.'

Anger and outrage ripped through Anne to have her deepest fears confirmed in so callous a manner. 'You cannot do that!' she exclaimed. 'You cannot simply march in and take my land!'

Simon's jaw set hard. 'My men will be staying at Grafton until this land is secure for the Parliament,' he said. There was a thread of steel in his tone now, beneath the silky courtesy of the words, and it made Anne furious to hear it. 'This area is rife with civil disturbance and Grafton will make a fine base for Parliamentarian control. I regret that you have no choice in the matter, my lady.'

Anne turned abruptly away from him. Her head was

aching already. She wanted to sleep. She wanted her father's strength and wisdom to draw upon, but she was alone now. She rubbed her brow hard.

'You cannot *steal* my inheritance like this!' she burst out. 'You have no right!' She looked at him beseechingly. 'Surely once the current threat is past the estate will once more be mine?'

Simon shook his head. 'I took Grafton and it is mine now,' he said. His tone was grim. 'It is forfeit to me and to the Parliament. You have nothing, Lady Anne. No fortune, no estate and no authority here. It is now my decision and that of my commanders as to what happens to you.'

Anne felt a blinding rage. She had struggled so long and so hard, endured the occupation of Grafton by the hated Malvoisier, watched him destroy her lands and bring siege and war to her home, and had lost her father during the fight. She locked her fingers together so tightly that they hurt.

'So you are telling me that Grafton is your property now, Lord Greville?' Her voice shook. 'And so am I?'

'Grafton belongs to the Parliamentarian cause.' Simon sounded so calm that she wanted to scream at him, 'but I shall be petitioning my superior officers to be allowed to rule here. After all, it was once promised to me—and so were you.'

Anne made a gesture of fury. 'I know this "petitioning" for the pretence it is! You have already decided that you have the right to determine Grafton's future and *my* future with it!' She glared at him. 'You hide behind notions of legality. This is intolerable! I am merely exchanging a house under siege for one under occupation! I am a prisoner in my own home!'

Simon did not reply. Anne put her hands briefly to her face. She was blinded by anger. Damn Simon Greville, and damn her too, for thinking that his victory might bring her freedom. She felt a fool.

'I will never accept this,' she said slowly.

Simon pushed away from the fireplace and came towards her slowly. 'I am sorry to hear it.'

Anne's expression was stormy. 'Can you not see that it is out of the question that I would welcome your annexation of this estate?' she demanded. 'I will oppose you to the very end.'

Simon smiled. 'Then we have a battle on our hands, Lady Anne.'

Their gazes locked. Anne could see respect in his eyes, but she could see determination as well, and the strength of a man resolved to win.

'And,' Simon continued softly, 'I fear that the first thing I must tell you is that you are confined to the castle for the present. It is for your own safety as much as for any other reason.'

Anne made a sound of disgust. 'You waste little time in asserting your rule, my lord! I had thought that at the least we should be free to come and go about the estate as we pleased, now that the siege is lifted.'

Simon was shaking his head. 'It is too dangerous,' he said bluntly. 'There are masterless men on the loose, Lady Anne. Malvoisier is an outlaw now; until we hunt him down and capture the remnants of his army, it would be too perilous for anyone to venture far from the castle.' He drove his hands into his pockets. 'Besides, I cannot permit you, of all people, to have your freedom.'

'Because you do not trust my loyalties,' Anne flashed. 'You imagine that I would be running to the King's aid as soon as your back is turned!'

Simon laughed. 'Would you not?' he queried. 'You have just refused to submit Grafton to Parliamentarian control. It would be foolish of me to trust you at all.'

'I hope,' Anne said hotly, 'that the King will send troops from Oxford to retake Grafton—' She broke off, outraged, as Simon laughed again.

'There is not the least likelihood of it,' he said. 'You may as well give up that hope now.'

Anne gritted her teeth. Despite her defiance, she knew deep within that Simon was correct. It simply would not happen. King Charles had had ample opportunity to come to their aid during the months of siege and had not chosen to do so. The tide of the war was turning against the Royalists, slowly but inexorably. King Charles had suffered several military defeats in the region only recently and now General Cromwell had established a battery just outside Faringdon, a mere five miles away. No, Charles was fighting for his kingdom now, fighting for survival, and Grafton was small and insignificant in such a scheme. Anne knew that he would sacrifice her and the estate for the greater cause. And, although it broke her heart, she understood why. She was on her own now.

She turned aside so that Simon would not see the misery she could not hide.

'Well, you will not find Gerard Malvoisier,' she said, more to conceal her feelings than for any other reason. 'He is probably back in Oxford by now, coward that he is.'

Simon took a swift step towards her and caught her by the arm, swinging her around to face him.

'Did Malvoisier tell you his plans for escape?' he demanded. His eyes were narrowed intently on her face.

'Of course not!' Anne snapped. 'He would never confide in me. He would have killed me with no compunction when he fired the Tower. That was the measure of his regard for me!'

Simon's gaze searched her face for a moment and then he nodded. He dropped her arm and turned away, and she absentmindedly rubbed the place where he had held her. His grip had hurt.

She watched as he strode back across to the fireplace, his boots ringing on the stone floor. He was very much in command of the situation and Anne felt her frustration rising. She was also cursing her unwary tongue. She had spoken without thinking, but she was going to have to be a great deal more discreet than that if she wished to keep all her secrets from Simon Greville. He was too quick and his intelligence too sharp. There were matters she simply could not give away. There was no one else left who could take the King's commission at Grafton and the whole future course of the war could depend upon her keeping the King's treasure safe.

'I was merely guessing about Malvoisier,' she said, her cool tone belying the nervous beating of her heart as Simon turned back to look at her. 'Since he deserted us so swiftly,

I imagine that he will wish to get safely to Oxford and put his case to the King, before his Majesty hears a less flattering version of his cowardice from another source.'

Simon smiled grimly. 'From you, perhaps, my lady? I can imagine your opinion of his actions.'

'I shall certainly write to the King if I am permitted to do so.' Anne inclined her head in ironic obedience. 'I would wish to reassure my godfather that I am safe and well. I trust that that will be acceptable to you?'

'Of course,' Simon said.

'If I permit you to read my correspondence first?'

'Of course,' Simon said again, with a smoothness that made Anne want to stamp her foot in frustration. 'I regret that I must peruse all the letters you write and those you receive as well.'

'I doubt that you regret it at all!' Anne snapped. For a moment she stared angrily at him and he looked steadily back at her. The frustration bubbled up inside her again and she turned on her heel and marched across the chamber, as far away from Simon as she could get. Suddenly the rooms that had been hers all her life felt intolerably small and oppressive. There was a prickle of tears in her throat. Her family had been at Grafton for hundreds of years and now it was all but lost to them. If only there was a way in which she could throw Simon and his men out! But without military force she was powerless. She could refuse to sign Grafton away, but it was a hollow victory. The King could not come to her aid. She doubted that there was a single Royalist commander who would think Grafton worth fighting for now.

'So,' she said, 'what is to become of me, Lord Greville? You have said that you would petition your commanders to be permitted to keep Grafton. Am I then to be married off to some convenient supporter of your cause to get me out of the way?'

'No,' Simon said, 'I will take Grafton and I will take you too.'

The hot colour ran under Anne's skin at his words. She remembered the way that he had held her that night in his quarters. His desire for her had been plain then and it had called forth an echo of a response from her. It was impossible. She ought to hate him. A part of her *did* hate him for what he was doing, but a deeper, undeniable part wanted him too. It always had done. She could recognise that now. From the very first, when he had come to Grafton to court her, she had been his.

She crushed down the frightening thought and stood straight with defiance.

'Never!'

Simon came towards her slowly. His tread was measured, inexorable, across the stone floor. Anne found herself retreating instinctively until she was standing with her back to the window.

'I would not expect you to fall into my arms, my lady,' Simon said softly. 'A woman who will fight for her freedom by turning my own sword against me will not let me take her patrimony—or her person—without a struggle.'

Anne tilted her chin up proudly. 'I give you fair warning, my lord. I shall do everything I can to be rid of you.'

The lines at the corners of Simon's eyes deepened as he

smiled. A cool shiver ran along Anne's skin to see it. She knew she had just thrown down a challenge—and he had taken it up.

'I believe you, madam,' he said. 'I am on my guard.' He took a step closer, trapping Anne within the stone window embrasure. She backed away, feeling her gown brush the edge of the window seat. There was nowhere to run to. She felt her breath catch.

'Stand back, my lord.' Her voice sounded too weak and in response Simon moved in even closer. She could feel the press of his thigh against hers through the material of her skirts. Her breasts brushed his chest and an arrow of pure sensation pierced her, turning her inside molten.

'How far would you go to be rid of me?' Simon's voice was relentless. 'Would you seek my life?'

'Why should I not?' Anne demanded, a little breathlessly. She wanted to escape. At such close quarters his physical presence overwhelmed her. The way that he looked at her was deeply disturbing.

'You are my enemy,' she said, pressing her palms against the rough stone of the wall behind her in an effort to be calm. 'Nothing can ever change that now.'

'Need we be enemies?' Simon bent closer. She could feel his breath stir the tendrils of hair at her neck, causing the quivers of feeling to run along her nerves. Her whole body felt sensitive. The goose flesh brushed her skin. Her legs were trembling. She felt hot and cold, light-headed and weak.

'I saved your life,' Simon continued. 'You owe me something for that.'

'You gave me my life and now you take away my future,' Anne said, as coldly as she could. 'I owe you nothing.'

She saw the flare of heat in his eyes. 'We were not always enemies,' he said. 'When I came to Grafton courting you—'

'That was years ago,' Anne snapped. She tried desperately not to think of how sweet the memory had been. 'Everything is different now.'

'And yet that night when you came to my quarters,' Simon said, 'there was a moment when I held you in my arms and I swear you saw me as more than an enemy then…'

A pulse beat in Anne's throat. 'That was…' Her voice trailed away. Her mouth was dry. The memories danced before her eyes. It had been terrifying yet deeply, absolutely right to be held in Simon's arms like that. It had felt right—but it was wrong.

'It was the night before battle,' she said. 'You wanted a woman, any woman, and I was afraid and sought comfort—'

'Not so.' She felt the instinctive denial in him and it shook her because she knew he spoke the truth. He was so close now that she could smell the muskiness of his skin, the scent of laundered cloth, and the tang of fresh air and leather. It made her head spin.

'I wanted you, Anne of Grafton,' he said. 'I still do. And you wanted me. There is more between us than enmity and there always has been.'

'No!' Anne said. She folded her arms about her for protection, standing still and stiff before him.

'You are lying,' Simon said drily, and she knew that he was right.

He stepped back at last and Anne was free to breathe again. 'Circumstances make me master of Grafton now,' he said, 'and none will blame me when I take both the Manor and its mistress as my own.'

The outrage burned hot colour into Anne's face. 'Hell will freeze over first!' she snapped.

A smile tugged the corners of Simon's mouth. 'We shall see.'

'I scarce know whether you are proposing marriage or to make me your mistress,' Anne said, 'but be assured that I will not legitimise your theft of Grafton by consenting to a marriage between us!'

Simon laughed. His dark eyes were bright with challenge. 'Then will you consent to be my mistress?'

Anne gave him a look of searing scorn. 'There is even less likelihood of that.' She drew a deep breath. 'Your arrogance is astonishing, Lord Greville. If our business is complete, then I will bid you good day.'

Simon shook his head. 'It is not complete.' He drove his hands into his pockets and his tone changed completely.

'There is one other thing that I require from you,' he said. 'I want to know about the King's treasure.'

Chapter Five

Simon had given her no warning and Anne knew it was deliberate. He had undermined her defences and then he had sprung the surprise upon her. He had wanted to see how she would react, had wanted her to give herself away. He was a ruthless man and what made him even more dangerous was that his ruthlessness was not brutal and open like Gerard Malvoisier's, but clever and subtle and merciless. One mistake and he would pounce. He was watching her now, studying her response to his words. Anne knew that there was not the slightest chance that he would be fooled by protestations of ignorance on her part. He was not the sort of man to believe that women could play no part in affairs of state. He would not overlook the possibility that her father had confided his plans and his secrets in her.

Anne closed her eyes briefly and opened them again. Her father's words pounded in her head. *'Hold the treasure safe. Keep the secret. Tell no one. Trust no one…'*

'Well, my lady?' Simon asked, with deceptive gentleness.

'I fear,' Anne said, 'that I can tell you nothing at all about the King's treasure.'

For the life of her, she could not prevent a slight change in her voice and she knew that Simon had heard it too. He raised a quizzical brow.

'You can tell me nothing or you *will* tell me nothing?'

Anne was silent.

Simon sat down on the corner of the desk and swung one booted foot casually. His gaze was watchful.

'Let me tell you a tale,' he said slowly, 'and then you will have one chance to tell me whether it is true or not.'

Anne sank down into the chair. She kept her gaze lowered, but she was aware that she had no protection from the penetrating intelligence of his gaze.

'A week before Gerard Malvoisier came to Grafton, in November of last year, we received reports that King Charles was awaiting the arrival from Bristol of a fortune to swell his coffers,' Simon said. 'The cache was en route to Royalist headquarters in Oxford from supporters in the West Country. We immediately set out to intercept it. We came upon the King's troops close to Grafton, but they had no treasure with them.'

He looked at her. Anne kept her face quite expressionless. The story was very familiar to her.

'They fought like the very devil,' Simon said. 'It seemed to me that none wanted to be captured alive and be made to tell the tale of the whereabouts of the treasure.'

He paused. Anne avoided his eyes.

'Five men were killed and the rest escaped that day,'

Simon continued. 'We could not be certain, but we believed that when the troops first became aware of our approach a small party broke away and came to Grafton and entrusted the treasure to your father.'

He stopped. And waited. Anne did not speak.

Simon sighed. 'I believe that your father told you of the treasure when he knew that he was dying,' he said, 'and that you, Lady Anne, and your most trusted servants, are the only ones who now know its whereabouts.'

A silence fell over the room.

Anne pressed her hands together hard. She felt hot and disturbed. This, she knew, was only the start. Simon was shrewd and relentless and he would question her and question her until she made a mistake and he had the answer he sought. He was no Malvoisier, to torture the truth from his prisoner, but in some ways he was more dangerous, for he missed nothing and he would not let her go until she told him all she knew. And in the meantime she had somehow to restore his treasure to the King and preserve the lives of those innocents caught up in the story.

The silence was becoming heavy. 'Do you deny it?' Simon asked gently.

'I cannot help you,' Anne repeated. She could feel her fingers clenching on the arms of the chair and forced herself to relax them. He could ask and she could refuse and they could continue playing the game for as long as it took. Except that she was very afraid that sooner or later he would catch her out.

Simon got to his feet. 'I will give you a few days to think

on it,' he said, and Anne shivered to hear the threat implicit in his words. 'If you remember anything that might be of use…' He let the sentence hang.

There was a stiff silence.

'My memory,' Anne said, 'is unlikely to improve in the near future.'

'Then your situation is also unlikely to change,' Simon said. He shook his head. 'Come, Lady Anne, pray be practical. What can you achieve by opposing me? You are my prisoner and would fare better if you surrender your secrets rather than resist me.'

Anne's lips tightened. 'There is nothing to tell.'

'I believe that there is,' Simon said. 'Should you recover your memory, you will always find me happy to speak with you, madam.'

He walked over to the door. 'I shall be watching you,' he added. 'I have the strangest feeling, my lady, that you know far more than you divulge. We both know that King Charles trusted your father, and in his turn your father would, I am sure, have the good sense to confide his secrets to you rather than to Gerard Malvoisier.' Simon paused. 'I would give much to know those secrets.'

Anne turned her face away and did not answer. Her nerves were stretched to the limit.

'I want three things here at Grafton,' Simon said. 'I want the estate, I want the King's treasure and I want you, Lady Anne. And I intend to gain all three.' He closed the door gently behind him and Anne heard the key turn quietly but inexorably in the lock.

* * *

That afternoon, Anne, Edwina and Muna watched from the window as Simon Greville's men turned Grafton upside down in their hunt for the King's treasure. Byres, barns, storerooms... None was left untouched. The church was searched whilst the priest threw his hands in the air and berated them for their sacrilegious ways. In the kitchens the cook had a tantrum and threw flour over the soldiers when they broke some crockery. In the stables one of the horses bit them.

The troops were thorough. And within ten minutes they were filthy as well.

Muna pressed her hand to her mouth and giggled as the soldiers emerged from the stables festooned in hay, dirty, sweaty and bad-tempered.

'At least Lord Greville does not send his men to do the jobs he would not do himself,' Edwina said, as Simon came out into the courtyard with Guy Standish. 'Some commanders would not get their hands dirty.'

Anne thought that Simon looked worse than dirty. 'That uniform was clean this morning,' she said, unable to keep a quiver of amusement from her voice. 'The laundry will be kept busy.'

'And to think,' Edwina said, with a sideways look at her, 'that you could have spared him the trouble, madam.'

Anne glanced towards the door. She knew there was a sentry on the other side. Not only was she locked in, but she was guarded as well. Simon was making his point with very little subtlety.

'Hush,' she said. 'Someone might hear you.'

Edwina dug her in the ribs. 'You must agree, madam,' she whispered, 'that Lord Greville is a fine figure of a man.'

'Hmm,' Anne said. She had already noticed for herself, but she was certainly not going to tell her maid. In the weak February sunshine, Simon's hair gleamed conker brown. He was laughing at something that Standish was saying and picking the strands of straw off his uniform. It gave her a small pang to see him so at ease. It was like looking at a different man. It reminded her of the brief time that they had spent together all those years before, hunting, hawking, dancing... Once again the memories stirred, disturbing her.

'Such good humour,' Edwina said slyly. 'Such an attractive man, madam.'

'Such nonsense,' Anne said shortly. 'You forget, Edwina, that Lord Greville is no more than a renegade soldier who betrays the King.'

She was about to turn away from the window when Simon looked up and raised a hand to her in salute. He gave her a brilliant smile, one that conceded rueful defeat. There was so much feeling in it that before she could help herself, Anne felt an answering smile twitch her lips. She pulled herself together hastily.

Simon turned, exchanged a quick word with Standish, and took the castle steps two at a time.

'Here he comes,' Edwina said.

'I hope not,' Anne said. 'Not dressed like that.' Nevertheless her heart had started to race.

A moment later there was a knock at the door and the sentry ushered Simon into the room.

'You are somewhat dishevelled, my lord, to come calling on a lady,' Anne said coldly, looking down her nose at him. He did not actually smell of the stables, but there was no harm in implying he did. Since their meeting that morning she had pondered long and hard on the best way to thwart him, both in his plan to take Grafton and in his desire to discover the King's treasure. She had eventually concluded that it was best to take refuge in the fact that he held her imprisoned; the less she saw of him the better. She would keep her own counsel and keep her distance until the King's treasure was safe. That was of paramount importance. Only when the treasure was off her hands would it be time to fight for her patrimony.

Simon did not seem remotely discomfited by her coldness. He laughed. 'I beg your pardon, madam,' he said. 'I came directly to tell you that our search is concluded for now.'

'Ah.' Anne fidgeted a little with the needlework she had left on the table. She could feel Edwina watching her with bright, speculative eyes. It put her even more on edge in Simon's presence.

'We found nothing,' Simon added.

Anne felt a surge of amusement. 'No? I am sorry,' she said insincerely. 'But I did warn you, my lord, that your travail would be in vain.'

'You did,' Simon agreed. 'I regret that you were proved correct.' He straightened up. 'However, we have not yet searched your chamber.' He looked around at the wooden box chests and the carved oak dresser that had been a part of Anne's mother's dowry. 'With your permission, my lady.'

Anne's amusement fled. 'You do not have my permission, Lord Greville. It would be an impertinence.'

Simon looked unconcerned. 'Then without your permission, madam. Standish, Jackson… Search my lady's chambers.' He shot Anne another look. 'Gently, mind.'

Muna came across and put a comforting hand on her arm, but Anne stood stiff with outrage as Simon's men emptied the chests and the drawers, scoured under the bed and peered into the garderobe. She was very aware of Simon, who made no effort to help this time, but merely stood watching her. She knew he was measuring her reactions to this invasion, waiting to see if she would intervene, almost willing her to lose her temper and to give something away. She gritted her teeth and kept very still as her mother's jewellery was tumbled unceremoniously on to the bed and her underclothes scattered for all to see. She knew that they would find nothing and it gave her some comfort and the strength to keep quiet as the solders picked over her possessions. Simon Greville was defeated for now, but she knew it was the barely the beginning of their battle.

One of the soldiers gave an exclamation and grabbed a fine pearl necklace from the jewel box, holding it up to the light.

'That was my mother's,' Anne snapped. 'It is *not* the King's treasure.' She swung around on Simon. 'Surely you do not mean to take away my own jewellery, my lord? Or are you so much a brigand that you will steal it on the pretence that it might not be mine?'

Simon raised a brow. 'I have only your word that these jewels do indeed belong to you, Lady Anne. They might well be part of a hoard intended for the King. In fact, I am shocked that you have not already donated them to his cause. Such reluctance shows a certain lack of loyalty.'

'Do not presume to lecture me of loyalty,' Anne retorted. She knew that he was deliberately goading her, but she could not seem to help herself. Her temper was in shreds whenever Simon was near her.

'I have already done my part,' she snapped. 'The King knows my loyalty is unquestioned—' She broke off as she realised that he had provoked her to within a breath of indiscretion.

Simon's gaze was very bright. 'Have you, indeed? I would dearly love to hear more of how you have served your King.'

'I dare say,' Anne said. She turned away, schooling herself to calm again. 'Is that all, my lord?'

Simon cast a swift glance about the chamber. 'For now,' he said.

He signalled to the soldiers and went out, and Edwina gave a gusty sigh as the door closed behind them. 'He'll find out, ma'am,' she prophesied. 'You mark my words. He is too shrewd.'

'No, he will not,' Anne said. She tried to calm her breathing. Her hands were shaking a little. It was all Simon Greville's fault. She found it impossible to be indifferent to him.

She joined Muna at the bedside. Her cousin had already started systematically to fold the tumbled clothes and replace them in the chests. Now she looked up and her gaze was troubled.

'Do you truly believe Lord Greville will not guess the truth, Nan?'

Anne paused, her hands full of linen. 'He will never guess,' she maintained stalwartly. 'He is looking in all the wrong places and for all the wrong things.' She smiled. 'Lord Greville thinks that treasure is nothing more than gold or silver. He does not realise that sometimes the things men value are worth far more than money. He has already seen the King's treasure. He merely does not know it.'

It was late that evening when Simon Greville went to speak with his brother. Henry had been so weakened by exhaustion and loss of blood that as soon as Grafton had been secured he had been put back to bed, much to his disgust. It had been a whole day before Simon had been able to snatch some time with him alone and hear from him at first hand the detail of his capture and imprisonment. What Henry had told him had hardened his already murderous resolve to capture Gerard Malvoisier. He had already started the slow process of searching the surrounding countryside for the Royalist general. His spies told him that Malvoisier had not run back to King Charles at Oxford, nor had he headed south to join the Royalist strongholds in the West Country. That meant that he was still at large and probably close by. And there had to be a reason. It might simply be that Malvoisier dared not show his face in Oxford when he had betrayed the Royalist cause by running away at Grafton, but Simon doubted that this was all there was to it. He suspected that Gerard Malvoisier had a stronger reason for remaining in the vicinity of Grafton and he suspected that it was something to do with the King's treasure.

Simon was still pondering where the treasure might be when he knocked on the door of Henry's chamber and his brother's voice bade him enter. Henry had sent him a message earlier in the day, asking to speak with him urgently and apologising for being unable to come to him. Simon had been curious as to the pressing nature of his brother's information. He had thought that Henry had told him all he could about Malvoisier and the siege of Grafton.

He went in to find Muna sitting at his brother's bedside. The two were deep in conversation. Henry was laughing at something the girl was saying and Muna was leaning towards him, her face alight with more animation than Simon had ever seen in her. He had thought before that Anne was the one with fire and spirit. Now he began to see what his brother might have found in Anne's cousin. She had a warmth and gentleness that were very appealing.

When she saw him, Muna stood up at once and the happy light died from her face. She slipped away with only a shy word of greeting. Simon sighed. It seemed that in his brother's company Muna could forget that they were on opposite sides, but that he, as conqueror of Grafton, was the personification of that very conflict. There were plenty of others in the household who avoided him too. Their Royalist sympathies could not be overturned. All he could expect from them was a wary respect, and that would have to be earned. He knew this was a difficult time for them as one man's rule gave way to another, enemy occupation. They had seen at first hand Malvoisier's depredations and he had purported to be their ally. Perhaps they were afraid of what the new order would bring and it would be a long time before they came to trust him.

He took the chair by Henry's bed that Muna had so recently vacated. There was a book of love poetry on the table beside the bed and he picked it up, turning it over in his hands. He remembered that Henry had had some pretensions to be a poet himself and that he had once caustically suggested that his brother was on the wrong side; it was the cavaliers who penned sonnets between battles.

'Mistress Grafton is devoted to your comfort,' he observed, settling down with a heartfelt sigh. 'I find her here every time I visit you.'

Henry blushed, looking suddenly very youthful. He had Simon's dark good looks, but they were softer on him, and despite all he had experienced he had not acquired the hard edge that soldiering had given his brother.

'She is an angel,' he said. 'I owe her much.'

Simon raised his brows. 'Enough to make you forget that she is a Royalist?'

Henry grimaced. He turned his head on the pillow so that he could look Simon straight in the eyes. 'We do not forget it, Simon. Simply, we do not speak of it.'

Simon did not reply at once. He was remembering the split from their father. In some ways it was different, but he understood how such a huge matter could lie submerged between Henry and Muna. They knew that once either of them raised the subject of their opposing loyalties they could never ignore it again. It would tear apart the tentative bonds between them and they could never go back. They were cherishing this first, tender revelation of love for as long as they could, both knowing that one day, inevitably, they would be forced to choose between their cause and their love. It reminded him of his youthful feelings for Anne and for a moment he felt a strange pang of loss. He knew it could never be like that for them again.

'I hear that you owe Mistress Grafton your life,' Simon said heavily. 'Did she not nurse you through the worst of your fever? Such an obligation places a burden of gratitude on a man and much besides.'

Henry nodded. He was plucking at his coverlet a little nervously and avoiding his brother's eyes now. There was a flush along his cheekbones that Simon thought might be a recurrence of that very fever or else a sign of something else amiss. As a child Henry had often put off telling him the worst until the last moment, whether it was a nursery escapade or something more serious that would incur their father's wrath. Then it was inevitably Simon who would take the rap for him.

'So,' he said deliberately, 'what was it that you wished to tell me? You said that it was an urgent matter.'

'Yes,' Henry said. He stopped. 'I asked you to come for that very reason—the burden of gratitude—' He stopped again and started again. 'Devil take it, I am as nervous as a schoolboy,' he said ruefully. Suddenly he looked up and met Simon's eyes directly. 'There is something I have not told you,' he said, 'and I feel I must. But it is not to do with Muna. It concerns Lady Anne.'

Simon waited.

'It is not Muna who saved my life,' Henry said in a rush. 'At least it was not in the first instance. It was Lady Anne who saved me from Malvoisier's vengeance.'

Simon frowned. 'I thought that—' He stopped. Henry was shaking his head. His look was almost pleading and there was a feverish brightness in his dark eyes.

'I understand what you have to do here at Grafton, Simon,' Henry said rapidly. 'Believe me, I understand better than most. You must secure the Manor for our cause and you must find the King's treasure. I know that makes you Lady Anne's enemy. But…' He paused. 'You should also know that were it not for her Malvoisier would have killed me.'

Simon felt a cold rush of hatred through his veins. 'Tell me,' he said softly.

Henry closed his eyes wearily and opened them again. 'Lady Anne saved me from branding,' he said simply.

Simon stared, a feeling of sick revulsion in his gut. 'Branding? Malvoisier sought to *brand* you? Burn you in the fire?'

'Aye. He wanted to mark me with his emblem. He boasted that he would show everyone the Parliament's man, subjugated like a slave.'

Simon gripped his hands together so hard that the knuckles showed white. 'Tell me what happened,' he said again.

Henry shifted on the bed. He looked young and tired. Simon was forcibly reminded that he was only nineteen years old. The careless youth who had set out with him from Harington eighteen months before had never thought that war would bring him to this. In contrast Simon felt old and cynical and worn with the horror of it all. All his life he had protected Henry, but, when this had befallen him, he had not been there.

'The night that I was taken prisoner, Malvoisier had me dragged from jail and taken to the Great Hall,' Henry said. His dark gaze was fixed on the red heart of the fire where it glowed in the grate. Simon suspected, however, that it was another fire he was seeing, one that had scarred him to the soul.

'Malvoisier was drunk and jubilant that he had fooled you into making a declaration to attack. The place was as hot as hell and full of the fumes of drink and smoke. Malvoisier paraded me before his men and their whores and then decided to have some sport with me.'

Henry closed his eyes briefly and swallowed hard. 'It was not pleasant. I was bound hand and foot and could not escape the lash. I knew they wished to humiliate me.' His shoulders moved beneath his shirt as though he could still feel the bite of the whip on his flesh. 'Then, as I said, they took a brand from the fire.'

Simon moved uncontrollably. 'Of all the sickening and brutal things—'

'They were frenzied with excitement and drink and lust,' Henry said. 'Malvoisier more than most. He kicked me as I was lying there at his feet. He was ablaze with revenge.' Henry shook his head sharply. 'I knew then that I would likely not survive. I lay there and looked at him for what seemed for ever. He had the brand in his hand and he was smiling. Then he leaned forward, so close that I could feel the heat against my cheek.'

Henry looked up and Simon saw the fierce light of memory in his eyes.

'I closed my eyes then. It was the only defence I had.' He blinked rapidly. 'But then *she* came. Lady Anne. Every sense I had was screaming aloud as I waited for the brand to touch. I remember feeling the cold rush of air as the door opened and then I heard the sound of her footsteps on the stone floor. The feeling in the room changed then. It is hard to describe, but I remember it so well. Everyone seemed to be holding their breath.'

Henry stopped and swallowed convulsively. 'Lady Anne's voice was so sharp it cut almost like the whip itself. She said, "What in God's name do you do here?" and I swear that when Malvoisier saw her he seemed to shrink in stature like a slug shrivelling before the salt.'

Simon's jaw hardened. He remembered the vulnerability that he had seen in Anne the night she had come to him to tell him that Henry was safe and to bargain for Grafton. She had not told him that his brother was alive only because of her courage. Everyone thought her invulnerable, but he knew that she was not. He knew she would have been terrified. Yet she had done that for Henry, at great personal risk. He had not been there to help his brother, but Anne had.

Simon felt a wash of anger and protectiveness so fierce that it shocked him.

'What happened then?' he said. His voice was grim.

'There was a long silence,' Henry said. 'No man dared speak. Then Malvoisier started to shout and bluster and smash the glasses, but for all his violence I knew that I was safe. I felt it. Something had changed.' He swallowed again. 'Lady Anne gave the instructions for me to be taken to her rooms and my injuries tended. Malvoisier was shouting that I should be taken back to the dungeons, but she countermanded his orders and he did not dare gainsay her.'

Simon found that he was clenching his fists so tightly they ached. He released them slowly and felt the tension drain from him. Anne, alone and unprotected, fighting every step of the way for Henry and for her home and her people as well as herself... He felt his heart wrench with an emotion he did not recognise.

'I am deep in her debt,' he said gruffly. 'She never told me.'

'She would not tell you herself,' Henry said. 'I doubt she would ever speak of it.'

'No,' Simon said. 'I do not suppose she would.' He looked at his brother. 'Why did *you* not tell me this when we first met, Henry?'

The bright colour mantled Henry's face again. 'I was ashamed,' he said simply. 'I was powerless and she...' he sighed '...she had no one to protect her and yet she saved me.'

Simon nodded. It went against the natural order of things. He felt the guilt stir within him. Anne Grafton was a tigress for those she cared for. She would risk everything for them and for justice. It seemed the cruellest of ironies that she had no one to defend her and he was the man set on taking all she held dear away from her.

Henry looked at him very directly. 'So, although I understand what you must do here at Grafton, Simon,' he said, 'I beg you not to ask of me anything that would hurt Lady

Anne, for then I would have to refuse you. I would go further—' he swallowed convulsively '—and ask that you would not hurt her. You owe her too much.'

A smile curved Simon's lips. 'Your loyalty is torn,' he observed. 'I am sorry for it.'

Henry shrugged. 'You have my loyalty, Simon. You always have and you always will. I am the Parliament's man and I am sworn to support you. But when it comes to Grafton I cannot help you.'

Simon rubbed his brow. He could understand Henry's difficulties well enough when they echoed his own. He was the one who had taken Grafton from Anne. He owed her his brother's life and he had repaid her with nothing but misery.

'I respect your feelings,' he said. 'God knows, I owe Lady Anne a great debt.' He sighed. 'But I will not give Grafton back to her. Even if I wanted to, Cromwell and Fairfax would never agree.'

Henry looked troubled. 'Is that certain?'

Simon nodded. 'Grafton is too rich a prize and too strategically important. Now that it has fallen to Parliament, they will not wish to make a gift of it back to the Royalists.'

Henry frowned. 'And Lady Anne herself? She is to be dispossessed and left with...what?'

Simon shifted in the chair. 'I will wed Lady Anne. I intend to take the estate for the Parliament cause and its mistress—for myself.'

Henry made a choking noise, part-laugh, part-disbelief. 'Through guilt, Simon, for taking her birthright?'

Simon shook his head. 'Once before I was promised Grafton. I made no secret of the fact then that I wished to marry Lady Anne.' He paused. 'I want her in my bed. If I wed her, I get all that I desire.'

He rested his head against the wooden back of the chair and closed his eyes. His body was tired. He wanted to sleep, but these days his dreams were haunted, not by images of battle and slaughter, but by Anne Grafton. He had not stopped thinking of her since that night she had come to his quarters. He could not. He wanted her with a desire so acute that he tossed and turned in restless slumber. He wanted her and he was going to take her.

There was a silence between them, heavy with unspoken thoughts. Then Henry shifted a little.

'You know that Lady Anne will never accept you now, Simon. It was different before. Now she holds fast to her loyalty to the King. She will never compromise her allegiance through marriage to a Parliamentarian.'

'I know,' Simon said. A reminiscent smile curled his lips. He quoted wryly, 'Hell will freeze over before she legitimises my theft of Grafton by agreeing to marry me.' His smile died. 'Nevertheless, I will have her.'

'Would you force a match if the lady was not willing, Simon?'

There was a long pause. Simon scuffed the wooden floor with his dusty boots. Would he force Anne to marry him? He was not a man who had ever had to force anything from a woman that she was not prepared to give freely. And yet Anne Grafton was enough to drive all sanity from his mind.

He was accustomed to making decisions based on reason, not emotion. Anne had changed all that.

'Yes,' he said softly. 'I would.'

There was a sentry yawning outside Anne's doorway, but he snapped to attention quickly enough when his commander appeared. Simon dismissed him to the guardroom for ten minutes. A line of light showed beneath the door and from within came the murmur of voices. Simon raised his hand and knocked softly.

It was Edwina who answered and her brows shot up into her lace cap when she saw who it was.

'My lord!' She sounded scandalised. 'Lady Anne is about to retire. Surely this can wait until the morning?'

'I require no more than a brief word,' Simon said. He opened the door wider. 'If you please.'

The maid shot him a distrustful look, but she stepped out into the corridor, folding her arms and taking up a seat on the wooden bench outside as though prepared to sit there for the duration of the war. Simon smiled at her, received a threatening scowl in return, went in and closed the door softly behind him.

Anne was sitting with a book in her lap, but she set it aside and rose to her feet as he came in. She wore no cap and the candlelight gleamed on the midnight black of her hair, making it look rich and dark, darker than the mourning gown that she was wearing. Simon itched to touch it, to loosen it and bury his face in its silken strands. Memories stirred; he had held her in his arms, kissed her, nearly—so very near-

ly—made love to her. He felt his body tighten in response
to that remembered passion.

'Good evening, my lord,' Anne said, and her coolness
was in stark contrast to the fire that threatened to consume
him. 'Is it your habit to call on ladies in their chambers so
late at night?'

Simon cleared his throat. 'Never before I met you, Lady
Anne,' he said.

A faint smile touched Anne's lips. 'So what urgent
business can this be, that it could not wait until the morrow?'

Simon hesitated a moment. Truth to tell, he was not
entirely sure. He only knew that, after he had spoken to
Henry, he had to see Anne immediately. He wanted to thank
her. He was obliged to, for he was deeply in her debt. But
he also wanted to know how she had felt about the confrontation with Malvoisier.

'I have been with Henry,' he said slowly, 'and I needed
to speak with you at once.'

A flicker of surprise touched her eyes. 'Is it to do with
Muna?'

Simon was momentarily distracted. He had not thought
how it would be for her with a younger cousin to care for as
well as her own interests to protect, but now he suddenly understood her fears. Muna was only eighteen and she had been
the Earl of Grafton's ward. No doubt Anne felt the respon-
sibility of her cousin's future keenly. And no doubt she was
as aware as he of the conflict in Henry and Muna's loyalties.

'At the least you may have no fear of Henry's intentions,'
he said. 'I suspect that they are entirely honourable.'

Anne frowned slightly. 'I am not sure that that reassures me, my lord. Henry is not a good match for my cousin. He is a younger son and a Parliamentarian to boot. I cannot approve and I will not give my consent.'

Simon laughed. 'Henry is a Greville,' he said. 'He may be young, but he knows his own mind. If you oppose him, he will take what he wants anyway.'

Their eyes met and locked and then Anne glanced ostentatiously away at the hours marked on the candle. 'Was that all you came here to say, my lord?' Her voice was cold. 'To tell me that, like you, your brother is a pirate who will simply walk in and take whatever he wishes?'

'No,' Simon said. He took a deep breath. 'I did not come to speak of that. I came to thank you. It seems I am in your debt.'

Anne moved away from him with a soft swish of black silk. 'How so?' She still sounded cold.

'On the night that you came to me in my quarters,' Simon said slowly, 'you said that if I stormed the Manor I would kill Henry along with all the rest of the inhabitants. I asked you if you cared about saving his life and you said that you cared for him like a brother.'

Anne was watching him intently. Her face had been expressionless, but now he thought he saw a flash of feeling in her eyes. He saw her swallow nervously.

'Well?' she said.

Simon followed her across the room. 'What you did not tell me,' he said quietly, 'was that you had already saved Henry's life once. You saved him from Malvoisier's torture. He told me about it this evening.'

Anne had turned away, but now she glanced up at him sharply. He thought that she seemed taken aback.

'Henry told you that?' she repeated.

Simon gave her a quizzical look. 'Did you expect that he would not?'

'No, I—' Anne broke off and started again. 'I did not realise that he remembered what happened. He was very ill. I had thought…hoped…that he had no recollection of that night.'

'Oh, he remembers,' Simon said grimly. He knew that the memory of that night would haunt his brother for a long time. He would probably never forget it. Such violence and such fear etched themselves on a man's soul.

'Then I am sorry,' Anne said. 'It cannot be pleasant for him to remember such things.'

They looked at one another for a long moment. The candlelight was gentle and in its glow Simon thought that Anne looked very young. In that second he saw all her loneliness and grief mirrored in her eyes and then, as though she thought she had revealed too much, she turned away from him.

'It was very courageous of you to help Henry,' he said softly, 'and very dangerous. Malvoisier could have hurt you badly.'

Anne had stopped when he spoke and now she put her hands up to her face in a brief, betraying gesture before she let them fall again and straightened up. Simon knew that for her, too, the memories of that night were intolerable. 'What was I supposed to do?' she whispered. 'Sometimes it is not possible to put aside the ties that bind us to the past. All I knew was that I loved your father greatly and that I could not let Gerard Malvoisier kill his son in cold blood.' She swallowed convulsively. 'Muna came to me in floods of tears that night. She had already fallen half in love with Henry's courage and gallantry, and she hated Malvoisier for striking him down when he had come under the flag of truce. She knew what they were planning to do to him. Was I to tell her I did not care? Was I to say that we were Royalists and Malvoisier should not be opposed?' Her voice broke. 'Was I to walk past the door and pretend that I could not hear?'

Simon took her hand. 'So you took it on yourself to intervene,' he said. He felt angry. Angry with her for taking such a terrible risk, angry with himself for letting Henry walk into such a situation and more than angry with Gerard Malvoisier for the pleasure he took from such callous and casual cruelty. But he also felt a protectiveness towards Anne that was deeply disturbing; far more troubling than the lust that prompted him to take her to his bed.

'It was folly,' he said roughly, his fury whipped up by the complicated desire he felt for her. 'He could have killed you too.'

'There was no one else who could save Henry,' she said simply. Her eyes were very candid. 'When a man's very life is in such danger I do not have the inhumanity to think of him as my enemy, my lord, and to walk away.'

Simon looked at her downbent head. He felt a savage need to keep her safe. 'You do not have to be alone any more,' he said abruptly.

Her gaze flew to his. 'Yes, I do.'

Simon made a slight gesture. 'Trust me. Let me help you.'

He saw her close her eyes for a moment as though in despair, but when she opened them again her gaze was steady.

'I cannot,' she said simply, and once again her honesty wrenched his heart. He knew what she meant. She had a duty to serve the King just as he had a duty to prevent her from doing so; until that was resolved, they were locked in a conflict with no respite. His rational mind knew that; it was his instinct that told him so urgently that such scruples mattered nothing when he wanted to shield her from all harm. To feel this way troubled him. To want Anne in his bed was simple enough to understand. It was a matter of lust. But to want to protect her was an entirely different emotion.

From his pocket he took the jewel-handled dagger.

'You left this behind when you fled from me the night before the battle,' he said, weighing it in his palm. He held it out to Anne, hilt first. 'If you truly believe that I am your enemy, then take it and be rid of me in one blow.'

Anne's eyes were suddenly huge. She made no move to take the knife. 'You are inviting me to strike you down?'

'Aye,' Simon said softly. 'You say that I am your enemy. I have taken your birthright. I oppose your cause. You saved my brother's life and still I will not give you back your freedom or your lands. So strike now and be rid of this conflict for good.'

The silence in the room was absolute. He saw Anne swallow convulsively.

'This is some trick,' she said.

'No trick,' Simon said steadily. He spread his arms wide. 'I am unarmed. We are alone. Take the knife. If you dare.'

The challenge lay between them like a gauntlet flung down. He saw the anger and the frustration flare in her eyes, saw her put out a hand to take the knife, and wondered if he had made the worst miscalculation of his life. And then, abruptly, she turned her back on him.

'You jest,' she said, over her shoulder. 'If I tried, you would overpower me easily enough.'

Simon caught her wrist and spun her round to face him. 'You hide behind excuses. The simple truth is that you do not dare strike me because you know in your heart that you care for me. You said it yourself when you spoke of saving Henry's life. You cannot be rid of the memories of the past.'

Anne's eyes narrowed with temper. 'That was different,' she said. She tried to free herself, but he tightened his grip. He could feel her pulse hammering beneath his fingers.

'I am not afraid to do it,' she flung at him.

Simon smiled a challenge. 'Then what are you waiting for?'

He could feel her shaking now. 'If I strike you down, every Parliamentarian soldier in Grafton would be waiting to take my life,' she said. 'You try to tempt me to folly, Lord Greville.'

'I try to show you that you could never do it,' Simon said. 'You may hate my cause, but you do not hate me, Anne. Admit it.'

He saw the confusion in her eyes. She wanted to hate him; she hated all that he stood for, but she would not take the knife and make an end. She could not. He loosened his grip, holding her in no more than a gentle caress.

'You see?' he said. 'You will accept me. You will sign Grafton over to the Parliament cause.'

Anne's free hand made contact with the side of his face in a resounding slap that made her response clearer than any words could. He dropped her wrist instinctively, his hand going up to his cheek, and she grabbed the knife and pointed it at his throat.

'Out!' she said. 'Tempt me no further, Lord Greville, or you will feel this knife between your ribs.'

Simon felt his lips start to curve into a smile of reluctant admiration. 'My lady—'

'Out,' Anne repeated. 'When the time serves, I shall have my revenge.' And as Simon closed the door behind him he heard the sound of the knife embed itself in the oak and splinter the wooden panels behind his back.

Chapter Six

Anne was alone in her chamber. She had sent Muna and Edwina away. She needed a little time on her own.

It was the night of her father's wake and for the first time she was accepting that the Earl had gone. She was truly alone.

She wanted to remember him as the strong and powerful protector of Grafton rather than a man weakened by fever who had slipped away from life with barely a protest. That was the true measure of the Earl of Grafton. That was the man she wished to commemorate now. She took one final look around the chamber. Tonight it was a sanctuary, but she knew she could not linger there. She had to face her people. They would expect it.

She took a deep breath, smoothed the skirts of her black gown with a quick, nervous gesture, and opened the door.

The guard whom she had become accustomed to see posted outside had gone, and in his place stood Simon Greville. For a moment they looked at one another in silence.

Tonight Anne knew that the hostilities between them were suspended, if only for a little. Tonight was a night to show respect for the old Earl.

Simon bowed. Rather than uniform, he was dressed all in black tonight, and its stark simplicity suited him.

'Good evening, my lady. Are you ready?'

'As I shall ever be.' Anne repressed a slight shiver. She would never truly be ready to accept this change in Grafton's fortunes. But she had no choice.

Simon offered her his arm and she placed her hand on it lightly. Though she was barely touching him, she was very aware of the feel of him beneath her fingers. The material of his sleeve was slightly rough, but beneath that was solid muscle. He felt strong and reassuring. She wanted to tighten her grip, to draw on his strength, and she had to stop herself from doing so. It was so tempting. It felt frighteningly inevitable. And yet she had to fight it with all of her being.

They descended the stairs in silence and when they reached the door of the Great Hall Simon stopped and stood back to allow her to go in alone. Anne shot him a questioning look and he nodded towards the doorway.

'You are the Lady of Grafton this night. It is right and proper that you should go alone.'

She appreciated the gesture even through the blanket of misery that wrapped her. There was a lump in her throat that prevented her from speaking, but she nodded and swept through the door, head held high. Tonight was hers. She was mistress of Grafton, if only for a short while.

Everyone fell silent as she entered. The hall was packed

to the rafters. Every inhabitant of Grafton, the Manor, the village and the surrounding area, had found a place at the wooden trestles where the ale already flowed. As she walked through the multitude, Anne noted that Simon's men were sitting amongst the crowds in the Greville livery of scarlet and black. They looked a fine sight, but their presence was being tolerated with wary respect. The banners of black hanging from the beams were sufficient to remind everyone of the heaviness of the occasion and also the significance of the Parliamentarian troops amongst them.

It was a long, lonely walk to the dais. Anne mounted the steps and took her place at the centre of the table. The quiet that fell over the hall then was sufficient to hear a pin drop. She took a deep breath.

'I thank you all for coming here this night out of respect for the late Earl of Grafton,' she said. 'Throughout his life my father valued your loyalty most dearly and he bade me say that he wished for no grieving on his death, but for all to celebrate his life with great thanks.' She raised her glass and the torchlight sparkled on the deep ruby red wine.

'The Earl of Grafton,' she said. 'God rest his soul.'

The hall took the toast solemnly, but then someone lifted their tankard again. 'And to his daughter, Lady Anne of Grafton, a righteous and goodly lady!'

There was a buzz of approval as the crowd took up the pledge. Anne smiled. Their loyalty touched her, piercing the cold loneliness that encased her heart. She looked around for Simon. He had stood back so that she could speak to the crowd alone, but now she gestured that he should join her on the dais, signing him to the seat at her side. She knew it was a move that could well be misinterpreted by the people of Grafton, but she had little choice. Simon was giving the orders now and the least that she could do tonight was set a public example of courtesy, no matter her private rebellion.

The servants were already carrying in platters of steaming roast meats and all the delicacies that the Manor had been starved of during the siege. The atmosphere eased into good cheer and the noise rose to a good-humoured roar. In life the late Earl had been a good lord to his people and it was only fitting that his death should be marked by such a show of respect and a prodigal feast.

'Meat, my lady?' Simon was holding the dish for her. 'You must eat a little or you will take ill.'

Anne's mouth felt like sawdust. 'I do not think I can,' she said. She looked at her half-drunk glass of wine. 'Nor shall I take any more wine. On an empty stomach that would be most foolish.'

Simon smiled, and for a moment his hand covered her frozen fingers, too quick for anyone to see. The warmth of his touch penetrated her unhappiness.

'You are more than brave,' he said. 'Grafton is fortunate to have you for its lady.'

Anne drew her hand sharply away from his and toyed with the bits of food on her plate. 'Then they had better make the most of their good fortune,' she said drily, 'for it will not be for long, will it, my lord?'

Simon's eyes met hers in a challenging look. 'You know my mind. Grafton could be yours—'

'Should I please you as either wife or mistress.' Anne looked scornful. 'Thank you, my lord, but you know my mind as well as I know yours, and there shall be no such agreement.'

Simon turned away then to speak to Muna on his other side; to her surprise and irritation, Anne felt rather put out.

As the meal progressed, she could see that not everyone shared her abstemiousness. From her place above the hall she could tell that the meal was becoming more like a wedding than a wake. Literally starved of good food and drink for months, the people of Grafton were now making up for it in full measure and were becoming somewhat rowdy. Still, Anne reflected that it was what her father would have wanted. A celebration was more appropriate to his life than some miserable banquet at which no one spoke a word.

She nibbled a bit of food and watched the scene below. There was danger here too. Some of the villagers were becoming decidedly inebriated by now, and she knew that with inebriation could come truculence and aggression. And even as she thought it she saw what she had dreaded: a scuffle at one end of the table, where two of the yeoman farmers were having a small disagreement. One of Simon's men stood up to intervene. Blows were traded and the knight drew his sword.

Immediately the hall erupted into uproar. Men leapt to their feet, shouting with anger, women cried out and the children and babies started to wail as they sensed the threat suddenly in the air.

'How can there be peace at Grafton when men wear their swords to a wake?' someone shouted. 'For shame! Disarm!'

A menacing mutter of agreement ran around the hall, swelling to an ominous roar.

Anne was on her feet at once to quell the disturbance. She knew that the scene, poised as it was on the edge of grief and drunkenness, could turn nasty. She wished she had remembered to tell the kitchens not to serve so much ale.

She took a breath to shout for order, but then Simon's hand was on her wrist and she fell silent. He was standing beside her now. His eyes blazed. His voice brought instant silence to the hall.

'I have sworn to bring peace to Grafton! Does any man here doubt my word?'

There was a nervous pause and then one of the villagers, stauncher than the rest, shouted back, ''Tis deeds, not words, that matter, my lord! We have had a deal of fine words.'

There was a soft, deadly scrape of steel. The hall took a collective breath as Simon drew his sword. The candlelight flickered off the murderous blade.

Everyone seemed frozen into immobility. Anne put a hand on Simon's arm. She could feel the tension in him, taut as steel.

'My lord, this is not seemly—'

'Nay, my lady, I mean no disrespect.' With a lightning reversal of mood, Simon turned to her and gave her his flashing smile. 'Here is my pledge to the memory of the Earl of Grafton. I will bring peace and prosperity to his estate and to its people.' He took a deep breath. 'Once before I promised my protection to this estate and to its lady. Now I repeat my pledge.'

He reversed the sword and held it out, hilt first to Anne, in a gesture of homage. An astonished whisper fluttered through the silent crowd like the ripple of wind over water.

Anne looked down at the shining blade and from there to meet the bright challenge in Simon's gaze.

Everyone was looking at her, awaiting her response. Simon's men lounged between the villagers, apparently at ease now but with watchfulness in their eyes. The air was heavy with anticipation. And Anne knew that she was neatly trapped.

To refuse Simon's gesture would seem churlish and would cause offence. It would seem disrespectful to her father's memory to behave so ungraciously. On the other hand, to accept would be foolhardy in the extreme, for she understood that Simon was offering far more than fine words and the actions to match. Her people understood too. Simon Greville was offering protection and peace to a land that had been exhausted by loss and war. He was high in Parliament's favour and could defend them from the further depredations of unscrupulous men such as Gerard Malvoisier. He was strong and they sensed that he was just and fair. Not for them the intricate complications of loyalty to King or Parliament. Their unswerving allegiance was to a lord who could protect them, and to Anne, who had stood by them through the grim days of her father's illness and Malvoisier's brutality. And now they were looking to her to lead the way. She felt the weight of their expectation.

She put out a hand and took the hilt of Simon's sword. It slid smoothly into her grip, light and powerful and terrifying, as it had done once before, on the night she had threatened to take Simon's life with it.

A ragged breath ran through the hall, half-shock, half-hope. Anne saw the light flare in Simon's eyes, the satisfaction, the triumph and the power of conquest. Their eyes met and a curious feeling shot through her, as though she was tumbling into darkness. She steadied herself.

'You do Grafton much honour, my lord, in offering your protection,' she said formally. 'Alas that we hold allegiance to the King and cannot accept.'

There was a babble of voices, some raised in support, others not. 'And where is the King when we need him?' shouted the farrier, red-faced from resentment and drink. 'He leaves us here to rot! I say be damned to him!'

'That is treason,' Anne said sharply. The voices were instantly quelled, but the atmosphere in the hall was sullen now. Anne knew she was walking a tightrope. Courtesy she would show to Simon in public, but not by one word or deed would her allegiance falter. If the people of Grafton did not care for that—and she knew that there were many now speaking of supporting Simon and the Parliamentary cause—then it was too bad. *Her* fidelity was not for sale.

Anne saw Simon's smile deepen and her heart turned over. 'Lady Anne,' he said, 'when you accept my hand in marriage, then will you hold allegiance to me.'

'A match!' someone shouted. 'A match to secure the future of Grafton!'

Anne's eyes narrowed. She remembered her father saying that Simon Greville would offer for her and that she should accept him because he was a good man, a strong man, and she needed his protection. She understood her father's fears. He had known he was dying and had put her future and her security above all other concerns. But she was damned if she was going to accept the Earl's will, dying wish or not, especially as Simon had manipulated this very public proposal.

With deliberation she reversed the sword and held it out to him. 'Now you do me too much honour, Lord Greville,' she said. 'I beg you will forgive my refusal of your suit. Excuse me.'

She pushed back her chair and, gathering her skirts in one hand, stepped down from the dais and made for the door. The noise swelled behind her. She caught snatches of conversation; those arguing for peace and protection at all costs, those holding out for allegiance to the King. People looked at her out of the corner of their eyes, some hostile, some sympathetic. Anne felt the tears close her throat. This was supposed to be her father's wake and already the loyalty of his people was torn. She could not hold them together as he had done. The bitter injustice of it wrenched her heart.

The pages threw the doors of the Great Hall open for her and she hurried out into the passage. It was dark here, quiet and cold, lit only by flaring torches. Anne needed the solitude of her room. She wanted nothing but to be alone now.

There was a step beside her and she whirled around. Simon was behind her, his long, easy stride catching her effortlessly. Anne did not acknowledge him and quickened her pace, but as she reached the oak staircase leading to the sanctuary of her rooms he put one arm out, blocking her way.

'One moment, my lady.'

'Lord Greville—' Anne managed to hold her voice steady '—I am very weary. And I am perfectly capable of finding my way to my own chamber. Further, you need have no fear that I shall be creeping out to count the King's treasure tonight. You may safely leave me in peace.'

'Of course.' Simon spoke with the same courtesy he always displayed, courtesy that did little to mask his inherent authority. 'I merely wished to request an interview with you tomorrow, Lady Anne, if you feel strong enough.'

'Of course I am strong enough,' Anne snapped, made irritable by the fact that she felt anything but robust at that moment. 'I am not certain, however, that there is anything that we may usefully discuss.'

Simon smiled. 'The future of Grafton is very much on my mind,' he murmured. 'And that of its mistress. It needs to be settled soon.'

'So I understood from your remarks in the Hall,' Anne said. She drummed her fingers on the banister rail. 'You need have no fear that I shall require you to make good your promise, Lord Greville. I rely upon the King to secure my future, not the Parliament.'

'The King is scarce to be relied upon in these matters.' Simon's voice was dangerously soft. 'He was the one who consented to your betrothal to Gerard Malvoisier, lest you had forgot.'

'I do not forget,' Anne said. She kept her voice expressionless.

'I assure you,' Simon said, 'that I would make you a far

better husband than Malvoisier, and I suspect the people of Grafton agree.'

A cold breeze rustled along the corridors and made Anne shiver. 'I need to be careful in my future choice,' she said, 'no matter the wishes of my people.'

She saw the flash of Simon's teeth as he smiled. 'Their only wish is for you to be safe—and happy, my lady,' he said, 'and for your husband to hold Grafton in a strong hand.'

'It astounds me that they think that I could be either of those with you,' Anne retorted, arching a disbelieving brow. 'You are the most dangerous man that I have ever met.'

Simon shifted slightly but he still barred her way. 'Accept my suit,' he said and once again Anne knew it was a challenge, not a request. 'I am offering you my protection. You once said that you would do anything to save Grafton.'

Anne glared at him. 'This is my father's wake,' she said coldly. 'I'll not discuss such matters now.'

'Then tomorrow,' Simon said. 'You need to decide. You saw what happened tonight, my lady. You cannot hold Grafton together and defend it. I can.'

Anne pressed her fingers to her temples in a brief, desperate gesture. 'I will not submit!' She stared at him. 'I will find a way of my own.'

Simon shook his head. 'There is no other way,' he said relentlessly.

'There has to be!'

Simon slammed his open palm against the stone of the wall. 'How? The King has forsaken you! You have no men to fight! Already your people are talking treason.' He lowered his voice. 'If you want to help Grafton, then this is the price.'

Anne's shoulders slumped. 'No,' she whispered. 'It cannot be.'

Simon caught her arm. 'At least with me you would know passion,' he said fiercely, 'not the dull shadow of a marriage you would have with another man.'

His mouth was on hers, robbing her of speech, and beneath the fierce demand of his kisses her lips parted and opened to him. His tongue plundered her mouth. She felt shaken, on fire, desperate for his touch. Her mind screamed that he was an enemy and her body betrayed her, pressing closer into his embrace.

Then he broke away.

'Yield to me,' he whispered against her hair. Anne shivered, remembering the last time that he had held her thus and used those words. 'You know you must.'

'I know no such thing,' she said stubbornly, trying to push away.

He held her face between his hands and feathered tiny kisses across her cheekbones and down the sensitive skin of her neck. She shuddered as pride, loyalty and desire warred within her. His words echoed in her ears.

'I am offering you the protection of my name. No other man will be able to take you or take Grafton from you. You will be safe.'

'I need neither your name nor your protection,' Anne said. She could feel herself weakening, hear the tremor in her voice.

His touch was so damnably seductive. She wanted his strength and, no matter what she said, she wanted his protection. She needed him. But she also knew that she was vulnerable.

'You need me.' Simon's whispered words echoed her thoughts. 'Grafton needs protection and you cannot provide it alone.'

His mouth took hers again with a savage hunger, his tongue tangling with hers. Anne could feel her body start to melt in the heat of his passion. She remembered this. It was blissful, but dangerous. If once she permitted herself to surrender, he would possess her, body and soul. She would betray her allegiance to the King as though it were no matter, dust in the wind.

'Accept me because you want me,' Simon said roughly when he let her go this time. 'For that is the truth.'

It was true. Anne wanted him desperately. Her whole body ached for him. She was tired and lonely and she wanted to find oblivion in his arms—and she knew that those were all bad reasons for giving herself to him on this of all nights. She wanted to recapture the past, but she knew that it could never be.

She pulled away from him in a welter of black velvet. 'You may be winning the support of my people, Lord Greville,' she said, 'but it takes much more than pretty words and gestures to make me forget my loyalty to the King.'

Simon released her. He was breathing fast and there was a hard light in his eyes.

'You are mine,' he said. 'You cannot deny it. You will marry me.'

Anne shook her head. 'Oh, no, Lord Greville. You took Grafton, but you will not take me.'

And she ran up the stairs to the sanctuary of her room before she could reveal her weakness by begging him to stay with her.

In the long, painful days that followed her father's wake, Anne had tried her best to drown her grief in work. She rolled her sleeves up in the kitchens, pulled up weeds from the iron-hard earth, exercised her mare in the paddocks, helped to churn the butter and knead the bread. No one tried to stop her. They seemed to understand that she needed to be busy. And sometimes she also needed to be quiet. They knew that too.

Simon did not trouble her and occasionally his patience would fill Anne with dread, for she knew that he was waiting—waiting for her to lead him to the King's treasure, waiting for her to give something away, waiting for her to weaken and accept his suit. It was at such times, Anne knew, that Simon was at his most dangerous, for he had all the time in the world and she did not. Sooner or later the word would come from his commanders confirming his possession of Grafton. Sooner or later he would force a match. And sooner or later she would have to try to reunite the King with his treasure.

Simon's searches of the house and estate had continued in pursuit of the King's treasure and Anne had shuddered with fear as she saw the painstaking nature of his quest. It gave her nightmares that one day he would find what he was looking for. He was also hunting for Gerard Malvoisier. Anne had written to King Charles to beg his help in bringing the renegade general to justice, but so far there had been no sign. And in the meantime Simon had started to rebuild Grafton, working with the villagers to restore all that they had lost. Anne felt torn to see it, for Simon worked with a will for the good of her people and with each day she could feel them slipping further from her. With each day her own loyalties were strained as she saw the fairness of his justice and the generosity with which he helped them. She told herself that it was in his own interests, and those of the Parliament, to make Grafton strong again, but the contrast with Gerard Malvoisier's brutal rule could not have been more marked.

It was on a bright February morning that Anne cut some stems of blackthorn and winter jasmine for the church, and went to sit for a while in one of the pews to think about her father and try to find some comfort. She missed the Earl sorely with each day that passed, and the ache of loss still seemed all too raw. Time and again she found herself drawn to Simon, attracted by his strength and apparent integrity, forced to an unwilling respect for him when she saw with what patience and consideration he set about establishing peace and prosperity at Grafton. She remembered her father's wish that she should accept Simon's offer of marriage, and only her desperate desire to keep the treasure safe and keep the Royalist faith kept her from faltering.

As she sat in the cold shadows of the church she tried to put this from her mind, drawing her cloak closer around her and burrowing her hands within the fur of her gloves. The church was cold and smelled faintly of dust and incense. It was a smell that was as familiar to her as the lavender scent of her clothes chests or the beery fumes of the brew house. It was one of the constant themes of Grafton, as comforting as all the other memories of her childhood. Yet now it felt lonely. Anne knew that she was not alone—she had Muna's quiet companionship and Edwina's outspoken support and she had John's silent loyalty. She thought that she also held the love of her people still, but she had to do what was right for them. And the ache left by her father's death could not easily be assuaged—and this was one of the things that frightened her because it tempted her all the more to accept Simon's offer.

Anne sat back, feeling the hard wood of the pew dig into her shoulders. There was no chance of falling asleep in this church. The seats had been designed to remind sinners of the need for penance by making them as uncomfortable as possible. Anne shifted on the seat.

She knew that she did not have many choices left. She could marry Simon Greville, keep Grafton, and resume her rightful place as the lady of the manor. It would be no mere marriage of convenience—she knew that there was an attraction between them that could not be denied. Here in the cold emptiness of the church she could acknowledge it and feel its warmth. Simon could give her seduction and passion and desire. He had the strength and courage she had so admired in her father. He could fill her life and eventually make her forget her grief.

And he would make her forget her loyalties.

And one day he might march to battle and never return.

Anne shivered violently. The thought of Simon cut to pieces on the battlefield was terrifying. She did not even want to think on it.

'Would you seek my life?'

'Why not? You are my enemy...'

Her enemy was even now rebuilding Grafton and making it a safe place to live. He was bringing in supplies to feed the populace, he was restoring order and he was offering a strong defence. And her defiance was weakening. Even if he put the knife in her hand again now, she knew she would never be able to kill him. Already her feelings for him had gone too far and her fealty to the King was half-compromised by her desire to succumb.

How Simon felt, she had no notion. She thought that she was just another conquest to him, like all the challenges that had gone before, like defeating Malvoisier, like taking the Grafton estate. And once she had surrendered to him, what then? She was too proud merely to become his chattel.

There was a creak as the door from the vestry opened and Father Michael bustled in, surplice askew, white hair standing on end. He appeared even more absentminded than ever. Anne smiled at him. The poor man had barely recovered from the search of the church by Simon's troops when they were searching for the King's treasure. They had been respectful, but they had not been able to persuade the priest that they had any right to be there.

'Good day, Father Michael,' Anne said. 'You are well?'

'As well as can be expected with those vandals pulling the place apart,' the priest grumbled. 'Did you know, madam, that they have started searching again today? They were looking down the well this morning. Down the well! As though any man in his right mind would hide treasure in such an inclement place!'

Anne smiled. 'It keeps them occupied,' she said, 'and they find nothing.'

'True.' Father Michael pulled a face. 'Their commander, Lord Greville, seems a good fellow, but his men are buffoons.'

'Thank goodness,' Anne said. Nevertheless the news of the renewed search disturbed her. She had known that Simon would never let the matter rest.

She threw a look over her shoulder. Guy Standish was lurking at the back of the church, desperately looking as though he was not watching them. He had appeared at the same time as Father Michael and it was fairly obvious why. Simon still did not trust her. He thought she would not be above passing messages via her most reliable servants and colleagues. Well, Anne thought wryly, he was right. Her lips twitched. Even though Simon gave her the run of Grafton now, his guards followed her around like puppies. Anne hoped Standish would be easy to deceive.

'I have a message for you,' Father Michael said under his breath. 'It was in the usual place by the bridge. The messenger must have been in the night.' He rummaged beneath his surplice and came up with a prayer book, which he placed in Anne's hand. He raised his voice.

'There are words here to comfort you. Go in peace, child.'

'Thank you, Father,' Anne said softly. She waited until his

footsteps had died away before she opened the book. There was a shred of parchment between the pages.

'It will be within the month. Be careful. Keep the treasure secret.'

Anne's heart fell. A month seemed like an inordinate amount of time to keep the treasure safe. Each day stretched like a lifetime. And yet she had no choice. To deliver it up to Simon was not possible. To keep it hidden from him was essential.

She folded the little shred of paper and slipped it within her glove just as Guy Standish reached her side. She prayed that he would not have seen the surreptitious gesture. Father Michael's actions would have made him suspicious and now she tucked the prayer book under her arm, daring him to challenge her.

'I imagine that you have quite exhausted your interest in here, Captain,' she said with a smile. 'If it is any consolation, I intend to go to the kitchens now. You may even get something to eat if you follow me there.'

Standish reddened to the tips of his ears and Anne felt sorry for him. It was no sport playing games with Simon's captains. Unlike their commander, they did not know how to deal with her.

'My apologies, madam,' he said awkwardly. 'I must ask to see the book the priest gave to you.'

Anne sighed, but handed it over. She thought Simon's men would probably spend an unprofitable few hours trying to find non-existent coded messages in the text.

They fell into step as they walked up the nave. Standish opened the door of the church for her and the lozenges of bright winter sunshine fell coldly across the tiles. Anne was halfway down the steps to the courtyard, with the guard behind her, when it happened.

There was a swish like the sound of feathers through air, and an arrow sliced through the sleeve of Anne's cloak and embedded itself in the door of the church. She felt a sharp, ripping pain in her shoulder and put her hand up to touch it. She felt dazed. The sun was in her eyes and she could not see, and she felt a little dizzy. Standish was shouting and pulling her down to the ground, his grip urgent on her wrist, and she saw blood on her gloves and the pain worsened and her head started to spin.

Another arrow skidded across the cobblestones and another deflected off the prayer book in Standish's hand and pierced his side. He crumpled up with a groan. Anne crawled over to his side, tearing off her cloak, trying to staunch the blood. She looked up to the battlements and saw a lone figure silhouetted for a second against the sky. He was running along the stone walkway between the towers and down the steps towards the moat. She caught her breath on a painful gasp. Malvoisier… He had penetrated Grafton's defences.

The church bell was ringing a warning to the whole castle now. Soldiers spilled out from the guardhouse and into the yard. Father Michael was there now, flapping about in front of them like a great white bird, wringing his hands but doing very little of use. People were shouting and running across the courtyard.

Anne gave a gasp of relief as she saw Simon racing down the steps from the guardhouse towards her. The cloak in her hands was already sodden with Standish's blood and her head was aching with the effort to stay conscious. The sound seemed to ebb and flow around her. She tried to stand, but fell back on the snow with a gasp of pain. She could see Edwina pushing her way through the crowd, all the while tearing up Father Michael's surplice to bind Guy Standish's side. Tears of shock and pain filled her eyes.

Simon knelt in the snow in front of her and took the collar of her gown in one hand, ripping it open to expose the wound to her shoulder. Anne tried to push him away.

'I am not hurt!' she protested. 'It is only a scratch. See to Captain Standish! He is more badly injured than I…'

Simon did not reply. His fingers moved gently over the wound, but, when he pressed a wad of cloth to it in a make-shift bandage, Anne could not quite prevent a gasp of pain. Simon heard it and his jaw tightened murderously.

'You were fortunate,' he said grimly. 'It is a nasty cut, but no more than that.'

'I told you so.' Anne was starting to shake with a combination of cold and shock. 'Please…' She tried to sit up. 'Let me get up now.'

Simon wrapped her about with his cloak. It was still warm from his body and Anne clutched at it gratefully. Simon's hands were gentle, but his dark eyes burned with such a fierce light that she shrank to see it.

'Stay still,' he said. 'You are losing blood.'

'It is nothing,' Anne repeated, but her legs were trembling and she doubted that she could stand. She shrank within the warm folds of the cloak.

'Malvoisier,' she said, through chattering teeth. 'He was on the battlements. I saw him. He ran towards the moat…'

Simon snapped around. 'Jackson, Mason, Clegg, take the east stair! Go! Verney, Aston, take your men and search the house! Double the guard on the gate!'

They were bringing a stretcher for Guy Standish. Anne watched as they lifted him on to it and carried him off. His face was a chalky white and there was so much blood on the snow. Anne felt her throat clench.

'It was my fault,' she said brokenly. 'Malvoisier wanted to kill me and he has killed Captain Standish instead.'

A muscle moved in Simon's cheek. 'Standish will survive,' he said grimly, but Anne did not know if it was a promise or merely a hope.

Simon swung her up into his arms as easily as he had done once before and started to walk towards the house. Anne turned her cheek into the hollow of his shoulder and tried not to let her tears soak his jacket. She felt weak and sick and outraged by what had happened.

Malvoisier had walked into their midst. How could that have happened? Her mind was hazy with pain and grief as she tried to work it out.

There was a shout from the battlements. 'Two dead up here, my lord!'

Anne caught her breath on a gasp. She felt beyond bitterness and anger. She felt shattered. For she had realised that the only way that Gerard Malvoisier could have entered Grafton was through the secret path she had used the night she had slipped out to visit Simon's camp. She had thought he was in ignorance of it. She had thought it was her secret alone. But now she knew that either she had a traitor in her camp or Malvoisier had known all along. And if he had known one secret, did he know them all? Did he know about the King's treasure? Anne had been so certain he did not. Now she was painfully unsure.

'My lord, Simon—' She grasped his sleeve urgently and he slowed his step on the stairs and looked down into her face.

'What is it?' he asked.

'There is a tunnel,' Anne said, speaking rapidly. 'It lies at the end of the laundry cellar and leads beneath the moat. It was the route I took when I came to you that night.' She saw Simon's expression harden and hurried on. 'It may be that Malvoisier knows of the passageway. I would have sworn that he did not, but…' Her voice trailed away. There was such a wealth of bitterness and recrimination in Simon's face that she could not continue. She could feel it in his touch; suddenly he was holding her as though he hated her.

'I see,' he said and his voice was like the chip of hammer on stone.

'I swear I did not tell him of it,' Anne said again, and her voice broke. She could see Guy Standish's fallen body before her eyes, leaching away its lifeblood into the snow. Was that her fault? She had kept the tunnel a secret and now two men were dead and another fighting for his life.

Simon kicked open the door of her chamber and placed her on the bed. He did not look at her again. He did not even say goodbye. She could feel his scorn and anger as he turned away. He was already issuing the order to find and block the tunnel. He went out of the door and he did not look back and Anne rolled over and turned her face to the wall.

She knew that not long ago she would have been pleased to see the Parliamentary cause at Grafton suffer such a blow. Simon was her sworn enemy and she should not care how many men he lost. But Gerard Malvoisier was a dangerous renegade. He had forfeited the King's commission when he had abandoned Grafton. Worse, he had tried to kill her twice now and Anne thought that could only mean one thing. Malvoisier knew about the treasure and he wanted her dead so he could claim it for himself.

The rest of the day was a blur to Anne. She lay still whilst Edwina and Muna bound her wound and then she agreed listlessly to stay in bed to rest, but she did not sleep. She stared up at the canopy of her tester bed, thinking about what she had done and the guilt she bore. Muna and Edwina stayed with her, talking softly to one another and occasionally coming to check that she was not developing a fever.

Simon's troops were searching the house in case Malvoisier had concealed himself within, but word came later that he was nowhere to be found. As she lay in her room, Anne heard Simon's troops ride out in a furious clatter of hooves to comb the surrounding area for the fugitive. They returned as darkness fell, empty-handed. It seemed that Malvoisier had vanished once again. Word of the outrage had gone about the villages and the whole area seethed with unease.

'They are saying that Malvoisier is the devil's general, never mind the King's general, madam,' Edwina reported, as she brought Anne some soup for her tea, 'and that Lord Greville cannot fight the forces of evil.'

'Nonsense!' Anne said angrily, but she felt sick in her heart. 'Malvoisier is no ally of the devil, nor is he the King's man any more. He is no more than an outlaw.'

It was late that evening when Simon came to see her again. Anne was sitting in the solar, her tambour frame on her lap, having won the battle with Edwina over whether or not she should stay longer in bed. She did not want to lie there, doing nothing but thinking. She sat by the fire, but she could not seem to feel its heat. The thick curtains were drawn against the winter night, but still she did not feel safe. She felt as though someone was watching her. Muna, frightened by the pinched coldness in her face, had gone to make her a hot cup of milk.

Anne was holding the wooden edge of the tambour frame so tightly that it scored her fingers. She did not notice. She had not moved for at least an hour.

Darkness had brought an uncomfortable quiet to Grafton. The guard had been doubled, but it was too little too late. Anne knew that. She moved stiffly in her seat. Her wound hurt, but she knew she had been the fortunate one.

She looked up as she heard Simon's step in the doorway, and shook off her reverie. She thought that he looked tired, as though he had aged ten years since the morning. The candlelight was rich on the conker-brown darkness of his hair. He looked grave and sad, but not as angry as he had done earlier. Anne's heart turned over. Enemy or not, she did not want him to hate her.

He came across the room towards her and she stood up at once, moving to meet him.

'I am sorry,' she said, before he could even greet her. 'I am so very sorry for the loss of your men.'

The lines settled deeper into Simon's face. For a moment she thought he was about to spurn her sympathy. Then he took her hand and drew her back down to the settle.

'Such things happen,' he said, 'in a war.'

Anne shook her head. 'Malvoisier did not do this for the Royalist cause. He is enemy to both of us now.' She sighed. 'I have been naive. I did not think… When I kept the tunnel a secret from you I never realised that he would benefit from my silence.' She stopped. 'I have no excuses.'

Simon smiled, a brief, tired smile. 'You are very honest. I do believe that that is one of the things I admire about you, my lady.'

Anne's heart leaped. She looked down at their clasped hands and then back at his face.

'So you do not hate me,' she whispered.

Simon's expression hardened and he released her hand. 'No, I do not. But I have lost two good men.'

Anne nodded. She understood what he meant. Such wanton loss was impossible to forgive.

'You are too hard on yourself,' Simon continued. 'We found no trace of Malvoisier's presence in the tunnel.' His face was grim and hard in the firelight. 'I suspect that there is another explanation. Someone from within Grafton is a traitor to both your cause and mine. Someone let Malvoisier in—for a price.'

Anne sat up straight. 'No!' The denial was instinctive and now she shook her head stubbornly. 'I cannot believe it.'

'Men will do many things for money,' Simon said.

'I know,' Anne said. 'But not here at Grafton. Every last man and woman hates Malvoisier. They would never aid him.'

'You cannot know that,' Simon said.

Anne looked up at him. 'I will not believe that of the people I trust,' she said, but she could hear the plea in her own voice. She did not want it to be true. She could not bear to think that one of her own people had betrayed her for money.

Simon did not reply. Anne knew that in a little he would ask her for the names of all those who shared her secrets. Muna, Edwina, John, Father Michael... They were the only ones who knew of the secret passage and of the King's treasure. Anne shook a little. She trusted them all and she would have to defend them all against Simon's vengeance. He was stung by the loss of his men and by his inability to protect her. She understood that. First there had been Henry and now this. With each new outrage Malvoisier perpetrated, Simon hated him a little more and he would stop at nothing now to hunt him down.

Simon had shifted a little and the movement drew her attention back to him. He was watching her with brooding eyes. 'Why would Malvoisier wish to kill you?' he asked. 'Twice he has sought your life. That I do not understand.'

Anne shifted. For a moment she thought of the King's treasure and then she tried to push the suspicion aside. There was no chance that Malvoisier could have known about that. In all of Grafton there were only a half-dozen people who knew the secret and all of them were loyal to the death. There had to be another reason.

She shrugged. She had forgotten the wound to her shoulder, but now the movement made it ache and she bit back a gasp of pain. 'He had many reasons to hate me,' she said. 'I humiliated him before his men. He was proud. He bore a grudge.' She turned towards the fire, trying to draw on its warmth. What she wanted to say was that Gerard Malvoisier had desired her and that she had scorned his suit. She knew that he had never forgiven her the snub.

Simon moved slightly, touching her hand softly. 'Explain to me,' he said. 'Malvoisier was betrothed to you. Was there truly nothing but hatred between you?'

Anne shook her head. 'It was not as people think. There was no formal betrothal between us. He wanted it and the King promoted the match. But I refused.' She fidgeted with the skeins of silk on her lap. ''Tis true that Malvoisier told everyone we were betrothed.' She looked down. 'It suited his purposes. And it suited him to tell everyone that we were bedded as well. I heard his calumnies. They were not true.'

Simon's dark gaze held hers. 'I am glad,' he said quietly. 'Though it means Malvoisier hated you, still I am glad of it.'

Anne bit her lip. 'That night when I came to you,' she said softly, 'I was afraid that you might think that I…that he… I responded to you with such passion that I was afraid you would believe the tales and think me his whore.'

Simon's hand closed sharply over hers. 'I would never have thought that of you, Anne. Even had there been a betrothal and a bedding, I would have known it was none of your doing.'

There was silence, falling softly between them. Anne did not want to break it. This fragile peace seemed so precious. For a little while they could forget that they were on opposing sides and bitter civil war would come between them again all too soon.

'You asked me once whether all men were afraid of me,' Anne said, wanting Simon to understand. 'Well, Gerard Malvoisier *was* afraid of me. He was afraid of me and of the chance that my father might recover and call him to account, and of the fact that the King is my godfather. And I told him I would kill him if he laid a finger on me.' She grimaced. 'Those were reasons enough to want me dead, in all conscience.' Her expression crumpled. 'But instead of me, he has taken the life of others.'

Simon was silent. Anne knew that he could not give her easy absolution and she did not expect it. In a way he was treating her with the respect that he would accord another commander who had made a difficult decision, as a result of which men had died. He would not offer consolation, but neither did he condemn her. But she was not so hardy as he. She blamed herself. She had made choices and men had suffered for it. She jumped up, unable to keep still under that burden.

'I do not understand why Malvoisier took such a risk in coming into Grafton itself,' she said. 'It was madness.'

'He came to Grafton because he wanted to send me a message,' Simon said. His tone was rough. 'He wanted to invade my stronghold and show me that I have not yet won. He wanted to destroy all that I had tried to build, damn him.'

There was so much venom in his voice that Anne

shivered. 'Yes, I understand,' she said. She hesitated. 'The men who died… You will help their families?'

'Of course.' She saw a flicker of expression cross Simon's face. 'Miller had a wife and two small children and Sugden had only married six months ago. I believe his wife is pregnant.'

Anne felt a lump on her throat. So many lives had been devastated by Gerard Malvoisier's casual brutality. She knew he would care as little for that as he had when he had tortured Henry Greville. His was no devotion to a greater cause. He worked for the profit of himself alone.

'Malvoisier was always a fine marksman,' she said. Absentmindedly she rubbed the place where the arrow had caught her shoulder. 'He would practise for hours in the butts each day.'

'He used arrows because they were more accurate at that distance,' Simon said. His lips thinned. 'It was clever of him, but still he was not clever enough to succeed.'

Anne wrapped her arms about her to try to ward off the cold that was seeping into every cell of her body. 'I moved at the last moment,' she said. 'Something warned me. I know not what.' She shuddered to think how close she had come to death. 'I am fortunate,' she said softly.

She moved towards the door. 'I think that I shall retire now, my lord. I am very tired.' She did not wish to be alone. Fear lurked in all the dark corners. But she was practically falling asleep where she stood.

Simon had also risen to his feet. 'I have doubled the guard on your door,' he said. 'There is nothing to fear.'

'I would feel safer with my pistol by my bed,' Anne said

with a faint smile. 'Unfortunately your men took it away lest I used it on you.'

Simon smiled too. The dark shadows veiled his expression. 'If only you could take me to your bed in place of the pistol, my lady,' he said, 'I would swear to protect you.'

The silence shivered along Anne's nerves. Simon watched her, his eyes shadowed and dark. She could feel the temptation as powerfully as a physical blow. To feel the touch of his hands on her skin and the strength and hardness of his body against hers; to feel the comfort of not being alone and the passion that would drive the darkness from her mind… She made an involuntary move towards him and saw the flare of desire in his eyes.

'I confess that I do not wish to be alone,' she said softly, 'but, Simon, you know I cannot…'

There was a taut moment when the emotion between them stretched as tight as a cobweb about to snap, and then Simon nodded. When he spoke, though, his question surprised her.

'You said that you told Malvoisier you would kill him if he touched you,' he said quietly. 'Would you truly have done so?'

'Yes.' Anne spoke adamantly. 'I would kill any man who presumed to touch me.'

She saw the smile start in Simon's eyes. 'You are a wild cat,' he said. He shifted a little, raising a finger to her cheek and letting it trace a gentle path along the line of her jaw and down her throat. Anne stood very still. Her blood was beating in thick, heated strokes and she felt a little dizzy.

'Would you kill me if I touched you?' Simon whispered.

Anne's heart was racing now. 'You have already done so,' she said.

'And I am still alive.'

'For now.' Anne raised a hand and brushed his away. 'You are too sure of yourself, Simon Greville. We are allies in this one thing only, so have a care.'

Simon smiled again. 'We are more than allies,' he said. 'I will take you to my bed soon, Anne of Grafton.' He raised his hand again and touched her cheek. 'Do not make me wait too long. I am not a patient man.'

He bent and touched his lips to hers, a featherlight touch that barely grazed her mouth and he was gone, before Anne could contradict him.

Simon frowned as he read the letter on the desk before him. Anne's page had delivered it a half-hour before with the request that she should be permitted to send it to the King immediately. She had been anxious to apprise her godfather of Gerard Malvoisier's attack on Grafton and to press for his help in bringing the outlaw general to justice. Simon doubted that there was much that King Charles could do. Anne had written to him before, when Malvoisier had first abandoned Grafton to its fate. That letter had received no response at all. The King had evidently lost control of his rebellious commander some while ago.

Simon chewed the end of his quill. That morning there had been reports of a gang of masterless men terrorising a village to the east of Grafton, smashing buildings, burning and looting. Simon was certain that Malvoisier was respon-

sible and that the men involved were his disaffected troops.
By his actions Malvoisier had put himself beyond the law,
attacking Royalist and Parliamentarian lands alike, looking
only for personal gain. Simon knew that King Charles could
no longer afford to let such matters go when Malvoisier had
once been his own general. There would be Royalist troops
on the road soon trying to hunt the man down and that could
mean trouble for Grafton as well. He doubted that the Royalists would try to take the Grafton lands back again, but he
wanted to make sure that there could be no legal dispute over
their ownership. That meant that it was time that he secured
the estate formally for the Parliament. And that meant
formally securing the hand of its mistress in marriage.

Simon smiled a little ruefully. Anne would continue to
refuse him, of course. She had a commission to fulfil for the
King and she would not compromise that loyalty. But if it
were a matter of desire alone then he was certain he could
overcome her scruples. She was his match in every way.
They both knew it.

He sighed and returned his attention to the letter. A part
of him felt deeply ashamed at trespassing on Anne's private
thoughts, but he knew that he had to do so. He perused the
letter once, and then again, and finally he rested his chin on
his hand as he tried to decipher the message within.

At first glance there was absolutely nothing suspicious
about the letter at all.

'May it please your Majesty to know that I am in
good health although still deeply affected over the loss

of my father. General Malvoisier's shameful desertion of the garrison here, and his subsequent renegade behaviour, condemn him absolutely and I beg your Majesty as a matter of extreme urgency to do all that you may to arrest him for his crimes. Whilst greatly dismayed that Grafton has fallen to the forces of the Parliament, I can confirm that we are all treated well under the occupation and I would like to take this opportunity to reassure your Majesty that everything and everyone entrusted to us here at Grafton is quite safe. I remain your Majesty's most loyal servant
Anne Grafton.'

Simon rubbed his head and poured himself another beaker of ale. His instinct, which he trusted, told him that there was something here, something he was missing.

'I would like to take this opportunity to reassure your Majesty that everything and everyone entrusted to us here at Grafton is quite safe...'

That had to be the relevant sentence. Anne was telling King Charles that none of Grafton's secrets had yet been revealed. The treasure was safe for the time being.

Simon frowned. He had scoured Grafton from top to bottom looking for silver plate, jewellery, coinage, *anything* that could conceivably be intended to finance the King's cause. Yet there was no treasure to be found. It was a complete mystery.

He could force the secret out of Anne, of course, but such action was not his way. He detested men like Malvoisier who would torture prisoners for pleasure as well as profit. He had been hoping that one day, in her own good time, she would trust him sufficiently to tell him the truth. Simon sighed. Perhaps he deluded himself. He thought that Anne was very close to trusting him, yet her promise to the King still stood between them. Perhaps it always would.

He sealed the letter and gave it to his garrison captain with orders that it be despatched to the King in Oxford with all speed. Then he sat back to think about Anne again. The day before when he had come running down the steps of the guardhouse to see her crumpled on the snow he had thought his heart would stop. The relief he had felt when she had moved again had been so powerful it had stolen his breath.

A man needed to have a cause to fight for, but he also needed a reason to return from the wars. Previously he had had the first, but not the second. Now he had Anne. He wanted her. He needed her. So now he had to plan the capture not of Grafton, but of its mistress.

Chapter Seven

❧❧❧

February went out with another snowstorm like the one that ushered it in, but then the weather mellowed into the beginnings of spring, the snow started to melt and the first green shoots of new life began to push their way through the earth. Anne took to walking again in the Grafton gardens and from there to exercising her mare, Psyche, in the paddocks and to flying her father's hawk in the fields beyond the moat. Muna came with her. She was learning to fly Anne's merlin; although she had been apprehensive at first, under Henry's patient tutelage both her confidence and her falconry skills were improving.

It was on one of these deceptively peaceful mornings that Simon had sent a page to summon Anne to his study. Word had arrived from his commanders, as Anne had known it inevitably would. The future of Grafton—her future—had been decided.

Now her fingers beat an impatient tattoo on the parchment

that lay on the desk before her. It was from General Fairfax and it was the military submission that Simon had spoken of, prepared for her signature. The anger fizzing inside her made the words appear to dance on the page.

The Lady Anne Grafton swears her allegiance to the Parliamentary cause and promises to hold Grafton Manor for that cause in perpetuity, renouncing all other alliances now and for ever...

She had liked Lord Fairfax when they had met in the past. He was a good man, fair and moderate. She respected him. But he was not going to persuade her to sign Grafton away.

She pushed the document from her and swung around in her seat to glare at Simon Greville. He had been sitting across the desk from her, head bent, quietly reading one of the pile of documents in front of him. Now he looked up and a rueful smile quirked his lips to see her indignation.

'This deserves to go in the fire!' she said.

Simon's gaze was steady.

'Fairfax is at least giving you a choice,' he said. 'I would not be so generous.'

'Submit the estate to the Parliamentarian rule—or marry the man Fairfax has chosen for me?' Anne looked down her nose. 'What sort of a choice is that? Even were I to submit Grafton to the Parliament—which I shall not!—there would still be an *administrator*—' she invested the word with immense scorn '—here running the estate for me. It would be equally as bad as—' She stopped.

'As bad as having me here?' Simon enquired mildly.

'Almost!' Anne snapped. She was inordinately angry. So

it had come to this. Simon had warned her that when his political masters had their say she would see Grafton taken from her one way or another. She had hoped against hope that it would not be true. Now it was.

Simon laughed. 'So you will not submit.'

'Never!'

'In which case you will be obliged to marry a Parliamentarian. That is the choice on offer.'

Anne narrowed her gaze. 'Lord Fairfax has no right to make a match for me. The King is my guardian now my father is dead. He will decide my future.'

Simon threw down his pen and got to his feet. 'We have had this conversation before, my lady,' he said. 'We both know that the King is in no position to enforce his rights of wardship now.'

Anne glanced back at Fairfax's letter:

If you cannot see your way clear to signing the military submission, then I fear that we must consider an alternative course. It would please us greatly to see you safely married to an honest man who might protect you and your estate from the further depredations of war and hold it safely for the Parliament...

No names were mentioned, but Anne knew exactly whom he meant. She doubted that there were many candidates for her hand in marriage. Simon had already indicated his eagerness to wed her—and to hold Grafton for the Parliament. He was high in Fairfax's favour. No doubt his commander would wish to reward him.

She made a sound of disgust. 'I will not be parcelled off

to some…some Parliamentarian *squire* to wife and make him a present of my person and my lands!'

Simon straightened. 'I am scarcely a Parliamentarian squire,' he pointed out gently. 'One day you will be Countess of Harington.'

The colour rushed into Anne's face. 'Do you think I care about that?'

'I do not know.' Simon thrust his hands into his pockets. 'It was important once, when I came courting you all those years past.'

Anne shook her head. 'It mattered to my father and to yours,' she said now. 'It never mattered to me.'

Simon came to her. 'What did matter to you then?' he asked.

Anne bit her lip. She wanted to say that what had mattered to her was the undeniable affinity she had felt for him, the excitement of his touch, but, more important than that, the sense of something precious that had for ever slipped from her grasp. Simon's gaze was steady, demanding an honest answer. Almost she told him, but then the present jabbed her with its reminder of her current jeopardy and she turned her shoulder.

'Nothing mattered to me.'

'Then,' Simon said, an edge to his voice, 'it can scarcely matter now that you are to wed me at last.'

Anne glared. 'It is you—or no one?'

'No,' Simon said. 'You will wed me.' He smiled. 'No choices.'

Anne held all her emotions under tight check. This was so painful. This was what she had wanted all those years ago, but now it was twisted and spoiled beyond recognition. 'You will have to carry me kicking and screaming to the altar,' she said.

Simon shrugged. 'If needs be I will do that.'

Anne glowered at him. 'You will marry me because it is the Parliament's will?'

'No,' Simon said. 'I will marry you because it is my will.'

There was a silence heavy with confrontation, then Anne jumped to her feet. 'I told you once before that hell would freeze over—'

Simon leant forcefully on the desk. 'And I told you that I wanted you and would have you—you and Grafton, both—whatever you say.'

They stared at one another. The air crackled with mutual antipathy and something more, something that made Anne shiver. This was the real Simon Greville she was seeing now, the merciless conqueror, the man other men feared. All that charm and courtesy could not conceal his true ruthlessness. He had told her only a few nights ago, *'The Grevilles take what they want…'*

Now she trembled at that predatory intent. 'No,' she whispered. 'I'll make no match of convenience with you so that you can have my lands and I can have your protection. I will *not* give my consent to you taking Grafton.'

Simon took two steps forward and caught her in his arms. It was so sudden and unexpected that she had no time to escape him. His mouth came down on hers in a blistering kiss. It was a kiss of mastery and masculine power and all she could do was endure it until he released her.

When he let her go she stumbled and almost fell.

'Convenience, is it?' He was breathing as hard as she. 'At least have the honesty to admit to your desires, Anne.'

Anne drew in a painful breath. 'A little more of your courtship, Lord Greville,' she ground out, 'and I shall begin to hate you all over again.'

Simon laughed. He put up a hand and smoothed the tumbled dark hair away from her face. His touch scalded her.

'I do not believe you,' he said. 'I told you from the start that we could not be enemies. There is something else between us.'

'Well, we cannot be lovers.' Anne stared at him defiantly. 'You hold your allegiance and I hold mine, and it will always stand between us.'

Simon took a step closer to her again. His eyes burned darkly.

'And if it did not,' he said softly. 'What then?'

Anne's throat closed with nervousness. She knew she could find passion with him—she knew that every time he touched her. She could lose herself and her fine principles in Simon Greville's desire. She shivered at the thought. But in the end she would still have betrayed Grafton by giving herself to a man whose loyalties were so far removed from her own. Until she had discharged her duty to the King she could not even begin to think of her own future. And she could not wed her enemy no matter how hot the passion between them.

'Then matters might have been different,' she said. 'But that can never be.'

Simon moved away. She could tell that he was angry. It was latent in every line in his body.

'Very well, then,' he said. His tone was clipped. 'If you insist that we must be enemies, then so be it. Tell me about the King's treasure, Lady Anne.'

Anne clasped her hands together tightly. 'I have nothing to tell you.'

Simon brought his fist down hard on the table, making her jump. 'You have no choice now! If you do not accept me as husband, and insist on holding to your loyalty, you will be imprisoned and I will make you break your silence.'

He gestured to the parchment on his desk. 'You think that you do not care for Fairfax's dispositions? You should read my orders!' He spun round on her. 'I am told that if you refuse to wed me I must use any means in my power to make you sign the military submission and tell me where the King's treasure is.' His voice fell to a menacing growl. 'I suspect that you would dislike that experience even more than I would.'

Anne stared at him. 'So, unless I am to be your wife, you will force me to submit and torture the truth from me? How scrupulous you are!'

Simon clenched his jaw. 'You give me no choice,' he repeated.

Anne felt a sense of dread and a creeping sympathy for him. She could see from the bitterness in his face that he was torn. He was not a man who would make war on women. His honour was too strong for that. But she was defying him and denying any true feeling there might have been between them. She was forcing him to be less than the man he should be.

'You would not do it,' she said slowly.

Simon's face was set. 'I will do everything I have to do,' he said. 'You put me in an impossible position, madam.'

Anne felt cold. She clutched after hope. 'You do not wage war by torture,' she said. 'You are not like Malvoisier, enforcing your will through power.'

'I have not done so until now,' Simon agreed. 'However, you hold the key to what I need to know.'

He put a hand on her arm and drew her to her feet, and his very gentleness this time was frightening. Anne trembled with tension and apprehension. At such close quarters Simon's proximity stirred her senses. It confused her. She felt so close to him and yet frustratingly distant as though there was forever an invisible barrier between them. The conflict she sensed in him, the conflict that they were both locked into, was infinitely disturbing.

'I will not question you further,' Simon said softly. 'Instead I will speak with those in your confidence. I will interrogate your cousin Muna, and Edwina and John Causton, and force the truth out of them. I doubt that they will be as staunch as you are, at least not after a few hours.'

Anne felt herself turn pale. She felt sick at the thought of it. The images crowded her head: Muna, alone and vulnerable, Edwina afraid, John with his sullen defiance. Her voice shook.

'You would not do such a thing!' Suddenly she did not care that she was pleading. 'You could not be so cruel! Why, Muna is barely more than a child! She has nursed your brother devotedly. And Edwina—' Her voice broke.

'It is within your power to prevent it,' Simon said implacably.

'That is blackmail!' Anne flashed. She felt devastated. The thought of him interrogating Muna or Edwina or John was intolerable. They had shown her nothing but devotion. They did not deserve such a fate.

Simon nodded. 'It is blackmail,' he said. 'I concede it.'

Anne put her hands up to her cheeks. 'I cannot permit it. Question me! Lock me up if you will, but do not hurt those I care for!'

Simon shook his head. His expression was dark. 'I can make no such promise.'

Hope flared in Anne's heart. 'If I were to agree to marry you—' she began.

But Simon was already shaking his head. 'I still require your submission,' he said, 'for then you could not take any action to restore the treasure to the King, on pain of death.'

Anne looked across at the desk, where the hated document of military submission lay, taunting her. She was standing on the edge of the precipice. If she refused, Simon would take Muna or her servants and question them about the King's treasure until they broke. If she agreed to sign the submission and to marry him, she could spare them that intolerable torture. But it would mean renouncing her Royalist allegiance and that would destroy her integrity.

'I will sign,' she said slowly, the words forced from her. 'I will hand Grafton to the Parliamentarian cause and I will wed you to seal the bargain and make your sequestration legitimate.'

Simon went very still. 'And will you tell me of the King's treasure?'

Anne shook her head. 'At the very beginning you told me

you wanted three things,' she said. 'You wanted Grafton, you wanted the King's treasure and you wanted me.' Her voice shook a little. She felt as though she was tearing apart the very principles on which she had based her whole life, betraying her father to her soul and all she believed in with it.

'I will give you two of those things,' she said, 'and it will have to be enough. Further, I will swear to do nothing to restore the King's treasure to him. More than that I cannot do. I will never break my silence. One day—' She swallowed the tears that threatened to close her throat. 'One day I may be able to tell you the whole. I pray that that day will come. Perhaps when this country is no longer at war with itself.' Her voice broke. 'But for now those are my terms and you may take them or leave them as you please.'

The room was heavy with tension. Simon came very close to her. 'You would do this to save those you love?' he questioned harshly.

'Aye,' Anne said. 'I would do it for them—and to ensure peace at Grafton, and to keep the King's treasure out of your hands.'

Simon was as pale as she. 'If you sign that document,' he said, 'you are signing away your very allegiance.'

Anne held his gaze. 'I know,' she said. Her heart was breaking. 'I will agree to take no active part in supporting the Royalist cause, on pain of death. But you must agree to leave Muna and Edwina and John alone, and to abandon your pursuit of the King's treasure.'

This time the silence seemed to stretch for hours. And then Simon shook his head.

'No,' he said. 'It is all or nothing.'

The anger and the relief combined in Anne in a huge tide. She had been prepared to surrender her allegiance to save those whom she loved and to protect the King's treasure, but she would never, ever, give up its secret. The entire course of the war could depend on her holding the peace.

'Then we have no agreement,' she said. She drew herself up. 'And I swear, Lord Greville, that if you touch my cousin or a single one of my servants to make them break their oath, I will personally take your life even though it cost me my own in the process.'

She stumbled from the room. All she wanted was to find somewhere quiet and dark where she could hide for a little while. She had come so close to betraying almost everything that she believed in. She would have struck a bargain to save those whom she loved and to keep the secret of the King's treasure. She would have done whatever she had to do. But it would have broken her heart. And now she was terrified that Simon would fulfil his threat to question Muna, Edwina or John, and break them because she would not submit. If he chose to do so, there was nothing that she could do to save them other than tell him the truth. And that she could never do.

Simon sat at the desk in silence for a long time after Anne had gone out. He had started to pen a letter to General Fairfax, but after only two lines he had stopped and laid down the quill. Now he unfolded the parchment and stared at the military submission that Anne had come so close to signing.

She had been within an inch of betraying her Royalist allegiance and Simon knew that in the process she would have torn her principles and her life apart.

He rubbed his brow. He could understand the agonies she had gone through, choosing between her loyalty to those whom she loved and to her cause. He had pushed her hard, threatening to hurt those closest to her, resorting to blackmail. Guilt stirred within him. He told himself that it had had to be done, for the Parliamentarian cause, for the war. Yet he felt a blackguard.

Anne was not like him. She had offered to sign away her birthright and her allegiance for love. He had turned his back on the love of his father for his principles. The decision still gave him nightmares.

He got to his feet abruptly and strode across to the window. Yet again a contingent of troops were quartering the Manor, searching for the King's treasure. He could see them now in the stables, shovelling out the dirty straw, searching the feeding troughs, looking above the rafters and down the drains. The grooms were watching in amused bewilderment. Simon sighed. He would continue to search Grafton—take it apart stone by stone, if necessary—until the treasure was found.

And that was the final thing that puzzled him. He could understand Anne agreeing to sign the military submission to save those she loved, but he could not understand her doing so to save the King's treasure. In the end, treasure was only jewellery, or silver plate, or money. It was not worth laying down one's life for. Yet to Anne it was more important than anything. He had heard the desperation in her voice as she had bargained for him to abandon his search and he did not understand it.

He went back to the desk, folded up the submission document and stowed it away in the drawer. He would write to Fairfax and explain that Anne had refused to sign and that he would continue to try and persuade her and to discover the whereabouts of the treasure. But he knew that he would not question her servants or her cousin to get to the truth. Such gallantry as Anne Grafton possessed called for an equal response from him. Maybe he was a fool, but he could not use them to hurt her. He closed the drawer and picked up his quill. He had been very close to achieving all that he wanted—the Manor, the treasure, and Anne Grafton herself. Yet he recognised that a part of him was relieved that Anne had not surrendered. He had always respected her. He could not break that very thing that he had admired.

Anne opened the door of her chamber very quietly and looked out into the corridor beyond. It was not long since the church bell had tolled a half-hour past one in the morning. The night was quiet and she had work to do. It was time to go to the King's treasure.

That morning, Father Michael had delivered another note. Like the last one it had counselled caution, but it had also promised hope. A message would come soon with instructions for the handing over of the treasure. A week, two… Anne knew they must all be ready.

At night there were two guards outside her door and when she stepped out into the corridor they both looked astounded, and, she thought, rather nervous. One was a fresh-faced youth whom she knew was a junior recruit, but the other was Will Jackson, who had taken Standish's place as Captain of the garrison. It seemed that Simon was taking no risks if he was putting his captain on guard.

'Captain Jackson.' She smiled at the young soldier in precisely the way she knew made him feel most uncomfortable. 'I do apologise for disturbing you. I fear I could not sleep and thought that a period of reflection in the church might soothe me.'

Jackson looked flustered, but determined. Anne suspected that he had hoped against hope that she would not do anything suspicious on his watch. His luck was clearly out tonight.

'Madam.' Jackson bowed stiffly. 'I regret that I must ask you to return to your chamber. It is not safe for you to wander about at night.'

'What danger could there be in my own home,' Anne questioned, 'and with the house so well guarded?' She sighed. 'I merely wish to go to the church for a little solace.'

She could see Jackson frowning as he thought about this. Anne knew his instinct was to agree. A man would need a heart of stone to refuse the bereaved daughter of the house the comfort of prayer. But yet he would have his orders, orders that would definitely preclude permitting Lady Anne Grafton to go wandering about alone at night…

'I will escort you to the church, ma'am,' he said eventually.

Anne shook her head. 'Please do not, Captain. Grieving is a solitary activity. I am sure that you understand.'

Jackson blushed. 'I will escort you to the church and wait

outside,' he said doggedly. 'Curtis,' he turned to the young soldier, 'report to Lord Greville.'

Anne smiled to herself as she fell into step behind Captain Jackson. The young lieutenant evidently had an eye to making a success of his promotion and seemed content that he had done the right thing. He would no doubt be congratulating himself on having the foresight to report to Simon. It was his misfortune that he had done exactly what Anne wanted.

The corridor rang to the sounds of their footsteps as they walked towards the stair. Torches flared in the wall sconces as the wind rippled along the passage. The night silence in the house was illusory. These days Grafton never truly slept. There were always men on lookout.

They came to the top of the staircase, where another sentry challenged them, standing back with a clash of arms as he recognised Jackson. The captain made to start down the stone staircase, but Anne put her hand on his arm. 'There is no need for us to go down into the courtyard, Captain. I will use the church door from the long gallery. You may wait here if you wish.'

She did not wait for Jackson's acquiescence, but turned into the long gallery. It was very dark, for the wall sconces were not lit here, and cold, for the fires in the braziers were no more than glowing coals. The painted faces of Anne's ancestors stared down at her from the walls with deep indifference. She shivered and hurried on.

This, she knew, was the moment that might make or break her venture. Jackson was now realising the crucial point that he had forgotten earlier—namely, that there were two entrances to the church. He would be considering the fact that if he accompanied her to the long gallery door and waited outside, she might go in one door and out the other. And then he would realise the other difficulty, that if he let her go into the church alone and then hurried around to the main entrance in the courtyard, she might slip back out into the long gallery whilst he was away. She quickened her pace. The captain was now a good few yards behind her and was clearly uncertain what to do, for she heard his footsteps lagging. As she reached for the handle she heard him say, 'Madam' in a tone of sudden desperation, but she ignored him. She whisked through the doorway and turned the key in the lock, profoundly grateful that Simon had not seen fit to remove all the keys in the house. It was his first mistake.

Unless… She paused. Would Simon have a man permanently stationed on watch in the church? It seemed unlikely, for the church was built into the encircling wall above the moat and there was no escape. Simon's resources were not limitless and one of the things that she admired about the way he ran Grafton was the efficient way he used his troops. She knew that he had regarded the church as a prime hiding-place for the King's treasure and had scoured it from rafters to crypt. When his men had found nothing but mouse droppings and old candles, he had given up the search. She was banking on the fact that he would think the church not worth guarding now.

Anne paused to say a brief and heartfelt prayer both for her father and for the success of her scheme, then she crept down the nave and into the side chapel dedicated to Saint

Hubert. He was the patron saint of hunters. It seemed appropriate. She hoped fervently that he was on her side that night.

At the back of the church was a small door leading into the chaplain's vestry. The latch lifted silently. Anne had asked Father Michael to keep it well oiled. Again, she locked the door behind her.

The room was tiny, for it contained nothing but a cupboard for vestments and a small desk. What it did have, however, was a window that gave on to a dark corner of the courtyard by the kitchens. Anne climbed carefully on to the desk. It creaked a little under her weight. Her pulse was racing and her ears straining to hear the slightest sound. She put a hand out to the latch. This one had also been well oiled. Her fingers tightened on it as she prepared to slip it open. Then she heard noise—and froze.

It came quickly—the crash of the main door of the church opening, hurried footsteps on the stone flags, voices raised, then hastily hushed in belated reverence. The handle on the vestry door rattled as someone tried to open it.

'Locked, my lord! Shall we break it down?'

'No.' It was Simon's voice. He spoke from directly outside the door. 'Not yet. The priest generally keeps it locked. I do not wish to cause unnecessary damage.'

Anne kept very still. Jackson had certainly acted quickly in raising the alarm. He had been quicker than she had wanted. And Simon had responded with all the decisiveness that she would have expected.

Jackson's voice was low, urgent and nervous.

'We have done a quick search, my lord, but Lady Anne

cannot be found. She must have come into the church and gone straight out of the main door, just as I feared.'

Anne held her breath. She had a superstitious fear that the slightest move, the slightest breath, would give her away. Simon felt too close. She could almost feel him reaching out to her, searching her mind to discover what her actions might be. It was a terrifying feeling. She had known almost from the first that something closer than she could understand bound her to Simon Greville and now she felt as though she could not keep him out.

'My lord?' Jackson prompted. 'Do you wish me to order a full search of the house?'

'No,' Simon said, and a shiver ran along Anne's skin. 'Do not raise the alarm. Not yet.'

The cold intensified, bringing Anne out in gooseflesh. Her mind raced.

'You take the main door and check the hall and lower chambers. Take two men only. I shall go to the long gallery and search the upper floors,' Simon said. 'And Jackson—' His voice was a little further away, as though he had already started to move, 'Go quietly.'

Jackson's reply was indistinguishable and then Anne heard the muffled sound of steps on the cobbles, then silence.

She had only a few minutes. Once they had searched the castle again, with all the ruthless efficiency that Anne knew Simon was capable of, they would rouse the whole household. They would call on Father Michael to provide a key for the vestry. By that time she wanted to be back blamelessly in the church.

She opened the window a crack. All was quiet below. The courtyard was empty, exposed in the moonlight, and the corner below her window was dark and shadowed. Anne edged herself out of the window and on to the ledge outside, gripping the coping with her fingers. As a child she had swarmed over the roofs of Grafton without fear. Now a four-foot drop terrified her. A broken ankle would be well nigh impossible to explain away, out in the courtyard, in the middle of the night.

Blotting the fear from her mind, she jumped, landing a little awkwardly on the cobbles and smothering a gasp at the jolt. She pressed herself against the rough stone wall of the castle wall. No sound. No movement. There was a light in the church now. And above her the window gaped open. She had forgotten to pull it closed when she jumped.

Too late. There was the sound of a clash of arms from across the courtyard as the sentries changed, and Anne dived into the doorway of the kitchen. The darkness yawned within. It was fortunate that twenty-one years of experience meant that she could move about in the complete dark.

She scurried through the kitchen, where a servant yawned by the embers of the fire, past the larder, around the corner, past the storerooms, scuttling down the corridor like a mouse. Left, right, through the servants' dorter, out into the stable-yard and finally into the lodge where the grooms and coachman slept. There was a small tack room at the end of the hall and she stopped, out of breath, cold, nervous, aching still from the leap from the church window.

She knocked softly on the door.

There was a sound within, and then the door opened a crack and a young girl's face appeared in the aperture. 'Madam?'

'It is I,' Anne said. 'Open the door.'

The room was tiny. It contained two pallets, one for the nursemaid, who curled up again, looking at Anne with sleep-filled eyes. On the other slept a child of about ten, a rag doll clutched tight in her hand. She had long dark hair that curled prettily about her face. She shifted a little in her sleep, murmuring something indistinguishable before turning on her side and clutching the doll a little closer to her chest.

Anne looked at her for a moment, then spoke in a whisper. 'Her Highness is quite well, Meg?'

'Aye, milady.' The nurse glanced across at her charge, her face softening into a smile. 'She cries for her papa sometimes in her sleep, but no one hears.'

Anne nodded. 'A message has come. He will send for her soon. A week, two at the most.'

The girl's eyes widened. 'Praise be! At last!' She hesitated. 'I was so worried when I heard that General Malvoisier was threatening Grafton.'

Anne shook her head. 'Do not be afraid. Soon you will be going home. We shall be ready when the King sends.'

The maid snuggled down beneath her blankets once more. She was smiling. 'It will not be long. His Majesty will move heaven and earth to see his daughter to safety.'

'I hope so,' Anne said. 'In the meanwhile, is there aught else that you require?'

The maid shook her head. 'Your household has cared for us right royally, madam, for all that they do not know who we are.'

Anne smiled. 'I am glad.' She pressed the girl's shoulder. 'I am sorry. I must go. There is so little time. But if there is anything you need, speak with Edwina and she will come to me.'

The maid nodded, smothering a yawn. 'Thank you, milady. Goodnight.'

Anne went out and closed the door very quietly. Upstairs in the hayloft she could hear the rustle of the mice and the snores of the grooms. They were a stalwart bunch and they had accepted without comment the newcomers in their midst. Anne had told them that Meg was the widow of a Royalist soldier and that she and her daughter needed refuge at Grafton for a little. No one had questioned it, though Anne had suspected that everyone knew something was afoot. But they would never talk. She trusted them implicitly. So Meg helped in the kitchen and the Princess Elizabeth of England played with her dolls by the hearth and made friends with the pages and kitchen maids, and Anne reflected that the best place to hide something had always been right under the noses of those who were looking for it.

She went out into the stable yard and paused for a moment to take a deep breath of the cold night air. The stars were hard and bright in the black sky above her. All she had to do now was to get back to the chaplain's vestry unnoticed.

She edged her way around the stable block. There was a sentry on the battlements above, but he did not turn. She reached the long, cold passageway past the storerooms and crept forward. Past the larder, into the kitchen... The servant lad muttered in his sleep as he rolled closer to the warmth of the fire.

Anne let herself out into the courtyard. There was danger all about her now. If they found her too close to the stables, they would search again and perhaps this time someone would make the connection, someone would think that treasure came in all shapes and sizes and was not merely coin or silver… Every day she had lived with this secret and lived with the terror of Simon or one of his men realising the identity of the little girl in their midst. The King of England's daughter. If Elizabeth had been identified, it would have meant the end for the King's cause. For what would his Majesty give for his daughter to be saved? Very likely he would lay down his own life.

The cavaliers who had entrusted the Princess to the care of the Earl of Grafton that day six months before had done the only thing they could. They had been trapped by Simon's men as they were escorting Elizabeth from Bristol to join her father at Oxford, and had known that to stand and fight might well be to condemn the King's daughter to imprisonment or even death, and their sovereign to a cruel decision no man should ever have to make. So they had taken her to Grafton for refuge and the Earl had kept the secret, telling no one other than Anne and their most trusted servants. They had kept the Princess's identity a secret from Malvoisier and had maintained it throughout the siege of Grafton. Then the Earl had died and Anne had had to carry the burden alone. And she had known that no matter how Simon questioned her, she could not sacrifice the safety of a ten-year-old child for herself or for Grafton.

She dared not confide the truth in Simon no matter that

a part of her had desperately wanted to. She knew Simon was a good man who would never deliberately hurt a child or use her for his own ends, but she also knew that, if Elizabeth fell into his hands, he would surely have to send her to Lord Fairfax and the Parliamentarian commanders. He would never let her go back to the King. Princess Elizabeth would become a political prisoner—a child of ten would be a pawn in the game of Kings. If once Simon knew the Princess was at Grafton, her fate would be sealed.

Anne's eyes stung as she thought of the Princess calling for her father in her sleep. Her mother was abroad in France, her siblings scattered. She had nothing but the rather rough and ready kindness of Anne's household on which to rely, and an uncertain future in which she had to trust. Once again Anne felt the heavy burden of the King's commission all but crush her. He had written to her father:

'Keep my daughter safe and when the time comes, bring her to me…'

They were simple words, but the task was well nigh impossible.

Anne squared her shoulders. The time was coming soon and whatever she had to do to reunite Elizabeth with her father must be done. For a moment her heart almost failed her as she wondered what Simon would do if he found out the truth. She pushed the thought away. It could not happen.

The door of the church was in front of her. If she could creep through to the vestry before she was seen, then she would be safe. If not, she would have to bluff it out as best she could.

She was breathing quickly as she slipped into the church.

It appeared to be empty. The search for her must have moved on. She hurried down the nave towards the vestry door, praying that Simon had not changed his mind and broken down the door. Only a few more moments… She unlocked the door with shaking fingers, opened it…

And then the main door of the church behind her crashed open and Simon Greville, Will Jackson and a half-dozen soldiers stood on the threshold behind her.

Anne deliberately took her time in turning around. She blinked a little as though the flare of torchlight dazzled her. She pulled the vestry door closed again as though she were in fact emerging from the room rather than going into it. Then she rested her back against the reassuringly solid panels of the door and took a deep breath.

'Lord Greville?' Her bewildered tone was easy enough to assume. 'Is there something amiss? What are all these soldiers doing here?'

'Madam!' Jackson sounded shocked to see her. 'I…' He turned to Simon. 'I swear she…she cannot have been here when we searched earlier, my lord!'

Anne could almost feel sorry for him, he sounded so hurt. She looked at them all, arranging her expression to one of perplexity.

'Lord Greville?' she said again, politely. 'What is going on?'

Simon came forward slowly, his hands deep in his pockets, his casual demeanour belied by the watchfulness in his eyes.

'Where have you been?' he demanded.

Anne opened her eyes wider. 'What do you mean? I have been here. I told Captain Jackson—'

'Captain Jackson escorted you to the church a half-hour ago,' Simon said. 'You locked the door in his face and promptly disappeared. I demand to know where you have been.'

Anne tried to look suitably contrite. 'Captain Jackson, I apologise. I wanted to be on my own with my thoughts, as I am sure you are aware.' She turned back to Simon. 'I have been here all the time, my lord. In the chaplain's vestry.'

Jackson made a sound of disbelief. Simon silenced him with a look.

'You were in the vestry the entire time?' he repeated, his voice soft. 'Surely you must have heard us searching for you out here in the church? Surely you must have heard us at the door?'

Anne cast her gaze down. 'I heard nothing. I fear I was…somewhat distressed.'

Jackson and the others looked awkward. Simon looked disbelieving. There was a long, distrustful silence.

'I would like to go back to my chamber now,' Anne said. 'If you please.'

Simon raised his brows. 'Very well,' he said, 'there is no more to be said. Jackson, stand your men down. Send word that Lady Anne is found.'

Anne watched as the crestfallen captain drew his men up and marched them out of the church. Their footsteps died away. She was left in the flickering torchlight—with Simon. He was still watching her with unnerving closeness. She knew without a shadow of a doubt that he did not believe a word she had said. He had sent his men away only because he wanted no witnesses to their conversation.

'Since you have finished your devotions for the night,' he said coldly, 'I shall escort you back to your chamber.'

He stood back to allow her to precede him through the church door and then fell into step beside her across the courtyard to the main door. Anne's nerves were wound up tight. The urge to burst into speech, to say something, anything, to break the silence between them, was incredibly strong. She knew that was what Simon wanted. He was waiting for her to give herself away.

By the time they reached her door, Anne's nerves were in tatters but she had managed to keep quiet. She put out a hand to the latch and Simon put his hand over hers.

'A moment, my lady.'

Anne stopped.

'Why did you choose to go into the vestry rather than stay in the main part of the church?' Simon asked.

A pulse hammered in Anne's throat. 'I wished to read at the desk. Father Michael keeps the prayer book there.'

'And you locked the door after you?'

Anne raised a haughty eyebrow. 'I did. I had no wish to be interrupted.'

'The vestry window was open,' Simon said. 'Did you notice that?'

Anne hesitated. 'No,' she said eventually. 'Father Michael must have left it open. He grows absentminded in his old age.'

Simon's dark gaze was challenging. 'You must have

been unconscionably cold with a draught blowing through there,' he said.

'I had my cloak,' Anne pointed out.

'Ah, yes.' Simon took his hand from the latch, bent and picked something from the floor. He held it out to her.

'There is straw on your hem,' he said. 'Does Father Michael keep his horse in the vestry these days?'

Anne looked down. Her heart contracted. Treacherous strands of hay were indeed clinging to the material of her skirts. She shook them off.

'Perhaps the passageways are not as clean as I had thought,' she said lightly.

'Or perhaps your midnight wanderings took you further afield than you have led me to believe?' Simon suggested. He shifted slightly, still blocking her entry to the room with his body and his tone changed, became icy. 'Come, Lady Anne, you must take me for a fool. You were not in the church tonight. You were in the stables. I suspect it is where you have hidden the treasure.'

Anne's heart lurched. 'I was in the church,' she repeated. 'You found me there.'

'Now you are lying,' Simon said. He held her trapped between his body and the door.

Anne raised her chin and looked him straight in the eye. Her heart was pounding beneath the bodice of her gown.

'I will search the stables,' Simon said. 'I will find the treasure.'

'You have already searched there,' Anne pointed out, 'and you found nothing.'

Simon took a step back. His eyes were cold.

'One more escapade of this nature,' he said, 'and I will lock you up. I swear it.' He took her by the shoulders and his gaze raked her from head to foot. 'We shall be wed within a fortnight, Anne. I cannot go on like this. I will even take your hatred if I must for forcing the match. At least it would be better than your indifference and better than this torment.'

For a moment they stared into each other's eyes and then his arms closed about her and his mouth took hers, parting her lips, his tongue plunging deep. The kiss was fierce, his mouth hot and searching on hers. Anne stood helpless within his embrace, dizzy and shaken.

He let her go with an oath and stood back. 'One week, not two,' he said, turned on his heel and walked away.

Anne pushed open the chamber door and closed it behind her, leaning back against the panels for support. Her body still hummed with the force of Simon's anger and passion, and her response to it. She felt utterly bewildered and terribly alone. The affinity that she felt for Simon was unshakeable despite all the forces that threatened to keep them apart. The love that had developed its first, tender feelings in her girlhood had clung stubbornly to life through all that had happened since. She sat down heavily on the settle. She wanted to stay at Grafton and live there in peace and build a family. She had wanted to do that with Simon, but she did not want it to be like this, with anger and conflict.

She crossed to the casement and drew back the heavy drapes. The night was cold and dark. Never had the Earl of Grafton and his wise counsel seemed so far away from her.

She knew it had been his wish for her to accept Simon's offer of marriage, enemy or not. Her father had put her welfare and her future above all things. She was the one who had chosen to go against his wishes because of her own loyalties.

She let the curtain fall. There was one man who could, perhaps, help her. She would not ask him to oppose the match, merely to give her his advice and the benefit of his wisdom and experience. She went to the desk, withdrew a piece of parchment from the drawer, dipped her quill in the inkpot and started to write.

The following morning a messenger left Grafton at first light, heading for Simon Greville's family seat at Harington, a day's ride to the north-west. He carried letters from those of Simon's troops who were Harington men to their families at home. There was also a despatch from Simon to his father, Fulwar Greville, Earl of Harington, reporting on Henry's improving health. It had become Simon's habit to write weekly to Fulwar. His father never replied, much to Simon's grief, but he persisted obstinately in maintaining the contact.

On this particular morning the messenger also carried a letter to the Earl from Lady Anne Grafton. She had passed it to him in the stables, when he had been about to depart. He had not thought twice about it, for although Simon had impressed upon him that he should never carry any letters from Lady Anne to the outside world without express permission, he had assumed that this was different. This was a letter addressed to the Earl of Harington himself and the messenger reasoned that there could not possibly be any danger in that.

Chapter Eight

'You are distracted tonight, Simon,' Henry Greville said with a smile. 'Unless you are deliberately letting me win?'

He looked up from the draughts board and fixed his brother with a quizzical look. They were alone in the long gallery, with the board on a table beside the fire. Dinner was past and all was apparently quiet. Yet Simon felt restless.

He did not wish to acknowledge that it was because he missed Anne. He had not realised how he had come to take for granted her presence, whether it was beside him at dinner, or reading in the gallery in the evenings or exercising her mare in the paddocks during the lengthening spring days. Since the night when he had ordered her to marry him she had spent as little time in his company as possible, so that the reverse of what Simon had wanted was inexorably coming true. He had pushed her further from him. There was a widening chasm between the two of them. They were to marry, but they were already estranged.

Simon got up and strode over to the window, peering out into the ragged darkness. The wind was rising, ripping at the Greville flag on the pole and howling through the battlements. The brazier hissed, its flames dancing in the draught.

'I cannot concentrate.' He frowned. 'There is something in the air tonight. Something I do not like.'

Henry idly stacked the counters up. 'An attack?'

Simon shook his head. 'I do not think so. Not yet. I had news from Fairfax this morning, though. There are troops on the move and a number of skirmishes have taken place close by here. I think he will order me to battle soon, but he wishes the matter of Grafton—and the King's treasure—to be resolved before then.'

Henry pursed his lips in a silent whistle. 'He asks much. How is it possible to make my lady tell you of the treasure?'

'I know not,' Simon said shortly. He felt the frustration tighten within him. He would not compromise his honour and torture the truth from Anne's servants, but it was costing him dear.

They both turned at the sound of a scuffle at the far end of the gallery. Jackson was hurrying down the room towards them, his face strained.

'Outriders, my lord! Horsemen approaching! They carry Harington colours!'

Simon exchanged a look with Henry. His brother was suddenly looking very ill at ease.

'Harington arms?' he demanded. 'My *father*'s colours?'

'Aye, my lord!' Jackson stood to attention. 'Enemy colours! Do I lower the drawbridge, my lord?'

Simon's lips twitched. 'Of course you do, Jackson. For all my differences of opinion with my father, I am not going to refuse him entry to the Manor. He is not a combatant in this war and I doubt very much that he has come to conquer Grafton.'

'Sir!' Jackson saluted and sped off. Simon turned to his brother.

'Something in the air tonight indeed! Did you know anything about this, Henry?'

Henry looked amused. 'What, you think that I would invite our father here to Grafton? I would rather face the entire Royalist army single-handed than our father, after all that has happened.'

Simon grimaced. 'I share your sentiments, but I insist you join me in greeting him!'

Henry gave him a rueful smile and they fell into step along the long gallery. Simon noticed that Henry's limp was more pronounced now, no doubt through sheer nervousness. Fulwar Greville could do that to a man. He was known as the Iron Earl and the nickname was well earned.

'Courage!' he said softly, and Henry gave a wan laugh.

'So you did not invite him yourself?' he asked.

Simon shot him a look. 'Of course not! Do you think that I wanted him here? Now there will be all hell to pay.'

Together they went down the main steps and out into the courtyard. The torches and braziers were flaring, lighting the stormy dark. The first of the column of cavalry was clattering over the drawbridge now, the pennants of Harington blowing in the wind. In the centre of the column was the unmistakable figure of the Earl himself. Simon stopped on the top step and stared for a moment. Seeing his father again after so many months of estrangement was extraordinary. He realised, with a rueful grimace, that he was as nervous as a green youth in charge of his first command.

He saw Fulwar look up, raise a hand in greeting, and rein in the men behind him. The firelight glinted on the harness and the breastplates of his retainers. Even though Fulwar did not carry arms for the King as a result of poor health and great age, his men looked almost like an invading army.

The Manor was already buzzing with excitement. Word had gone around and even the cooks had emerged into the courtyard to catch a glimpse of the Iron Earl. Fulwar Greville of Harington was a man with the devil's reputation and everyone wanted to see him—from a safe distance.

There was a step behind him, and Simon spun around. Anne was standing in the doorway, a small upright figure clad in her deep, unrelieved black. He saw her face light up and her lips part on what seemed like a breath of relief. Fulwar had dismounted now, with much huffing and puffing. And Anne ran down the steps and cast herself into his arms.

'Uncle Fulwar!' she cried. 'I am so glad to see you!'

'I do not wish you to marry Lady Anne,' Fulwar Greville said. He brought the flat of his hand down hard on the oak panels of the table, making the pewter tankards dance. 'We may have our political differences, boy, but you are still my son and now the future of Harington is at stake. Forget the match! I shall never permit it.'

The argument had already raged for an hour. It had been apparent to Simon as soon as Fulwar had arrived that he was already in a towering fury. The Earl had put that anger aside for ten minutes whilst he greeted Anne, but then he had turned to his sons and the atmosphere had chilled. His icy greeting had withered Henry where he stood. Henry had muttered something about needing to retire to his room to rest and his father had looked suitably disgusted at this display of unmanliness. Simon, meanwhile, had set Jackson to arrange stabling and refreshment for his father's men, and had then taken the Earl's arm and escorted him into the Great Hall.

'The poor child,' Fulwar said now, shaking his grizzled head like the old bear he resembled. 'Poor Lady Anne. Barely two months bereaved, and already harried merci-lessly by Fairfax—and yourself, so I understand—to give up her patrimony. For shame!' His fist crashed down onto the table again. 'Have we come to this, that we must harass the innocent victims of this conflict? Fairfax has lost all sense!'

Simon winced. Ever since his father had arrived he had burned with curiosity to know what Anne had written to bring Fulwar hotfoot to Grafton to defend her. It was, he supposed, no real surprise. Anne Grafton was Fulwar's god-daughter and, despite the fact that the Earl was a non-com-batant in the war and was now old and relatively infirm, when she called for his help he would respond in all honour.

Fulwar was still grumbling about Thomas Fairfax and Simon sighed heavily. He knew that his father blamed the Parliamentarian commander for turning Simon to what he saw as the traitors' cause. Not for Fulwar the intricacies of politics. His loyalty to the King was absolute and unquestioned simply because the King was appointed by God. Simon had argued that the King had taken his exercise of royal prerogative too far and his taxes crippled the people. He had argued for reform. When Fulwar had discovered that his sons both intended to fight against the anointed sovereign there had been an almighty quarrel in which high words were exchanged and from which neither side had really recovered. The Earl had blustered and shouted and forbidden his sons to go to war, but Simon had known that, for all his threats, the split was breaking his heart. He had known it because he had felt the same. The Civil War had ruptured families and caused wounds he knew would never heal.

'The world has gone mad,' Fulwar grumbled now. 'None of this would ever have happened in my youth.'

'Some more beer, sir?' Simon said, pushing the jug across the table towards his father. 'Mayhap it will improve your temper. They brew a fine ale here at Grafton.'

Fulwar glared. 'There is nothing wrong with my temper! Nothing that would not be improved by having you back at Harington in your rightful place and knowing that your brother is avoiding a conflict that clearly he does not have the stomach to handle! I have only one heir and one spare and I do not wish to lose them both to a cause I do not believe in! Pah!' He drained his tankard and held it out reluctantly for more.

'I do confess I have a thirst on me after the journey from Harington,' he admitted, a little more quietly. 'These roads are not kind to old bones.'

'Then rest and take more ale,' Simon said. 'I am not hastening to either my marriage or my doom so fast that you need not sink your pint first.'

Fulwar regarded his elder son from under lowering black brows, took another draught of the fine ale, wiped his chin and sat back with a sigh.

'So tell me,' he said, 'what is in the air of Grafton that both you and Henry feel you must rush so heedlessly into wedlock?'

Simon rested his elbows on the table. The Great Hall was completely deserted. He had often observed that his father could clear most rooms with impressive speed. Servants were so fearful in his presence that they would turn white and run away. The scullion who had served them the ale had looked as though he would rather face the hangman's noose.

'I cannot answer for Henry,' he said, 'you will have to ask him yourself.'

Fulwar snorted. 'Fool boy won't speak to me! He's too afraid.'

'Henry has been extremely brave,' Simon pointed out. 'Gerard Malvoisier tortured him and he responded with great courage. You should give him some credit for that.'

Fulwar grunted. 'Malvoisier has no honour. I told the King months ago that he should dismiss him. If I get my hands on him—'

'You will have to wait in line, sir,' Simon said shortly. 'Mine is the privilege of killing Gerard Malvoisier.'

There was a simmering silence as Fulwar looked at him, brows lowered. 'Aye, well…' he said after a moment, 'you have my blessing in that at least.' He shifted. 'But this girl

Henry fancies himself in love with… What of her? Is she not Grafton's bastard niece with no name and no fortune?'

Simon pulled a face. He disliked to hear Muna disparaged so. 'Henry does not care about that,' he said.

'Then he should,' his father said testily. 'Younger sons have their way to make. They cannot afford to throw themselves away on a love match.'

'Henry is a Greville,' Simon said. He smiled. 'He takes after you, sir. He will fight for what he wants.'

Fulwar snorted, but he did not appear displeased. 'We shall see. I will give credit to the boy if he feels so strongly. Which brings me to you.' He glared at Simon. 'You took Grafton by force of arms and now you seek to legitimise your conquest through marriage.'

'It was my duty to take Grafton,' Simon said. 'I took the place for the Parliament and now I wish to hold it for them.'

'Aye, well…' Fulwar nodded, subsiding slightly. 'You did well to rout Malvoisier, boy, though I should not say it.' He chewed his lip. 'But you cannot put aside the betrothal between Lady Anne and Gerard Malvoisier. It was signed and sealed in word and deed, as I understand it.'

'You heard wrongly.' Simon spoke grimly. His father was trespassing now on matters that still touched him on the raw. Although he knew that Malvoisier had never touched Anne, he could not think of the man without wishing to break his neck.

'Lady Anne never gave her agreement,' he said. 'There was no betrothal.'

Fulwar was looking at him with pity. 'Yet men will say

that there was. A betrothal and more—a bedding between the two of them. Could you stomach those whispers about your wife?'

'No one will speak out with my sword at their throats,' Simon said. His knuckles showed white as he gripped the handle of his tankard.

'Yet supposing that it were true…' Fulwar paused. Simon appreciated with rueful amusement that this was his father attempting to be delicate. It was rather like watching a large carthorse trying to tiptoe around a room.

'Even were it true,' he said, 'which it is not, Lady Anne would deserve my protection, not my censure.'

'You are all honour and pride,' Fulwar said, 'but would you be prepared to give your name to another man's bastard child?'

Simon's patience broke. He stood up so sharply that the wooden bench rocked back and almost fell. It had driven him mad to hear other men speak slightingly of Anne but to hear their slander repeated by his father drove him to a white-hot fury. His hand slid instinctively to his sword hilt.

'Sir, I beseech you to be careful what you say.'

His father looked at him from under frowning brows. 'What's this? You would challenge your own father?'

'Aye, sir.' Simon spoke through gritted teeth. 'I have the greatest admiration and respect for Lady Anne Grafton and I will not hear any man disparage her, not even my own sire.'

Fulwar slapped his tankard down. 'So,' he said, 'you honour and respect Lady Anne. I confess it is more than I had expected. I thought this a matter of political expediency only. Sit down…' he nodded to Simon's chair '…and finish your ale.'

There was a silence fraught with tensions, then Fulwar sighed. 'I understand that Lady Anne holds fast to her fealty to the King?'

Simon nodded. 'She will never compromise it.'

Fulwar moved his tankard in circles on the table. 'Very laudable. The lady takes after her sire. He was a great man. Too many men hold their allegiance cheap.' There was a heavy pause and he added, 'I do not mean you, boy, so you may stop looking as though you were sucking on a lemon.' He sighed. 'To my mind you have chosen the wrong side, but where you give your allegiance you cleave fast and I admire that.'

Simon felt a huge lightening of spirits. 'Thank you, sir,' he said. 'You have no idea how I have wished to hear you say that.'

There was a moment when he could have sworn that his father almost smiled, but then Fulwar cleared his throat. 'But we were speaking on Lady Anne,' he said brusquely. 'A fine woman. One would wish for such a mother for one's sons.' He sighed. 'Grafton is a fine manor and a goodly estate, of course.' He cocked a brow. 'How much is it worth?'

Simon mentioned a sum.

Fulwar pursed his lips. 'So much? Well, well… I am remembering that I was once very anxious for you to marry Lady Anne Grafton.'

Simon raised his brows. 'That was a long time ago, sir,' he said. 'Times have changed. Should you not be reminding me that two people who hold opposing loyalties can never be united in marriage?'

Fulwar's bushy brows came down. 'I confess it was that

very thought that brought me to Grafton,' he said. 'That and the need to offer my godchild my protection.' He looked at Simon, and Simon could have sworn that there was something approaching pity in his gaze. 'I understand now that you wish to marry Anne for other than political expediency, boy,' he said, 'but it would never work. For as long as she holds her allegiance and you hold yours, you would be limping when you should run.'

Simon nodded. Knowing Anne and her loyalty to her cause, he could acknowledge the truth of that.

'Furthermore,' Fulwar said heavily, 'for either of you to compromise your fealty would be disastrous. It would make you become someone you were never meant to be.' He sighed gustily. 'Oh, to be young again, and have principles high enough to break my heart over!'

There was a silence between them. 'I hear what you are saying, sir,' Simon said, at length, 'but I cannot withdraw. I *will* marry her.'

'Because you desire her,' Fulwar said, nodding. A smile twisted his lips. 'That I understand. Oh, to be young and have not only high principles but blood hot enough to prompt me to rash action!' He lay back in his chair. 'I shall speak with her,' he said, at length, 'but it must be Lady Anne's decision alone. I cannot permit you to force her to the altar. If she chooses not to wed you I shall offer her a home at Harington.'

Simon gritted his teeth. It did indeed seem like rubbing salt into the wound of their estrangement for Fulwar to invite Anne to Harington, but he could understand his father's actions.

'What will you say to her?' he asked.

Fulwar gave him a very straight look. 'I will tell her what I have told you,' he said, 'and more besides. I am an old man now and I have seen many things. For the time being it may seem to us that this conflict will never end.' He sighed. 'Indeed, there is no way of knowing how it will end. But one thing I know, and that is that when the time comes it is alliance that we will need, not opposition, if we are to build the future.' He moved a little stiffly. 'So I shall tell my godchild not to throw away the chance of happiness now if she believes in her heart that she might be happy with you.'

Fulwar stood up. 'I will speak with her in the morning,' he said, 'if I may. For now I am old and my most ardent desire is for a bath and a rest.' He clapped Simon on the shoulder.

'I know it is awkward for you, boy,' he said, 'harbouring the enemy under your roof like this—'

Simon cut him short. 'First and foremost,' he said fiercely, 'you are my father, sir. And I pray neither of us shall ever forget it.'

They looked at one another for a long, dark moment, each recalling the conflict that had set father against son and torn families asunder. Then Fulwar nodded.

'So be it,' he said.

The following morning Anne rose early and went down to the falcons' mews. The grass was heavy with dew and the mist hung low over the Oxfordshire fields though the promise of sun was in the air. She took her father's tiercel peregrine on her wrist and went out into the paddock. The soldiers watched her go, but no one tried to prevent her.

These days they were becoming accustomed to seeing her go about the estate as she pleased. Anne was aware that there was an easing in the atmosphere at Grafton, almost an acceptance of the change in fortunes. The servants and the soldiers joked and chatted together as they worked the estate. One of Simon's sergeants was even courting a girl from the village.

Anne flew the falcon and watched it spread its wings and gather height, soaring up above the stand of trees that marked the western boundary of the estate. Muna had not accompanied her that morning. The Earl of Harington had expressed the wish to make her acquaintance; although Muna had been shaking in her shoes, she had gone stalwartly to breakfast with him. Anne smiled to herself as she thought of it. If Fulwar thought that Henry had chosen a quiet little mouse to wife he would soon be disabused of the notion.

Fulwar's apparent agreement to the match between Henry and Muna had surprised Anne. She had thought the Earl of Harington a man who would look high for wives for his sons. But Fulwar was in many ways an enigma. Grown men trembled at his footfall and yet Anne had heard that when his stallion had gone lame on the journey to Grafton he had tended it with gentle hands and soft words as he removed the thorn from its hoof. She knew from her own childhood that he was gruff and stern, but that his coldness hid a soft heart.

A shout from the field gate roused her from her reverie and she turned to see Fulwar approaching, with Muna and Henry at his side. Muna had the merlin with her and she and Henry waved merrily and walked towards the opposite end of the field to continue with the lessons. Anne sighed. They looked very happy.

Fulwar was coming towards her alone now. Anne had the strangest feeling of time slipping by, as though this was what Simon might look like in thirty years, when time and life had taken its toll. Fulwar's grey hair was still thick as a badger's pelt and he had the upright gait of a once-active man, for all that the lines of age were etched deep on his face. Anne felt a sudden longing to see the next thirty years through with Fulwar's son. They would be years rich in experience and action. They would be years of passion and feeling, warm and intense, unlike the cold loneliness that troubled her now. She needed to feel loved and involved; she wanted to have a family and surround herself with its laughter and tears. She wanted Simon. Over the past weeks she had watched him work to undo all the evil that Gerard Malvoisier had visited upon Grafton. He cared, both for the people and for the land, and she admired him so much for it. Besides, that was what was meant to happen. Anne felt a strong pang of nostalgia. Four years ago she had pledged her troth to Simon. Something had gone terribly wrong to turn the world upside down.

'Your cousin learns quickly,' Fulwar said with gruff approval as he reached Anne's side and turned to watch Muna patiently flying the merlin on its creance. 'She is a good girl, biddable and sweet. I have decided that Henry makes a goodly choice.'

'I am pleased that you approve,' Anne said. Privately she thought that if Muna had convinced the Earl that she was biddable, she had more deception in her bones than Anne had ever suspected.

Fulwar's blue eyes were amused as he watched her. 'You do not sound so approving yourself, Lady Anne. Is a Greville not good enough for your cousin?'

Anne laughed. 'The Grevilles are good enough for anyone, my lord! My cousin deserves to be happy.' She shrugged. 'Henry makes her so. That is sufficient to persuade me, although I worry about their opposing loyalties.'

She whistled for the tiercel peregrine and it came tumbling from the sky, landing on her gauntleted wrist in a flurry of grey. Anne scratched the top of its head and the bird made a faint cheeping sound.

'You treat that bird like a pet,' Fulwar grumbled. The peregrine turned its head and fixed him with a baleful look from its bright yellow eyes. Anne smiled.

'He is wild, my lord,' she said. 'He only comes to me when he chooses and because it pleases him.' She held out her wrist. 'He is an Earl's falcon. Would you care to fly him?'

Fulwar shook his head. 'You have taken your father's place. It is only fair and right you should fly his falcon.'

Anne held up her wrist again and the bird flew free, climbing higher and higher until they lost sight of it against the bright blueness of the sky.

'They say,' Fulwar said thoughtfully, watching its progress, 'that the female peregrine is more ruthless than the male.'

'''Tis often so,' Anne said, her face straight. Seeing Fulwar Greville trying to be tactful was rather amusing.

'You have proved the same in your stout defence of

Grafton, my child,' Fulwar continued, 'but now you must decide your future. I came to offer you a home at Harington should you find it impossible to remain here at Grafton.'

Anne sat down on the trunk of a fallen oak. 'Must I then choose?' she said, with a sigh.

Fulwar nodded. 'Grafton is Simon's now.' He shook his head. 'I cannot prevent that. The fool boy is misguided in his cause, of course, but where he fixes his loyalty he holds fast.' He looked at her. 'He wanted to marry you four years ago, Anne. He wanted you with honour. His opinion has not changed.'

Anne fixed her gaze on the clouds piled on the horizon. She could see the peregrine, a tiny black spot against the whiteness as it hunted higher and higher for its prey. There was a lump in her throat as she answered.

'He has a fine way of showing it,' she said bitterly, 'with his threats to harry my servants and his determination to force me to wed.'

'Simon does the work he has been given,' Fulwar said, 'and he does it with a heavy heart.' He sighed. 'The two of you are so alike, if you could but see it. Both so young, so passionate for your cause.' He shook his head. 'If only you could see that what truly counts is that you are both people who, once they give their faith, will keep it absolutely. If you could give that faith to one another above all things, then you would have the match of your heart.'

The March breeze tip-toed along Anne's skin. The pigeons rose flapping from the bare branches of the trees. Anne shivered for them. Somewhere above, the peregrine was waiting.

'I made a different promise first,' she said. 'I am sorry, my lord, but I cannot break my fealty.'

Fulwar nodded. 'I respect that, but there is something you should know, Lady Anne.'

His face was dark and sad all of a sudden, and Anne felt a clutch of fear. 'What is it?' she whispered.

'The King spoke to me of Grafton when it fell to the Parliament,' Fulwar said. 'He told me that he would sign the military submission himself. He was sorry for the loss, but he wanted to trade Grafton for Basing—a deal with General Cromwell to save the garrison there.' He took a look at Anne's stricken face. 'I am sorry, Lady Anne. There are hard decisions to be taken at times such as these. It is political expediency for a greater game.'

'No!' Anne said. She stood up. There was a painful burning in her throat. 'The King would not do that after all that we had done.'

There was pity in Fulwar's gaze. 'In the end he did not,' he agreed, 'though more than one of his advisers pressed him to it. But he was strangely reluctant. None of us understood why.'

Anne understood. With a blinding flash of disillusionment she could see it all. The King could not risk cutting Grafton loose whilst his daughter was in hiding there. It was the one thing that had stayed his hand. It had not been loyalty to Anne, or respect for her father or any of the things that she might fondly have imagined would move him. It was harsh reality. She held the Princess Elizabeth and whilst that was the case Charles could not use Grafton as a bargaining tool. Anne suddenly realised that if it had not been so, her fate would have been decided long since.

'I thank you for telling me, my lord,' she said, and her voice was thick with tears. 'I had not realised… What a fool I have been!'

She turned away so that Fulwar could not see the despised tears that fell from her eyes. 'Excuse me,' she said.

She dropped the gauntlet on the ground before his startled eyes and turned blindly away. She was not sure where she was going. She wanted it to be somewhere quiet, where she could lick her wounds in peace. But the words echoed in her head and would not leave her:

'He told me that he would sign the military submission himself. He was sorry for the loss but he wanted to trade Grafton… It is political expediency…'

A sob tore at her lungs. She had been so proud of her principles and her loyalty, little realising that in the struggle for the throne the King himself had no time for such things. And the terrible thing was that even knowing this of him, Anne still felt bound by her promise. She could not sacrifice Elizabeth, an innocent child, and the King had known this. He knew that despite everything, she would keep the faith.

'Anne?'

She realised that she had run further than she had thought and now she was in the walled garden with the sundial where she and Simon had met four years before. And Simon was here. She could see no more of a blurry outline through her tears, but she recognised the concern in his voice.

'What has happened?' he said. 'I saw you in the meadows

talking to my father. Has he…' Simon hesitated. 'I thought he was to offer you sanctuary at Harington,' he finished. 'Surely the thought is not so repugnant to you?'

Anne's breath caught on a laugh. 'No, my lord. It is not Uncle Fulwar who has so distressed me.' She rubbed the back of her hand against her eyes, smudging the tears. 'I realise that I have been very foolish,' she added, a little forlornly. She looked at him, then away. 'He told me that the King had thought to bargain Grafton away, sign the submission himself.' She gulped. 'He told me that it was politics. Politics! And there was I thinking it was a matter of trust.'

Simon did not answer at once. Instead he took her hand and led her to the bench that stood against the warmth of the south wall. He drew her down to sit beside him and retained her hand in his. It felt amazingly comforting.

'I am sorry,' Simon said, after a moment. 'I know that must have hurt you.'

Anne nodded. 'I feel very stupid.' She felt betrayed, for even though Charles had not used Grafton as a bargaining tool, she knew it was only because he was afraid of what she might have done if it had happened.

'You hold the King's treasure,' Simon said after a moment, and there was a note in his voice that made Anne realise he understood. 'He could not risk alienating you.'

'Yes,' Anne said. She realised it was the first time that she had actually admitted to Simon that the treasure was here at Grafton. But he did not press her to say more and she felt inordinately grateful.

'I think,' she said carefully, 'that had that not been the

case, he would have signed my life and my lands away without a thought.'

'Not without regret,' Simon said, 'but certainly for what he saw as the greater good.'

Anne flashed him a look. 'I suppose that you would have done the same,' she said angrily.

'Not without regret,' Simon said again. A shadow of a smile touched his mouth. 'Anne, this is war—'

'I remember,' Anne said bitterly, 'and in a war people will be hurt. Clearly I am too simple for such political games.'

'Do not,' Simon said, 'do not put down your own loyalty simply because those around you do not have your integrity.' He gripped her hand tightly. 'We are the ones who cannot live up to your example, Anne, not the other way about.'

There was a long silence and then Anne said stiffly, 'It is true that Uncle Fulwar has offered me a home at Harington. It is kind of him, but I should feel even more displaced there than I do here now. So…' she glanced sideways at him '…if your offer of marriage still stands, my lord, I should like to accept.'

Simon did not reply at once. She could feel the tension in him. 'I wish,' he said suddenly, fiercely, 'that it was not like this, Anne. It should not be like this.'

Anne turned to look at him.

'How should it be?' she whispered.

Simon bent his head and touched his lips to hers, gently, softly exploring. Anne held her breath, felt it mingle with his as his tongue delved a little deeper, courting a response from her. The irresistible tug of desire melted her. She rested one hand against his chest and eased away a little.

'That was how it once was,' she said.

Simon's lips traced a path to her throat, brushing aside her hair so that he could taste the tender hollow beneath her ear. Anne's eyes closed and her head fell back as the cool shivers of longing ran through her. Wherever his lips moved she felt her skin warm into life. He was tracing the line of her collarbone now and when he reached the place where it dipped beneath the neckline of her gown, he raised a hand to loosen the buttons that held her bodice together. One button, two, three… Anne shook as he gently eased the material aside and his lips and tongue continued their downward quest to the upper curves of her breast. The blood beat hot in her veins and her legs trembled.

Simon picked her up and placed her on his lap. Anne roused from her sensual spell. There were voices not far away…soldiers in the courtyard, scullions in the kitchen… The whole of Grafton was going about its business around them and Simon Greville was seducing her in the gardens in broad daylight…

'Simon,' she whispered, grasping the lapels of his jacket, 'we must stop. This is not seemly.'

'I told Jackson to allow no one to disturb us,' Simon said. 'The entire Royalist army could be besieging Grafton at this moment and I would not care.'

His mouth took hers, a little roughly now, stifling argument. Anne relaxed into the kiss, opening her lips to his, repressing a groan of pleasure as his hand came up to caress her breast inside the open laces of her shift. His palm was rough and calloused, a soldier's hand made hard with work, and it created the most exquisite sensation against the tender skin of her breast. When he lowered his head and took her nipple in his mouth she gasped and Simon looked up.

'Hush, sweetheart.' She could hear the undertone of amusement in his voice as he caressed her. 'You cannot make a noise—that *will* bring the household down upon us.'

Anne bit her lip. 'Then you had better cease your ministrations, my lord.'

'Simon.' He was rubbing his fingers lightly over the nipple he had aroused and Anne squirmed on his lap. 'Call me by my name,' he insisted, placing his hands about her waist and bending his head to her breasts again.

'Simon,' Anne said. Her head fell back against his shoulder as she felt his mouth tug gently on her nipple again. She could feel the hot sensation of desire all the way through her body. 'You had better stop if you do not wish me to scream the Manor down in my pleasure,' she whispered.

Simon laughed. He kissed her, rough, hard, demanding. His hand still rested against the hot bare skin of her breast and Anne caught her breath on another gasp.

'I am having too much pleasure myself,' Simon murmured, 'to stop now.' He drew her closer and Anne jumped in shock as his hand slid up her leg beneath her skirts, over her stocking, above her garter, creeping higher with subtle but merciless strokes until it skimmed the softness of her inner thigh. Slowly but surely he sought out the hidden inner recesses of her most secret place, and slowly but surely she melted to feel his touch.

She gasped aloud and he covered her mouth with his,

smothering her cries. One hand was on her breast, smoothing it with delicious strokes. His other was caressing with intimate insistence between her parted thighs and Anne thought she would smash and break from the sheer wanton joy of it. She gave a final gasp as the waves of pleasure broke over her and then he was holding her body still against his, as the spasms racked her and she buried her face in his neck and inhaled the scent of his sweat and his skin.

'*That* is how it should be,' he said, into the tangled skein of her hair. And Anne, trembling and quiescent in his arms, made a small sound of agreement.

She felt him smile against her cheek. 'I wanted to do that four years ago when I first came to you in this place to ask if you wished to wed me. I wanted to make love to you there and then.' He slanted a look down at her. 'We cannot go back, Anne, but we could try to go on.'

Anne put her hand up to his cheek. Already she could feel her happiness draining away as reality intruded. No amount of sensual pleasure could banish the unhappiness of feeling separated from Simon by such a gulf of secrets and lies.

'I will try,' she said. 'For Grafton.'

Simon looked at her for a long moment. She could see her own tangled feelings reflected so clearly in his eyes. 'Then that will have to be good enough,' he said. He kissed her again, but there was sorrow in it now and she felt his pain. It mingled with her tears. And when he walked away from her he did not look back.

Chapter Nine

The morning of the wedding dawned with a chill mist floating above the water meadows. Anne shivered as Muna and Edwina dressed her in the cloth-of-silver gown that had been her mother's wedding dress. It was old fashioned, but somehow it seemed fitting. Anne could not have gone to the altar in her mourning blacks, but nor did she wish to wear one of her everyday gowns. The long flowing sleeves of the dress were lined with scarlet and there was a matching scarlet braid on the hem and around the neck.

'Oh, madam,' Edwina wailed, trying to pinch some colour into Anne's cheeks, 'you are as pale and wan as a statue!'

'I know,' Anne said. Her teeth were chattering with nervousness and cold.

Edwina wiped away a surreptitious tear. 'It was not meant to be like this, was it, madam, to be wed amid war and bloodshed? I remember when we dressed you for your betrothal to Lord Greville all those years ago—'

'Do not,' Anne said. She could not bear to think of how it had once been for her and Simon. She wanted to grasp that happiness and hold it to her for ever, but she knew it had gone. Her voice broke. 'Please do not, Edwina.'

'Oh, Nan!' Muna hugged her close, then stepped back. 'The escort is here, Nan. They are ready to take you to the church.'

Anne looked towards the doorway where Will Jackson stood in the scarlet and black livery of the Grevilles. She knew that he was there to protect her, not to force her to the altar, but even so it was a stark reminder of how things were.

Edwina's expression softened. 'You look beautiful, madam. Your father would have been very proud of you. Remember that he wished you to marry Lord Greville.'

Anne swallowed the lump in her throat. 'I remember, Edwina. I am doing this for him and for the future of Grafton.'

The mist was lifting as Anne rode her palfrey through the gate of Grafton Manor and down the street into the village. Simon had decided that they should be married at the parish church of Grafton rather than within the castle walls. Anne knew it was a very public declaration, a sign that in taking Lady Anne as his wife Simon was also taking the whole of Grafton as his possession.

There was a pale sun peeping through and warming the crowds. Anne looked straight ahead along the old cobbled road to where Simon waited for her at the church door. She could see him from a great distance away and he stood straight and still, never taking his eyes from her for one moment. Anne felt a deep sadness. She was about to make this man her husband and master of her estate. Once that had been all she desired. Now everything between them felt twisted and strained.

Simon's hands, hard and sure, lifted her down from the saddle and set her on her feet. For a second she looked up into his face. He looked solemn and watchful, but his eyes were brilliant and bright. He took her hand and led her to where Father Michael waited. Anne took a deep breath. Her decision was made. For the sake of Grafton and for her father's memory she would become Lady Greville with all the grace that would have attended their wedding four years before. Only the joy would be lacking.

The wedding feast began after the service and was to continue for the entire day and most of the night. Every inhabitant of Grafton was present, from the oldest beldame to the youngest babe in arms. The Great Hall was packed with people and when it became too full the crowds spilled out into the courtyard and continued the festivities there, gathered around the braziers and the ale barrels.

There was music, masques and tumbling from a band of travelling players who had most happily heard of the nuptials and had come to offer their services. The roar of noise grew progressively louder as more and more ale was consumed and Anne soon gave up any attempt to converse with Simon since the din was simply too loud.

She was very aware of her husband's presence at her side in the place that had once been her father's. And, though she tried hard to block out the Earl's absence from the festivities, there were times when the thought of him would catch in her throat and make the candle flames blur as she blinked back a few tears. She wished that Fulwar had been there. He had left Grafton the day after they had spoken. Perhaps in that shadowy future that he had talked of Anne thought that there might be a time when Simon and his father could be reunited and there might even be an heir for Grafton and Harington…

Edwina caught her eye and gestured meaningfully towards the door. Anne caught her breath. She knew the nurse was trying to tell her that it was time to retire. She glanced at Simon. They were husband and wife and now—soon—they would become lovers. She shivered. She could give her body to Simon easily, oh, all too easily, but she wanted to give her soul and that was impossible.

'Excuse me, my lord.'

Captain Jackson was beside the table, touching Simon's arm to draw his attention. He threw an apologetic smile in Anne's direction, but she was not deceived. Something was very wrong. She could sense it. Suddenly nervous, she gripped her hands together beneath the table.

The chatter in the hall continued unabated, but Anne did not hear it. She was watching Jackson as he spoke urgently in Simon's ear, saw Simon's hand close tightly about his wine glass, heard the crystal shatter beneath the pressure of his fingers and saw the wine spread across the table like a bloodstain. There was cold in her heart.

Simon turned back to her and spoke in an undertone. 'There is an attack on the village. It is burning. It must be Malvoisier. I suspected he might take advantage of the feast to attack and I doubled the guard as a precaution, but they are hard pressed. I must go.' He was already half out of his seat, but then he stopped.

'Keep our people here and keep them safe,' he said. 'I will send word as soon as I may.'

Anne grasped his sleeve. Suddenly she was terribly afraid. 'You will be careful?' she whispered, and saw him hesitate as he heard the real anxiety in her voice.

'Of course,' he said.

'I fear for you.' Once before, she had said those words to him when he had been about to go out to do battle. She had meant it then and she meant it now. In that moment it mattered not that he held for the Parliament and she for the King; all that was good and true between them suddenly demanded that she speak honestly.

She saw the expression in Simon's eyes deepen and grow soft, and felt helpless to prevent the love in her unfurling and growing stronger with every moment. He bent and kissed her, a kiss that was sweet and deep and tender. Then he raised his hand to touch her cheek and was gone.

Anne felt bereft. She sat back in her chair, but only for a moment, for people were sensing that there was something wrong now and were looking to her for guidance. The music faltered and fell silent. The drunken carousing died down. All faces were turning towards her.

Our people, Simon had said and she felt a glow of pride in that. She got to her feet.

'Good people of Grafton, we are under attack.' She quelled the ripple of panic that spread through the hall. 'All able-bodied men to the armoury. Everyone else must stay here with me and prepare to nurse the wounded. Do not fear.' She raised her voice. 'My husband has sworn to defend Grafton with his life.'

There was a ragged cheer and then a scramble as the men and the boys ran to do her bidding, already fired up for the fight. The cold night air flowed through the hall, filling the spaces where only moments before had been merriment and celebration. The food on the tables was abandoned, congealing on the plates. The women were talking in low voices, but there was no panic. The people of Grafton had experienced warfare before. They were stolid and prepared.

Edwina and Muna came to her and stood by her, one each side of her chair. Anne put a hand out to each. She knew they wanted to give her comfort, but all she could think of for now was Simon riding out into the dark to meet Malvoisier's men in bloody confrontation.

Edwina squeezed her hand tightly. 'He will come back, madam,' she whispered. 'All will be well.'

Anne stood up. If she had ever doubted her feelings for Simon before this night, the imminence of death and the stark reality of danger made them all too clear.

'He had better come back,' she said fiercely. 'For, God help me, I love him and we must resolve this matter that stands between us before it is too late.'

A clatter of hooves echoed through the hall and they all listened as Simon's troop of horse thundered out across the drawbridge, and then there was nothing but silence and nothing to do but wait.

* * *

'Madam!' Someone was shaking her awake. For a moment Anne's vision and her mind was full of flame and she thought that she was back in the Tempest Tower two months ago, on the night that her father died. Then she blinked and realised she had fallen asleep curled in front of the fire. Around her the women and children of Grafton tossed in fitful sleep.

'Madam, wake up!' Edwina spoke again. In the firelight her face was set in deep lines of strain.

'What is it?' Fear clutched at Anne's heart. 'My lord? He is injured?'

'There is no word yet,' Edwina said. 'It is the Princess, madam. She has disappeared.'

Anne sat bolt upright. 'What? How? She cannot!'

Both the Princess Elizabeth and Meg, her nurse, had been bidden to the feast, for their absence might well have been noted and caused comment. Anne had made certain that they were part of the crowd that thronged the courtyard and were therefore well away from Simon's eye. When the alarm was raised they should have come into the hall for safety, but Anne realised now that she had not seen them. A sick dread caught at her.

'We do not know where she is, madam.' Edwina's eyes were red with tiredness. 'Meg and I, we have looked everywhere! We did not wish to disturb you before. We wondered if she had heard men talking about the attack, and, thinking that the soldiers might be King's men, had wandered off to try to find her father.'

A cry broke from Anne's lips at the thought of the little

Princess going to Malvoisier's men and thinking they would help her. 'No!'

'She is only a child, madam,' Edwina said miserably. 'She would not understand that there are some Royalist soldiers who could not be trusted.'

Anne scrambled to her feet. 'Where is Meg now?'

'Searching the stables again, madam.'

'Then we must go to help her.'

Anne looked around. 'Wake Muna. She must rule here whilst I am gone.'

The courtyard was ominously silent as they crossed to the stables. Simon had had to divide his forces and some men now patrolled the battlements and the gatehouse. The drawbridge was up and the castle secured. Anne shrank within herself and tried not to think about what might be happening in the village of Grafton itself. Pillage and burning… The estate had barely started to put itself back together after the depredations of Malvoisier's rule. And now it would all be lost…

Meg met them in the stable door, her face white with anxiety and her eyes puffy from crying. She caught Anne's arm and the words bubbled up in her throat, bursting out with a desperation to match that in her eyes.

'God forgive me, madam! I have searched everywhere and I cannot find her! We were in the bailey when the word of the attack came through and I only looked away for a moment, but she was gone…' The rest of her words dissolved into noisy sobs.

Anne thought quickly. 'I must go out there. If she is wandering alone…'

Edwina caught her breath. 'Madam, you cannot!'

Anne set her teeth. 'The Princess is my sacred charge! I cannot permit her to go wandering alone in the dark with masterless men on the loose. I will go after her.'

Edwina grabbed her. 'No!' Her voice was a wail of despair. 'The danger… And Lord Greville will find out! He will be so angry—you cannot!'

Anne shook her off. 'Nothing matters,' she said harshly, 'other than the life of the Princess.'

She turned to the darkened stalls behind her. The troops had ridden out, but one horse remained, Anne's own mare Psyche. She was watching them with her dark, intelligent eyes. Anne ran a hand along her neck and felt the warmth and familiarity comfort her.

'Help me saddle her up,' she ordered Edwina. 'Quickly!' She turned to the nurse. 'Meg, bring me the pistol you have in your chamber. And the knife.'

Meg went running. Anne's hands were shaking as she fastened the buckle on Psyche's saddle. Beside her Edwina worked in desperate silence. Meg brought her the pistol and she thrust it into the saddle pouch. The wedding dress had nowhere to conceal a weapon so Ann stuck the knife down her stocking.

They worked in silence and when they were finished Anne turned the horse towards the main gate. There was no time for subterfuge and deception now. When she reached the drawbridge she shouted for Jackson and the soldiers came running from the guardhouse.

'Open the gate!' she ordered.

Jackson goggled at her. 'Madam, I cannot! I cannot permit you to go out there!'

Anne glared down at him. 'Captain Jackson, this is a matter of life and death.' She took out the pistol. 'Open the gate or I swear I shall shoot you where you stand.' She took aim. 'Do it now.'

The young soldier's face was a petrified white mask. 'Open the gate,' he whispered.

Anne did not wait for the drawbridge to touch the ground. She was out of the gate and on the other side as she heard it thud into the earth and the clank and grind of the chains as they laboriously hauled it up again. She had no idea how she was going to get back in to Grafton. She did not even want to think about how she would explain this to Simon, or what he would say if—when—she saw him again.

There was the scent of burning on the wind, a scent so familiar it made her stomach churn. Before her she could see the village in flames. Psyche bridled and stamped at the noise and the smell and Anne put out a hand to soothe her. She could not hear any sound of armed fighting. She wondered whether Simon's men had chased off the attackers. They could be anywhere now, within a hundred yards or miles away. She was alone in the darkness with only the firelight and the moon to guide her and danger all about. But she had a child to find. She set off down the road.

An hour later Anne had circled back behind the village and discovered that it was empty. Malvoisier's renegades had fired the place and gone, and Simon's men had gone too. It was good because it meant that she could search the place unhindered. It was bad because she did not know where the enemy was and at any moment she could be discovered.

She had searched the buildings as best she could. Many of the fires were dying down now and some properties were untouched, but nowhere could Anne find the child. She called and called until she was hoarse with the smoke, but the night was silent. And all about her was Grafton destroyed again, her people's hope ground into the earth, their livelihood ruined. The hatred rose in her throat. This was Malvoisier's work and she would see him dead for it.

Eventually she was forced to accept that Elizabeth was not to be found. She had hunted until her voice gave out and her hands were chafed raw with burns. Her wedding dress was in shreds and there was despair in her heart. She had no options now. She would have to return to Grafton and mount a search in the daylight. Perhaps she should have waited for the morning anyway. She had been impulsive. Simon would certainly think so. If he was still alive.

She would have to tell him the truth about the King's treasure. The thought brought her some relief. But with it came the fear. She had no way of knowing how he would react to the night's events and she was deeply afraid.

She took a track out of the village that led back to Grafton by a longer route. She was growing tired, but not too tired to know that this was the time of most danger, when her guard was down. She walked Psyche along the grass to muffle her hoofbeats and kept the pistol in her hand.

She had almost reached the stand of trees that were visible

from the paddock and was about to skirt them and make her way down towards the castle when Psyche shied. Anne caught the scent a second too late. Men—and horses. They were close by and they would have heard Psyche by now. She dug her heels into the mare's side. With a head start she might just outrun them.

The sound of pursuit filled her ears. Psyche, picking up on some of Anne's recklessness, pounded straight down the hill towards the castle. The ground unrolled beneath her hooves. Anne could feel nothing but the cold wind on her face.

There was a shout behind her and she half-glanced over her shoulder to see Simon's black stallion thundering after her. Behind him the troop had spread out in a skein of men and were coming down the hillside like the horsemen of the apocalypse. Anne felt terror and relief combine.

Simon. He was alive. He was here. And he would be beyond fury.

She tried to rein in but Psyche was too wild now. She could sense the chase behind her and was out of control, veering away from Grafton towards the open hills. The troop of horse swerved away towards Grafton, leaving Simon the only one in pursuit.

The wind caught at the hood of Anne's cloak and snatched it away so that her hair tumbled free about her shoulders. The ground raced beneath them. They jumped one hedge and then a second. Ahead of them the ground began to rise and the fields give way to the springy grass of the Downs. Beyond the hill was the road to Oxford.

There was a narrow copse of trees between Anne and

the road and Psyche finally began to tire, enabling Anne to rein her in. Barely had she gained control when Simon's large black stallion crashed to a halt beside her. The moonlight glinted off his armour. His eyes blazed and he reached out and caught Psyche's reins in a grip of iron. He was breathing hard.

'Simon,' Anne said. Her voice broke. 'Thank God you are safe.'

Simon ignored her words. Behind the visor his eyes were cold and merciless.

'You ride well,' he said. 'In fact, you ride magnificently. But if you run from me ever again, my lady, I shall break your neck. Do you understand?'

Anne wrenched the reins from his grip. A combination of fury and relief flooded through her.

'I was not running away,' she snapped. 'Surely you could see that I could not stop her—' She broke off as Simon dismounted and lifted her bodily from the saddle, setting her on her feet, but keeping a tight grip on her shoulders. He shook her.

'What are you doing here?' he demanded. His grip crushed her bones. 'Where were you going? Whom were you running to?' His face was a mask of stone. He shook her again. 'Answer me! Was it Malvoisier?'

Anne stared at him in shock. Many times in that long night she had wondered how she would ever explain herself to Simon. The one thing she had never even considered was that he would think she was running to Gerard Malvoisier.

'Of course not!' she said. Her words came out as a horrified whisper that lacked conviction. She cleared her throat. 'I did not even know for sure that it was his men—'

Simon made a sound of disgust and disbelief. He let her go so suddenly that she almost fell. He took off his helmet and threw it down on the ground, running a hand through his hair. 'I do not believe you,' he said. 'God help me, you are a liar.'

The fury surged within Anne. 'Fine words on our wedding day, my lord!' She flung out a hand. 'What, do you think I am riding out to join Malvoisier with the King's treasure concealed on me? Perhaps you would care to search me to ensure that I tell the truth?' She turned away from him, outrage in every line of her body. 'To think I thought that one day we might be able to trust one another,' she said bitterly. 'You do not even trust me out of sight!'

There was a long bitter silence.

'I have lost three more men tonight,' Simon said between shut teeth. 'Malvoisier has burned Grafton village to the ground. I left you at the castle thinking that at the least you would be safe there and might rally our people. Instead I find you out here, alone... How did you get out?'

'I threatened to shoot Captain Jackson if he did not lower the bridge,' Anne said levelly. 'It was the only way. Simon, let me explain—'

The breath hissed between Simon's teeth as he cut off her explanations in their tracks. 'Then you are a fool as well as a traitor,' he said. 'A hundred men could have swarmed into Grafton at such a moment and killed all within. Did you think of that when you rode out to meet your paramour? Did you?'

'He is not my lover,' Anne said. 'Let me explain to you! Hear me out!'

'I heard you out when you told me that Malvoisier was your enemy,' Simon said, 'and even then you were playing me for a fool. I should have known you were no virgin.'

Anne's hand made contact with his cheek in a slap that hurt all the way up her arm. 'I told you before that my response to you sprang from my feelings for you, not from experience,' she said, her voice so harsh she barely recognised herself. 'And now you demean that too. You sicken me.' She turned towards Psyche, but Simon caught her arm, dragging her round to face him again.

'We are going back now, madam, and you will ride with me,' he said. 'And if you make a single move to escape me I will drag you back by the hair.'

He turned to her to throw her up into the saddle but in that moment there was a sudden sharp sound from the road beyond the trees. They both froze.

'Soldiers?' Anne whispered.

Simon's glance was blistering. 'Malvoisier's renegades. As you are well aware.'

Anne was not going to argue further. She knew that her only hope was to wait until Simon's temper had calmed and he might listen to her. Her feelings were raw at his lack of trust, but a part of her acknowledged and understood his anger. He had lost more men tonight and still Malvoisier continued to taunt him in a calculated gesture to bring ruin to the lands that Simon had so recently sworn to protect. This was no time to mention the King's treasure and damn matters between them further still. She needed to wait. Nevertheless, for Simon to think her Malvoisier's accomplice was unforgivable. She tried to smother the wretchedness inside her.

Simon was drawing the horses silently into the shadow of the trees. When he turned back he had his sword in his hand.

'I have a pistol—' she began, only to fall silent as Simon took it from the saddlebag and tucked it in his belt. She felt a dull shock. He thought she might betray them. That she might kill him, even. She could read it in his face.

He gestured with the sword.

'Be quiet or I shall use you as a hostage.'

He caught her arm and pulled her down into the undergrowth. The weight of his body on her held her still. One of his hands was over her mouth. The other held the sword. The blade was about an inch from her face.

The sounds of men and animals were growing louder now. The horses stirred nervously. Anne could feel every tense line of Simon's body against hers. She could feel the warmth of his skin so close to her own. She could see the way the night breeze teased the shadowy tendrils of chestnut hair in the nape of his neck. She remembered him holding her close in tenderness, not anger, and she felt sick at what had happened between them.

The sounds died away but still Simon did not move. An eternity later he shifted, raising himself on one elbow, and said quietly, 'They have gone.'

Anne lay still. It was very dark now in the lee of the trees. 'You were going to use me to buy your freedom,' she said dully.

Simon looked down at her. 'I would have used you

however I saw fit,' he said coldly. 'You are my enemy. I could not be sure that you would not betray us.'

It was as simple as that. Anne absorbed the blow of it and wondered why it should hurt so much. Simon held out a hand to help her to her feet, but she ignored him and scrambled up on her own. She was trembling and when he threw her up into the saddle before him she made no protest. They turned and made their way down toward Grafton at a sedate pace, Psyche following meekly behind. Anne did not speak again. She felt chilled to the bone, and not merely from the March cold.

The drawbridge was down and they rattled across and into the courtyard. The soldiers on the gate stood stiffly to attention, looking at her out of the corner of their eyes. A groom came out to take Psyche. As Simon swung down from the saddle and lifted Anne to the ground, Will Jackson came hurrying out from the guard post.

Simon turned to look at Anne and the coldness in his eyes froze her to the spot.

'Escort Lady Greville to the cells,' he said. 'Lock her up.'

Chapter Ten

For a long, tense moment, nobody moved. One of the guards gasped as though he could not quite believe his ears. Jackson looked shocked.

Simon's rage, which he had barely managed to contain during the ride back to Grafton, burst out.

'That is an order, Captain Jackson,' he ground out.

'Sir.' Jackson straightened. He looked at Anne almost beseechingly. Simon felt another great wave of fury. Damn the woman that all his soldiers were in awe of her! If Jackson did not move soon he would drag her to the dungeons himself.

But Anne was going to make it easy for Jackson. She made a slight gesture, indicating her willingness to follow him. Jackson looked hugely relieved.

'If you would come this way, madam…' He sounded as though he was offering to seat her at a banquet.

Anne cast Simon one long, unreadable look from her very dark eyes and then she turned her back deliberately and followed Jackson towards the door. Simon stood, watching tensely, as the torchlit shadows swallowed them. He would not put it past Anne Grafton to give his soldiers the slip on the way between the door and the prison cell.

He became aware of the night cold, and of his men looking at him curiously. He wondered what showed on his face.

'Lock the gate and double the guard,' he said. 'At first light we will assess the damage in the village, but for now no one leaves the castle. No one. Do you hear me?'

Without a further word he turned and stalked off towards the hall.

Henry caught him just as he reached the Screens Passage, took his arm and propelled him somewhat forcibly into his study. A fire was lit and the room glowed warm. Simon flung himself down into a chair and closed his eyes. The draughts board was still there set up from the night before the wedding when he and Henry had played a game together to help calm his nerves. It seemed a long time ago. He could not quite believe what had happened since then.

His face still stung where Anne had slapped him. He fingered it tentatively, welcoming the ache of pain. It told him that he was still alive.

'I heard what happened,' Henry said quietly. 'They say the damage to the village could have been greater—'

'The damage is in my failure to protect my people,' Simon said bitterly. 'Malvoisier has escaped again.'

Henry poured him a beaker of wine. 'Is it true that you have confined your wife to a prison cell?'

Simon looked up briefly. 'Aye, it is.'

Henry pulled a face. 'You are harsh, brother.'

'She tried to run away.'

Simon stared into the red heart of the fire. He did not want to explain to Henry that much of his anger sprang from disillusionment with himself as much as with Anne. Wanting Anne Grafton had been simple. How could he *not* want her, with her silky black hair and her slender, voluptuous body and that deceptive air of innocent valour? But this depth of feeling, this misery, this feeling of betrayal was entirely alien. He had let his feelings go too deep—he had loved her—and now he was paying the price.

'I do not believe it,' Henry said. He eased himself into the other chair. 'I do not believe Lady Anne would play you false.'

Simon glared at him. 'Do not be a fool. She has played me false from the first. She always intended to run away to Malvoisier. Likely they planned this attack between them.' He shook his head. 'I have been so blind! It was Malvoisier who sent her to me that night when she swore she was there without his knowledge to beg clemency for the people of Grafton. I wondered how he had managed to penetrate the defences that day that Standish was shot down. Likely he knew of the tunnel all along, or she let him through!' His fist crashed down on the table. 'And tonight she rides out to meet him while the estate burns!'

Henry's lips thinned. Simon saw his hand go to his sword and hover there for one revealing moment before he let it fall to his side.

'You are the fool here, brother, not I,' he said. 'What, you expect me to believe that Anne would betray her own people for Gerard Malvoisier? She has worked all her life to keep Grafton, to save Grafton, and now she would throw all that away? Your wits are gone begging!'

Simon made no reply. Henry had never challenged him like this before, but the grief and jealousy inside him was so great he did not think he could speak.

'You forget,' Henry said. 'I saw Lady Anne with Malvoisier the night she saved my life. That was no scene played out to deceive you! She hated him. Nor was she playing a part when she came to you to tell you that I lived. You have maligned her. You should be ashamed.'

Guilt stirred briefly in Simon and he repressed it. He did not want to think that he had made a mistake. He drank a glass of wine with one swallow and refilled the beaker, pushing the bottle towards his brother. 'Then what was she doing there tonight?' he demanded. 'If she had not run away to join Malvoisier, what was she doing outside Grafton?'

'I heard that there was a child lost and she had gone to search for her,' Henry said quietly. 'But surely Lady Anne is the best person to answer that question. Did you even ask her?'

Simon scowled at him. 'You are bewitched. Half my garrison is bewitched! She wraps you about her little finger.'

'And you are sick with jealousy,' Henry said hardily, 'and all for no reason.' He stood up. 'I do not wish to speak with you tonight, Simon, least of all drink your wine. I told you once that you had my loyalty.' He paused. 'Now I can tell you that you are very close to losing it. Think on that, brother, when you cannot sleep for what you have done.'

After he had gone out, Simon sat and stared into the fire. He was very tired, but not so tired that exhaustion had overlaid his hatred of Gerard Malvoisier. Once again the renegade General had marched into his stronghold and threatened all that Simon had sought to build. Simon had driven him off and had protected Grafton's people, but he could not save their lands. In the morning the charred horror of Malvoisier's work would be visible for all to see. And this time he would not have Anne by his side when he attempted to rebuild it, for he had driven her off too. Whether his doubts were justified or merely a ghost conjured by his hatred of Malvoisier, he could not be sure. He had had so little to bind Anne to him and he had always been up against her loyalty to her cause.

For a moment he thought of sending for Anne and demanding that she tell him the reason she had left Grafton that night. Henry had been right. He sank another glass of wine as he thought about it. He had not given Anne the chance to explain herself and now his feelings were so raw that he did not want to hear what she had to say. He was afraid to hear it.

With an oath, Simon tipped the glass to his lips again. Now, as the clarity the wine brought started to enter his brain, he could see the devastation he had wrought in his marriage before it had barely started. He had tried to make Anne break her allegiance by threatening to harm her servants if she did not tell him the whereabouts of the King's treasure. He had practically forced her into marriage. And now, in his jealousy and anger, he had shown how shallow his trust of her was. Every last vestige of the love she might once have borne him had been crushed in his quest to put principle before love and gain those things he wanted.

He called for Jackson, and when the captain came running he ordered that Anne be brought from the cells. A mere ten minutes later his captain returned, alone. He was shaking.

'My lord,' Jackson cleared his throat. 'Lady Greville bade me tell you that she will not obey your command. She said—' he swallowed hard '—that she would rather spend her wedding night in a prison cell than in your bed, my lord.'

After Jackson went out, Simon emptied the pitcher of wine into his glass. There was oblivion waiting for him, but even as he drank himself into it a small voice at the back of his mind told him that it would be no great wonder if his wife never wished to speak with him again.

Anne sat alone, curled up in the dark. The dungeon at Grafton was a tiny cell with a grille in the floor that opened on to the moat. The air that flowed in was bitterly cold and smelled of damp weeds.

The hour was late and Anne was hungry, but she doubted that Simon would permit her to have any food. She was too proud to ask for any, or for a few blankets to keep out the bitter chill. When Simon's message had come she had been so incensed that she would rather have cut her throat than do his bidding. So now she huddled in a corner, and thought about Simon.

She did not hate him. A part of her could even understand his treatment of her although her sore heart cried out against it.

As for the Princess Elizabeth, at least there her fears were allayed. Edwina had been in the courtyard when she had returned and Anne had sought her gaze as surreptitiously as possible. When Edwina had nodded and smiled at her, a huge weight was lifted from Anne's heart whilst another huge one plunged her further into despair. They had found the Princess. The whole escapade had been for nought. Now she need never tell Simon the truth of what had happened that night. She could keep the secret of the King's treasure for a few more days until Charles sent for his daughter. For send he would. And soon. Anne knew it.

And eventually she fell into a fitful sleep, trying to block out the cold and the unhappiness in her heart.

She was woken by the sound of voices outside the door.

'Lady Anne is not permitted any food? On whose authority?'

It was Edwina. Anne rubbed her eyes and sat up straight.

She heard one of the guards mutter a reply, then Edwina again, more strident this time.

'Ask Lord Greville? The porridge will be stone cold by the time you have done that! Don't spill it!'

The key squeaked in the lock and light flowed into the cell. Anne blinked. One of the guards was standing in the opening, a tray in his hand. He looked slightly sheepish. Behind him Anne could see Edwina standing, hands on hips.

'He would not let me bring it in myself, milady,' Edwina called indignantly. 'He asked me if there was a key in it!'

Anne laughed, her spirits lifting. 'Is there?' she enquired.

'No, madam. That would spoil the flavour.' Edwina's voice also eased into warmth and Anne saw one of the guards smile. 'The best bit is at the bottom, madam.'

'Enough,' the guard said. He held the tray out to Anne. 'Lord Greville will have my hide for this, but I do not like to think you hungry, madam.'

Anne smiled and thanked him, and took the tray from his outstretched hand. The porridge was still warm and smelled wonderful. She crouched down in her corner, took up the spoon and gobbled the lot with a great deal less finesse than became the lady of the manor. The guard had kept the door of the cell open and was watching her as she ate.

'It's good,' she said, with her mouth full, and saw him smile.

'Shall I take it away now, ma'am?' Edwina's voice came, innocently, from outside the door of the cell. The guard turned away for a second and in that moment Anne twisted the bowl over, read the message on the bottom and righted it again. The guard turned back and she held out the tray.

'If you would be so good,' she said.

He took it from her outstretched hand and passed it to Edwina. Anne's nerves eased a little.

'We miss you, madam,' Edwina called.

'Begone now,' the guard said, but his tone was friendly. 'Quick, before Lord Greville hears of this.'

The door swung to and Anne heard Edwina exchange more good-tempered banter with the guard before there was the scrape of the outer door closing on the stone step and silence descended once more.

'The child is safe.'

Anne pulled her knees up to her chin and curled up once more. This time she did not even notice the cold. It was the confirmation that she had needed. Princess Elizabeth was safe. Her own future was much less certain.

Anne rested her cheek on a fold of her cloak, thinking back to the time her father had called her to his chamber and told her of the great secret he was entrusted with. The Earl had known he was dying. Anne blinked back the tears as she remembered the strength in his hand as he had grasped hers and entrusted the secret to her. Such a heavy burden to lay upon the Lady of Grafton, with her father dying and her house overrun… And then Simon had taken the Manor and everything had changed, but some secrets still had to be kept. Anne rubbed her forehead. Her head ached—the whole of her body ached, and her heart ached most of all. She knew that she had loved Simon Greville and a tiny spark of that love still burned within her, but whether it would grow again or be snuffed out, she could not tell.

Simon marched up the staircase to Anne's chamber. He had had an exhausting day seeing at first hand the devastation that Gerard Malvoisier had brought on Grafton. His head was pounding from an over-indulgence in wine the previous night, he was tired, filthy and heartsore. He felt inordinately guilty to have kept Anne locked up all day whilst his anger abated. His first intention in returning to the Manor had been to order her release. And then Will Jackson had come to him and told him that Anne had demanded to be released earlier in the day, and he had let her go.

When Simon had first heard the news he was so incensed that he had almost thrown his Captain of the Guard into the cells in Anne's place. He simply could not believe that his men were so susceptible to Anne's persuasion. She could make them believe black was white and night was day. She asked to be released and they actually agreed... He flung open the door of Anne's chamber and stormed inside. He would have a reckoning with her now and he would not be so impressionable as those fools who made up his garrison.

At least she had had no intention of running off. Jackson had said that a bath was her most pressing request and it seemed she had spoken the truth. The room was warm and lit by candlelight. There was the scent of lavender in the air. For a moment Simon could not see anyone, although he could hear the sound of voices and laughter from behind the screen in the centre of the room. He pushed it aside. And stopped dead.

Anne was sitting in a huge wooden tub of lavender-scented water. Her hair was wet and sleek and black, streaming down over her bare shoulders. Her skin was pale and smooth. She looked innocently delectable and Simon wanted to pluck her from the water and make love to her there and then with all the anger, frustration and thwarted love that racked his body. The strength of his impulse, given all that had happened between them, shocked him deeply.

Edwina and Muna were on the point of pouring another bucketful of water into the tub, but when she saw Simon Muna gave a little scream and let go of her side of the pail.

Water splashed on to the rushes on the floor and spilled over his boots. Edwina staggered, grounding the bucket with a bang. Her face was red with exertion and outrage.

'My lord!'

'Lord Greville makes a habit of invading ladies' chambers, so I am told,' Anne said, sliding further beneath the water. Her dark eyes mocked him, but he could see the anger beneath her smile. 'I thought that you would be anxious to speak with me, Lord Greville, but not this eager.'

Simon looked down at her. Her chin was at water level now, but although the lavender turned the water a milky pale colour, he could still see the shadow outline of her body beneath the surface. The herb-scented steam filled his senses and clouded his mind with sensual thoughts. He folded his arms.

'I would be delighted to speak now,' he said softly.

Edwina gave a snort of disgust. 'You should wait outside, my lord,' she said, 'until Lady Anne is dressed.'

Simon laughed. 'My good woman, I am going nowhere. I do not trust my lady wife not to climb out of the window as soon as my back is turned.'

'Well you should do, my lord,' Edwina stated shortly. 'For shame, treating my lady like a criminal!'

There was a splash as Anne shifted beneath the water. 'That is enough, Edwina.' She gave Simon a look of challenge. 'Very well, my lord, we shall talk. Muna, the bathing sheet, if you please.'

She stood up. Once again the water spilled over Simon's boots, but this time he did not even notice. His entire attention was riveted on the pale, naked body of his wife as the water streamed off her.

Her skin was stung pink from the heat and smelled sweet and warm. Her hair was black as night. Her breasts were high and rounded. Simon was transfixed, his gaze travelling down the slender curve of her waist, over her buttocks to the line of her thighs. And down…

She wore nothing but a smile of wicked triumph.

Simon opened his mouth to speak, but no words came. He cleared his throat, turning to Anne's women.

'Get out.'

Edwina and Muna exchanged one long, frightened look. Simon grabbed the bathing sheet from Muna's hands.

'Get out,' he repeated. 'Now.'

They went. Not even Edwina objected. And through it all Anne stood pale and proud before him.

As the door closed behind them, he took the sheet, wrapped it about her and lifted her from the bath. He brought her close to him, sliding her body down the length of his so that his painful arousal could be no secret to her.

'You go too far.' He spoke roughly in her ear.

'I know.' Her voice was a whisper. 'But you deserved it. You provoked me to it.'

'You are wanton.'

She drew a little away from him, clutching the sheet to her, her chin tilted up at a haughty angle. 'No, I am not. You accused me of that yesterday. You were wrong—in that and in many other matters.'

Their eyes met and held. Since Henry had left him the

previous night Simon had had much time to think and he knew she was right.

'You are angry with me,' he said.

He felt a quiver run through her. 'For so many reasons,' she said. 'You locked me up. We are *married*, Simon, and you locked me up.'

He held her very tightly. 'We are married, Anne, and you ran away from me.'

She glared at him. 'I *told* you I was not running away, least of all to Malvoisier. You did not believe me.'

He ran a hand down her body over the tangled folds of the bath sheet. 'So now you are making me suffer for it.'

She smiled, a smile of feminine pleasure. 'Are you suffering?'

In reply, Simon drew her closer to his aching hardness. 'You know I am.'

Held close like this, her body answering the desire in his own, Simon did not want to think about war or loyalties or betrayal, or the complicated emotions they stirred. He took her face in his hands and kissed her, biting down gently on her bottom lip, sliding his tongue into her mouth. Her lips opened on a gasp and she responded to him fiercely. The bathing sheet fell to the floor between them. He ran his hands down her body, now cool from the air, but still scented sweetly with lavender.

'If you want to stop this, you must speak now.' Simon tore his mouth from hers. His voice was barely more than a whisper. 'I am no saint and I have wanted you every day that I have been here.'

Anne opened her eyes. They were black and dreamy with sensual pleasure, but he could see the flame of her anger was not yet quenched.

'I want you to want me,' she said, and there was an undertone of heat in her voice. 'You deserve to be on the rack.' She stepped back and looked him in the eye. 'You called me wanton,' she said again. 'You did not believe my protestations of virtue. Well…' she shrugged one bare shoulder '…it is for you to find out the truth now.'

Simon grabbed her, tangling his hand roughly in her hair as he tilted her mouth up to meet his again.

He scooped her naked body up in his arms and tossed her on the bed. Discarding his clothes seemed to take far too long. He was painfully afraid that in that time she would move—and escape him again. She would slip through his fingers as she had done from the first, tantalising him yet never truly his. He had to put his mark on her now. He had to claim her, indisputably, for his own.

He took the bathing screen in his hands and ripped the material into strips. He was so quick to tie her wrists to the bed rail above her head that she did not even move until he swung a leg over her, parting her thighs. He took one slender ankle in his hand and tied it to the post at the bottom, then the other. Her body was spread and open to him. He positioned himself between her legs.

Anne's eyes opened wide and she gave a wild cry. Simon put his hands on her bare waist, feeling the curve beneath his palms.

'So,' he said, 'you tempted me and now I will take you.'

He ran his hands up her body, over her breasts, rubbing the palms against her nipples.

'Perfect, sweeting. Now you are mine and I can do whatever I choose to you, when I choose.'

There was a mixture of nervousness and challenge in Anne's eyes, but she did not struggle against her bonds. Simon braced himself above her and leaned forward, cupping her in his hands, touching his tongue gently to her breasts this time, feeling the nipples harden in his mouth. He stroked upward over the curve of her breast and watched the goose bumps cover her skin. Anne's face was flushed now and she made small, convulsive movements upward against the restraints that held her, pressing herself into his hands. He leaned over her again and took her more fully in his mouth, tugging on her breasts until she cried out and the beat of his blood threatened to make him lose control completely. He was almost undone. He had wanted to do this since he had first seen her.

Her skin was slick and damp. He bent to kiss her, but she turned her head and bit his shoulder. The pain of it cleared his mind for a moment. She was not his yet. She was not seduced. She might be ravished—by him and by her own senses—but she had not given herself away.

His hand moved to her face, caressing her cheek and the slender line of her neck, dipping into the hollow of her throat, stroking down to her collarbone and further down to her breasts, laving away her anger with sweetness. This time when he bent to kiss her she accepted the gentle touch of his lips and curled her tongue against his. Her body moved, intuitively, irresistibly, up to meet him.

Simon sat back between her parted thighs. He was so hard it was unbearable. He touched his pulsing tip to her, briefly, gently, and she gasped and raised her hips again.

'Soon, sweeting…' His breath was ragged.

He caressed the soft skin of her inner thigh, each time moving subtly closer to her secret place. Now when he touched her she writhed within the bonds that held her, instinctively searching for the fulfilment she knew was waiting. He wanted to fill her and take her and make her truly his. But not yet.

He slid down the bed until he was between her thighs. His hair brushed her leg as he bent his head to touch his tongue to the very core of her. Anne gave another cry and squirmed within her bonds. Simon held her apart and touched his tongue to her again—and again until she cried out with each caress.

The rise and fall of her hips against his hands ruined any control Simon might otherwise have kept. He raised himself and covered her body with his own, braced himself above her and pushed inside her. He felt resistance; she cried out, but in surprise, not pleasure, this time and he sat back to caress her into response again. A huge, primal power shook him. She had said she was a virgin, had maintained it against all the calumnies and rumours, and now he knew she had told the truth. She had said she would never lie to him. She had not.

'Simon…' Her eyes were open, blurred with the vestiges of passion, but shadowed with confusion now.

'Hush, sweeting.' He leant forward to untie her hands and the movement brought him deeper inside her. She flinched a little.

He kissed her, smoothing the back from her forehead. 'It has to hurt. I am sorry.'

She nodded slightly, shifting to smooth her hands down his back to his buttocks. Her touch was light and wondering on him, exploring, relishing the touch.

'My legs—' she said.

'Must stay as they are for now.' He had no wish to pull out of her so that he could untie her ankles. He needed her to become accustomed to the feel of him inside her.

'I like you to be open to me,' he said.

He felt the jolt of sensation that went through her at his words and swiftly bent to capture her lips with his again, easing himself deeper inside her, moving gently at first then, as she started to respond, driving with quick, hard thrusts. He felt her twist and gasp beneath him, felt her hands on his back and buttocks, and lost the last shreds of his self-control as he felt the shudders of pleasure rack her body and heard her cry out. He emptied himself into her and lay, spent and still, entwined in her arms.

After a while she moved to loosen the bonds that held her ankles, and he watched her body in the fire glow, all creamy pale and bronze. Her expression was very grave and still. He rolled over, suddenly urgent.

'Anne…I…' He wanted to apologise for doubting her, but then he realised that she might take his apology to mean that he had been disappointed in her, and that would be worse.

She looked at him. She was sitting, her legs curled beneath her, like a naked statue.

'I thought that you came to talk,' she said, 'not to make

love to me.' She smiled slightly. 'Four years ago, Edwina told me that you might shock me on my wedding night. Little did I realise how right she would be.'

'I forgot about talking,' Simon said absently. He took a strand of her hair, twining it about his fingers.

'It can wait.' She rubbed her cheek against his hand like a cat. 'It has waited this long. I do not want to spoil matters.' She frowned fiercely. 'Just for this once, I *will* not.'

Simon looked at her. There was much he wanted to say to her, but for once he was uncertain. He had stolen her innocence in a most devastating way and had some shame for the way that he had done it, but he could not regret making her his. It had been the most shockingly perfect and exquisite experience of his life. Without her he was not whole.

'I was rough with you,' he began.

She gave him a shuttered glance. 'You were angry,' she said, 'but you did not hurt me.'

He had been angry. He remembered it with vague surprise, as though it had been a long time ago. Now he felt sated and almost content, but not quite. He struggled to work out what was missing. Once he had thought that if he had Anne in his bed then he would have all that he desired. Now he knew he had deceived himself. Without Anne's trust and her love, he had nothing.

'You were angry too.' He turned his head to look at her. 'Are you still?'

She did not answer straight away. She pulled the bindings through her fingers. 'I do not know,' she said. 'I do not know how I feel.' Her eyes were wide and thoughtful. 'I cannot accuse you of taking anything I was not prepared to give,' she said, 'so in that sense I am not angry.'

Simon put out a hand and pulled her down beside him again. He could still feel hesitation in her.

'But for doubting your word—'

'Yes,' she said. 'It pains me that we cannot trust one another.'

She lay next to him, the length of her nakedness pressed against his. She caressed his chest thoughtfully, gently. He felt a huge humbleness to see the innocent knowledge in her face.

'There are some things that we cannot change,' he said. 'Your allegiance and mine…' He felt an instinctive resistance in her as though such things were too painful to speak of, but he kept doggedly on. 'There is only one thing that I can promise you, Anne. I shall never ask you to give up your loyalty to the King's cause. I cannot ask it without asking you to change, to be a different woman from the one that I admire so deeply. I understand that now.'

Anne pressed her lips to his throat. 'Thank you,' she whispered. She turned more closely into his embrace.

'You asked what I feel,' she said, after a moment. 'I feel… interest.'

She threw one leg over him and slid up to sit astride his thighs, watching his face with bright eyes. 'I feel curiosity,' she said. She ran a hand over the hair of his chest. 'About this…' Her hand drifted down, 'and this…' She rubbed his thigh experimentally. 'And this…' Her hand hovered over his penis, which was already starting to stir and grow thick again.

'You approach everything with a great deal of passion, my lady,' Simon said, a little hoarsely.

Anne smiled. 'I confess it. I know that I do not seem shy, but…' she hesitated '…I do not quite dare touch.'

Simon groaned. 'Please do. I am begging you…'

Anne leaned forward so that her lips were just touching his. 'Perhaps I should tie *you* up, my lord, so that I might make my exploration at my leisure?'

Simon smiled. 'If that is your desire, my lady, I shall do all I may to help you learn.'

He watched the innocence, the intrigue and the dawning mischief in her eyes and felt his heart turn over with a strange sense of tenderness and lust.

'You are all goodness, my lord,' she said, and reached up to fasten the first of his bonds.

When Anne awoke it was dark and for a moment she was confused. Then the memories flooded her mind—heated, passionate, devastating memories—and she shot up in the bed with a mixture of shock and disbelief. Simon was lying beside her, one arm across her in casual possession, and when she moved he made a sleepy sound of protest and tried to pull her close to him again, but Anne was already fumbling for the tinderbox and striking the light for the candle. The small glow brought the room into dim focus. She could see it all now, the cold water of the bath, Simon's clothes in a discarded trail across the floor, the bedclothes half-tumbled by their rapture, and the bindings… She blushed to see the bindings.

She had always been aware of the wild spirit within her. It prompted her to courage and occasionally to rashness, but until she had met Simon she had not truly understood the other side of that wildness, the sensual will that had lain dormant within her, waiting for the man who was going to unlock it. And Simon had the same fierce spirit. She had recognised it in him when they were young, although she had not realised then what it meant. She had known they were matched as soon as she had stepped into his chamber on the night before the battle for Grafton. She had been resisting the truth ever since. They fought with a passion that was only surpassed by the fervour with which they made love.

She looked down at Simon. For once his restlessness was quelled and he looked wholly at ease in his sleep. He looked young. He looked peaceful.

Anne remembered all that she had learned of him—the hard planes and angles of his body, so different from the soft curves of her own, and the hidden, secret vulnerable places like the curve of his neck where the skin was paler and soft to the touch. She reached out a hand lightly to his lips. She could feel the stubble on his chin beneath her fingers and she could remember the sensation of it against her breast. She closed her eyes for a second.

When she opened them again Simon was looking at her, his dark gaze softer than she had ever seen before.

'You are well, my love?'

My love…

Anne's heart clenched. It was merely an endearment, but suddenly she wanted it to be true with every fibre in her being.

'I am well,' she said. Then, on a note of surprise, 'I am hungry.'

Simon laughed. 'Then let us eat.'

Anne put a hand out to catch his arm. 'Wait! You cannot merely call for food and drink here and now! Everyone will know what has happened!'

Simon looked at her. 'Sweetheart, unless I miss my guess, the entire castle will be aware of what has been happening between us. I have been with you for hours.'

Anne put her hands over her face, then pushed her hair back and sat up determinedly. 'Very well. I suppose I shall have to face down their disapproval.'

Simon smiled. 'I doubt very much that they *will* disapprove. We are married, remember. The entire population of Grafton will be relieved that our quarrel is at an end.'

Anne frowned. 'Well, what business is it of theirs?' she demanded.

Simon sighed. 'Our happiness will always be their business,' he said. 'They are our people.'

Our people. Anne felt a strange sensation, as though a part of her old life was slipping away from her. She was a little afraid of the new.

'We will eat together,' Simon said, 'and then, much as it grieves me, I must leave you.' He touched her cheek. 'But I will be back soon.'

Anne's skin grew warm as his caressing gaze travelled over her and she gathered the bedclothes closer. 'I feel shy,' she said crossly. 'Stop looking at me.'

There was a smile on Simon's lips as he swung himself

out of bed and strode to the door. He was utterly unselfconscious of his nudity. Anne looked at the compact elegance of his body and again felt the wrench of love, loss and strangeness inside her. She took the opportunity whilst his back was turned to grab her robe and wrap it about her.

Simon stuck his head around the door and issued a few brief orders.

'At least they will know we have worked up an appetite,' he said, with a grin.

'You are proud of yourself!' Anne said accusingly.

Simon gave her a bashful, boyish smile. He came up to her and held her lightly. 'I admit it. I wanted this. Of course I am pleased.' He gave her a quizzical look. 'But you, I sense, are not.'

Anne put one hand against his chest. 'I am sorry, Simon. It is that everything seems so strange and different, and—' She stopped. 'I cannot quite understand what has happened to me,' she finished honestly.

Simon's expression softened. 'I understand, sweetheart.' He drew her closer into his arms. 'I said once before that you need not be alone and now you will not be. Never again.'

Anne rested her cheek against the warmth of his chest. His heart beat strongly. She knew he would give her a strength and protection she could lean upon and in return she would give him her loyalty. Once the matter of the King's treasure was at an end there would be no more secrets between them.

She realised that Simon was kissing her again, scattering little persuasive kisses across her cheeks and throat whilst his hands were sliding the robe from her shoulders. She made a grab for it.

'You had better put your clothes on again,' she said, 'before the food is brought up.'

'Must I?' Simon was nibbling at her collarbone, nipping the skin of her breasts. 'We missed our wedding night,' he added. 'There is much to be done.'

Anne drew away a little and this time he let her go. His gaze searched her face. 'What is wrong?' he asked.

Anne hesitated. 'Simon, before when we made love…' She paused, the colour rushing into her face. What she wanted to say was that now she needed something different—tenderness, not passion. She was feeling vulnerable, acutely conscious of him and of the wildness with which she had responded to him. Whilst she groped for the words he read her thoughts in her face and swept her up once again to tumble with her into the centre of the huge feather bed. Then he took her in his arms.

'It is not always like that,' he said. The touch of his lips was gentle against hers. 'Let me show you.'

Anne smiled at him. 'With all my heart,' she whispered.

They had a week of almost perfect joy. Afterwards Anne was to remember that in the midst of the ruins of Grafton, nothing could touch her happiness. All day she worked with a will to help the villagers rebuild their lives and their homes and at night she lay in Simon's arms before the fire or in the big tester bed, and they made love, sometimes with wild passion, sometimes with gentleness, always with tenderness.

Then two things happened.

Fairfax wrote, summoning Simon to Northampton, where Cromwell's New Model Army was gathering to do battle with the Royalists.

And the King sent for his daughter.

Chapter Eleven

Simon lay his pen down upon the chaos of papers on his desk. There were requisitions for everything: provisions, horses, weaponry, all the equipment that an army needed. In the morning he would be leaving to join forces with Fairfax in Northampton. He did not want to go. It was too cruelly soon.

'How can I leave when I have found my only happiness?' he had whispered into Anne's hair the previous night, as they had lain together and made love. He had held her closer to him than ever before and made her a promise.

'I will come back to you,' he had said, 'for you were forfeit to me from the moment I saved your life. We belong together.'

He had seen the tears in Anne's eyes then and had teased her gently about them until she had stopped his words with her kisses. But it was difficult for them both and this final day before he left was agony. He was going to fight for what he believed in but in doing so he was going to fight against

Anne's cause. Neither of them spoke of it, just as neither of them had dared mention the King's treasure in the past week for fear of damaging the delicate happiness they had found. But the long shadow lay between them.

Simon got up from the desk and walked across to the window. The inner bailey was cluttered with provisions carts piled high for the journey. His men swarmed all over them like ants, fetching and carrying. But in a corner of the courtyard was something so unusual that it immediately caught Simon's eye. It was Muna and Henry, and they were quarrelling.

Simon raised his brows. It was difficult enough for anyone to argue with Henry since he was notoriously easygoing, though Simon did wonder if his exclusion from Fairfax's plans had put Henry in a bad mood. He had not been deemed fit to travel to Northampton, nor to fight, and, although he had seemed to accept the judgement with good grace, he might well feel embarrassed that he was not seen to be pulling his weight. As Simon watched, Henry turned away from his betrothed with a short, sharp word and Muna, the tears streaming down her face, shouted something at his retreating back and ran away to the shelter of the kitchens, ignoring the curious stares bent on her by soldiers and servants alike. A moment later there was a knock on the door and Henry walked straight in.

He was pale and breathing hard. Simon gestured him to a chair, but Henry shook his head.

'Thank you,' he said, his tone short. 'I prefer to stand.'

Simon inclined his head. And waited.

Henry took a deep breath. 'Lady Greville has taken the

King's treasure and gone to hand it over to a Royalist messenger in the Braden Forest,' he said baldly. 'I had the truth from Muna just now. She was fearful for Anne and could not bear to keep the secret from me any longer.' He clenched his fists. 'I told her that I would go directly to you and tell you of it. She begged me not to.' Henry made a violent gesture. 'I am sorry, Simon.' His voice shook. 'I am so sorry for both of us.'

Simon leaned both hands on the edge of the desk. He understood what his brother meant. In the final conflict between his loyalty to Muna and his loyalty to his cause, Henry had chosen to break his faith to her and keep allegiance to his brother. And Anne, it seemed, had done the same. She had chosen duty over love.

Simon felt sick and cold and old. He had hoped against hope that Anne would eventually trust him enough to tell him of the King's treasure. Had it only been the previous night that he had felt so close to her, loved her so wholly and completely? Yet he had known even then that they were playing a game of pretence, ignoring the huge secret that lay between them. He had known it, but he had not wanted to face it.

'There is more,' Henry was saying urgently. 'The King's treasure—it is a child. Simon, it is the Princess Elizabeth.'

This time the shock Simon felt was cold and hard and disillusioning. Anne had not thought he was a good enough man to entrust with the life of a child. She had kept the secret from him because she believed that he would use a *child* to further his own ends, or those of his cause. He stared blindly at his brother whilst the stunning blow wrenched him, so painfully that he thought he might be physically sick.

Henry was pulling his arm, recalling him to the present. 'We must go after her. It was madness for her to go alone.'

Simon did not reply. He felt so angry and hurt and betrayed that he thought it unlikely he could ever make Henry understand.

'Simon!' Henry was becoming impatient now. 'Do you not hear me? Anne is in danger and the Princess too—'

He broke off as the door slammed open and Will Jackson tumbled into the room.

'Malvoisier's troops have been sighted on Braden Down, my lord,' he gasped. 'General Malvoisier himself has been seen.'

'Braden,' Henry said. He was white to the lips. He grabbed Simon's arm. 'Anne is in the Braden Forest! Now will you interfere?'

Simon was already halfway to the door. And he prayed fervently that he was not already too late.

It was a long, frightening walk through the forest of Braden to the place appointed by the King's messenger. Anne walked briskly, holding tight to Elizabeth's hand. Meg, the nursemaid, had gone on before so as not to alert suspicion. They had not been able to ride, for that would have raised the alarm at Grafton. Instead Anne had waited until the bustle of Simon's war preparations was at its height and had slipped through the main gate when a provisions cart was passing out. No one had noticed. They were all too preoccupied with the battle to come.

There was a knot of fear in Anne's stomach, but strangely

she felt a sense of freedom as well. At last the burden of the King's commission was lifting. At last the Princess Elizabeth would be safe. At last Anne could go to her husband with a lighter heart and no more secrets.

The old leaves of the autumn crunched beneath their feet. The sunlight was dappled beneath the trees and the air fresh with the scents of spring. Elizabeth was starting to lag a little now. It was a long distance for a child to walk.

'Not much further now, poppet,' Anne encouraged her. She pointed ahead. 'You see the old charcoal burner's hut? There are soldiers waiting to take you to your father…'

There was no sound as they approached the hut. Anne trod softly around the outside, holding the child's hand. The doorway was overhung with ivy and the inside was green darkness. In the canopy of the trees the birds were silent. She felt Elizabeth's hand tighten in hers. Anne could feel her fear. She felt it too. There was no one here and something was dreadfully wrong…

Then the child gave a gasp and caught her sleeve. 'Madam—'

Anne had seen it at the same moment, the tumble of rags in the corner that was almost unrecognisable but for the cognisance on the sleeve.

It was the King's messenger. Beside him, almost as though she were sleeping peacefully, lay Meg, Elizabeth's nurse.

They were both dead.

Elizabeth gave a cry and backed out of the doorway, her eyes huge and dark in her pale face. A shadow fell across the bars of sunlight in the clearing.

'Steady, my poppet.' Gerard Malvoisier's arms enfolded her. 'You are safe now. I am here to take you to your papa.'

Anne froze. Over Elizabeth's head Malvoisier's eyes met hers and they were gleaming with triumph.

Anne stared at him. Here at last was the fugitive general who had deserted Grafton on the night before battle, who had tried to torture Henry Greville and had killed five of Simon's men. Here was the man who had fired Grafton village, and inflicted barbaric suffering on her people, the man who wanted her dead... And now he held a princess of England against him like a shield. Now he knew he was going to win.

Fury and hatred swelled in her heart, matched only by a fear and hopelessness that she had kept Elizabeth safe all these months, only for this to happen. The truth hit Anne with shattering power. Simon had never been the danger. He would never harm a child. But Malvoisier would.

Simon. If only she had told him. If only she had trusted him. She sent out a desperate plea to him, through the dark. If he knew that she was out here, then she prayed he would be guided to her.

'Well met, Lady Greville,' Malvoisier said. 'I had hoped that you would bring the child yourself. I wanted to see you again—one last time.'

'You cannot take her.' Anne spoke through stiff lips. 'I will never let you.'

Malvoisier's smile grew. 'You have no choice.'

Anne was shaking. 'You are a traitor and a murderer.' She gestured towards the hut. 'That was you.'

Malvoisier shrugged. 'It was necessary.'

Elizabeth gave a pitiful cry and Anne tried to moderate her tone to avoid frightening the child further. Elizabeth's face was strained, her eyes going from one of them to the other. Anne knew she did not understand, but that she had realised there was something terribly wrong. She held herself stiff and proud within Malvoisier's grip, every inch the princess, but Anne could see her trembling.

'You are going to use the Princess for your own ends,' she said carefully. 'I know it.'

'Of course.' Malvoisier smiled. 'I have plans, but they are expensive. This—' he looked down at Elizabeth '—is my guarantee of freedom.'

'I have a pistol,' Anne said. 'You must let her go, Malvoisier.'

Malvoisier laughed. 'If you have a pistol, then I suggest you use it on yourself. You cannot prevent me from taking her. She is my hostage.'

The breeze stirred the treetops, but it was the only sound on the air. It seemed that even the birds were quiet.

'How did you know?' Anne said. She cleared her throat. She had no plan other than to keep him talking and to hope that she would be afforded some help, some chance.

'How did you know to find us here?' she repeated.

Malvoisier looked contemptuous. 'That fool Father Michael gave it all away,' he said. He paused. Anne could tell that he wanted to talk. She knew him. He had to boast of how clever he had been.

'I knew where they left the messages for the old man to

collect for you,' he said. 'I found one of the King's messengers and made him talk. It was easy. I read them all first, before the priest picked them up for you. I was ahead of the game. I knew when they were coming for her.'

'I see,' Anne said dully. 'So you knew about the treasure? You knew all along?'

Malvoisier glanced down at Elizabeth again. 'I had heard that a troop of the King's men had left treasure at Grafton just before I arrived,' he said, 'but, like everyone else, I thought it was money.' He laughed. 'I went to your father one day and tried to force him to tell me about it. He cursed me for a knave and a traitor.'

'He was right,' Anne said steadily. 'You were sworn to the King's allegiance, sworn to obey and serve.'

Malvoisier shrugged. 'I serve no man but myself.' His arms tightened about Elizabeth and the child winced. 'This is better than any fortune,' he said. 'His Majesty will surely pay a King's ransom for this one, and if he will not, General Cromwell will.'

Anne stared at him in disbelief and fury. 'You would sell her to the King's enemies?'

'If I must,' Malvoisier said. His eyes gleamed. 'Do you want to kill me for my perfidiousness, Lady Greville? You, who are married to a Parliamentarian now?'

'That is different,' Anne said hotly. 'I never sold my allegiance!'

'No, you betrayed your husband to keep your pledge to the King,' Malvoisier agreed. 'How does that feel, Lady Greville? To be married to the enemy—'

'My husband is a finer man than you will ever be, Malvoisier,' Anne said, 'King's enemy or not.' The tears stung her eyes. 'I only wish that I had realised it sooner.'

'Well,' Gerard Malvoisier said, 'it is time that we were on our way.'

He looked at Anne and smiled. 'I have one bullet left,' he said, 'and it gives me great pleasure that it is for you.'

There was a sound from the ranks of trees on the left, the unmistakable clink of harness. Malvoisier froze, his head come up like an animal scenting danger.

'Troops,' Anne gasped.

'They will be my men,' Malvoisier said, but for once the swagger had left his voice and his eyes darted about like a hunted deer.

Anne's hopes were spinning dizzily, out of control. She had no reason other than instinct to know it, but she was certain that somewhere above them in the thicket of trees, Simon was waiting. He could not attack, for Malvoisier still held the Princess. And suddenly Anne knew exactly what she had to do.

She held Malvoisier's gaze.

'Simon!' She called his name with all her strength, praying that if he were there he would trust her and come out of hiding.

There were so many uncertainties.

These could be Malvoisier's men, in which case she was done for. Yet Anne was convinced they were not. She clung to blind instinct. The future hung by a thread. Elizabeth's life and her life, and most of all her future with Simon...

She saw Malvoisier spin around. She knew that she had

surprised him. He would not have believed that she would call his bluff and risk Elizabeth's life, or draw Simon into danger.

For a moment there was no sound but the silence of waiting. Anne felt the despair rise in her.

Then everything happened at once, in a welter of noise.

Simon came crashing down into the clearing behind her, a troop of his men behind him. He was not in armour and Anne realised that, in that first, desperate second when he had found her gone, he had not waited to arm up in case that precious time might make all the difference between life and death. But it meant that he was fatally vulnerable.

Malvoisier raised his pistol to shoot. Anne ran towards him, dragged Elizabeth from his loosened grip and turned to thrust her into Simon's arms. For a crucial second she was shielding both the little Princess and her husband with her own body.

'Take her!' she said. 'I trust you to keep her safe!'

Malvoisier's shot rang out and for a moment she felt nothing; nothing but a huge relief, for she had seen Simon's face and she knew he would not fail her and that Elizabeth would be safe.

Malvoisier had no opportunity to reload his pistol now. She knew he had wanted to kill Simon; that if it was the last thing he did, which surely it would be, he had wanted to take Simon's life. But she had prevented him. She had saved her husband too.

Then the pain struck her and took her breath away, and her legs seemed to lose all their strength and she fell.

By the time she reached the ground she could feel nothing at all.

* * *

When she opened her eyes the room was dark and she could see nothing. She knew that something was dreadfully wrong and for a moment she felt as desolate and lonely as when she had woken after the fire and known that her father was dead.

'Papa?' Her lips barely moved.

Someone moved beside her and spoke. 'God be praised! She is awake!'

But when she turned her head she could see no more than shadows and the effort to move was so great that she closed her eyes and welcomed the sleep once more. And after that she did not wake again for a very long time.

The next time she stirred, there was a fire blazing warmly in the grate and Edwina was sitting beside her bed sewing. Anne lay for a long moment watching her. She felt light-headed, as though she was in a dream. The maid looked older. Her face was thinner and her grave expression was not one that Anne remembered. She moved and Edwina jumped, then the joy lit her tired blue eyes.

'Madam!'

'I…' Anne's lips felt parched and the words that formed on her tongue felt strangely unfamiliar. She cleared her throat.

'How are you, Edwina?'

'I am well, madam, and so happy…' The maid sniffed, wiping a few rogue tears away with the corner of her apron. 'So happy to hear you speak again, madam… We thought you would never awaken! Here, take this water…'

Anne struggled to sit up and swallow a few sips, but she felt as weak as a kitten and fell back against the pillows.

'I am hungry,' she said.

Edwina nodded. 'I will send at once to the kitchens for some broth—'

'Wait,' Anne said. She stayed her with a hand. She had noted the brilliant sunlight that peeped about the edge of the curtains and the bunch of flowers in the pot by the bed. They were not spring flowers—bluebells or wood anemone—and the light was surely the bright light of a summer's day.

'How long have I been asleep?' she asked slowly.

'Eight weeks, madam, give or take a few days.' Edwina's eyes were still brimming. 'It is July, my lady.'

'July,' Anne said wonderingly.

'Aye, my lady.'

'And Lord Greville—where is he?' Anne was weak, but not so tired that she did not see the flicker of something in Edwina's eyes. Had it been anxiety, she wondered, or grief? Sudden fear gripped her.

'He is not… Gerard Malvoisier did not *kill* him?'

'No, my lady.' Edwina looked shocked. 'It is General Malvoisier who is dead. But…' She spread her hands in a helpless gesture. 'Lord Greville had to go away, madam. He went to fight. There has been a great battle, madam, at Naseby in Northamptonshire. The King was defeated and has fled to Wales. His army is destroyed, madam. They say he can fight no more.'

Anne frowned as she tried to assimilate all that the maid was telling her. Her head felt thick and fuzzy. She remembered vaguely that Simon had received his orders the very day that she had received the instruction to take the Princess Elizabeth to meet the King's messenger. It seemed a very long time ago now.

'The Princess Elizabeth—' she began and was immeasurably relieved when Edwina nodded.

'Safe, madam. Lord Greville sent her back to the King at Oxford before all the trouble started.'

The relief swept over Anne in a huge wave. 'Oh, thank God,' she whispered. 'But my lord…is he safe too?'

Edwina's face was troubled. 'Aye, madam, he is safe.'

Anne clutched her hand tightly. 'There has been word?'

There was an odd silence. 'No, madam,' Edwina said, avoiding her eyes. She leaned over to smooth the sheet, avoiding Anne's gaze. 'There has been no word from Lord Greville, but his father the Earl wrote to tell us that he had survived and was in good heart. So has Sir Henry. He has been fighting in the West Country, but neither of them have been injured.'

A cold chill seemed to settle on the room, seeping into Anne's very bones.

'Yet my lord sent no word to me,' she repeated dully.

Edwina bit her lip. She looked as though she wanted to cry all over again. 'He was angry, madam, about the Princess…'

Anne nodded. 'I understand,' she said wearily. 'Oh, I understand all too well.'

'He sat by your bed every day for a week, madam,' Edwina said, in a rush. 'Every hour of every day whilst you were asleep. He did not eat and he did not speak. I do believe that he cares for you, but—'

'But he cannot forgive me for deceiving him,' Anne said. 'I never trusted him with the truth of the King's treasure and in the end my deceit almost killed us all.'

She rolled over and turned her face away, pressing her cheek to the cool smoothness of the pillow. Her eyes were hot with unshed tears.

'It was always going to be the danger that I ran,' she said softly. 'I never wanted Simon to be obliged to make the choice between his duty to the Parliament and his humanity. For if he had known that the treasure was the King's daughter, what could he have done but betray her to his masters? If he had not done so, if he had helped her escape, very like they would have denounced him—tried him for his treachery, even.' A solitary tear slid from the corner of her eye. 'So I thought to spare him that decision.'

Edwina touched her arm. 'You did the right thing, madam,' she said stolidly. 'You saved Lord Greville's life, aye, and the Princess too. One day he will understand that.'

'And in the end,' Anne said bitterly, 'he was forced to make that choice anyway and he chose to save the child, to help her escape.'

'Aye, madam.' Edwina's voice warmed. 'He is a good man.'

'I know,' Anne said. 'I have lost a good man through my lack of faith.'

Edwina went out and closed the door softly, to return a few moments later with a bowl of broth and a hunk of bread and cheese. But although the maid tempted her to eat and her body, awaking to fresh life, told her that it was hungry, Anne felt too sick and dispirited to manage more than a few mouthfuls.

* * *

Harington looked both familiar and subtly different to Simon as he rode in through the gates. The long, low, Elizabethan manor, with its black beams and white walls sat amid the summer fields, drowsing in the sun. It looked timeless and yet so much had passed since he had been within its walls. Here he had quarrelled with his father and marched away to war. Now he was returning older and immeasurably more world-weary than he had departed. He had seen things that a man might reasonably hope never to see in a lifetime and had done things that he might prefer to forget. He had experienced the heat of battle and the coldness of lost love. And now, he ruefully admitted to himself, he wanted his father's counsel.

Fulwar Greville limped out on to the gravel to greet him as he slid from his weary horse before the door. The house was already buzzing with excitement. Word had gone around that Simon was home and everyone wanted to witness the reunion between the Earl and his son. Fulwar had the devil's temper these days and his breach from his sons had made his testy nature even more unpredictable.

For a long moment father and son stared at one another, then Simon said, 'Sir?'

Fulwar glared at him from beneath his shaggy brows. 'You look sick, boy. What's to do?'

Simon laughed. 'It is good to see you too, sir. You are well?'

'Can't complain,' Fulwar grumbled. He looked at Simon for a long moment. 'I have my health and my sons are alive.' His face darkened. 'Was it bad, boy?'

'Hellish,' Simon said. His followed his father through the passageway and out into the sunlit gardens. There was a bench beneath the spreading bows of the old apple tree Simon remembered climbing in his youth. He felt a sudden pang of nostalgia for all that had changed.

'So,' Fulwar said, easing himself down on to the seat, 'why are you here? I would have expected you to have returned to Grafton long since. A man needs a home to go to after the sickness of war.'

He stopped as he saw Simon's expression change. 'Fairfax has ordered me to London,' Simon said. 'There is work to be done. I go immediately.' He hesitated. 'It seems unlikely that I shall see Grafton again in a long while.'

Fulwar looked disgusted. 'London? Are you mad? Pah!' He swung around on his son. 'Do not seek to fool me. This is not to do with your work. This is to do with your wife— and the King's treasure.'

Simon shrugged. He had carried his anger and his grief with him through long months of campaigning. He had thought many times of the secret that Anne had kept from him and of the terrible consequences she had unleashed, that day in Braden Forest. In the end she had entrusted the child to him, but only when it was almost too late. He burned with fury and indignation that she had not come to him before. What sort of woman believed that her husband would harm an innocent child? He could not accept her lack of faith.

And yet when he had seen Anne fall that day it had felt as though his life had stopped. He had sat beside her bedside every hour, a part of him wanting to shake her unconscious body in a fury that she had done this to him, to all of them, another part wanting to weep at the futility of the sacrifice. The Princess was safe, Malvoisier was dead, but the price had been too high.

When Fairfax had called him away to battle it had almost been a relief. He was running from Anne and yet he could not outrun her. Her image had been beside him through the noise and bloodshed of the battle, steadfast and courageous, willing him on. He had tried to ignore it, to block her out, but she came to him in dreams and he would awake heartsore and lonely. His anger settled into a cold place within and he kept it locked away. And when he received the letter from Grafton telling him that Anne had at last recovered consciousness, he had thrown it on the fire.

Now he looked up at his father with every appearance of indifference, although he could feel the anger stirring within him.

'My lady did not trust me with the life of a defenceless child,' he said. 'No man would wish to go home to such a wife.'

There was an ominous pause, rather like the heavy moments before the first strike of lightning. Simon could feel the air grow leaden as though a cloud had passed across the sun. The birds still sang, the trees moved in the gentle breeze and behind them in the house he could hear the clatter of saucepans and the servants' chatter as they prepared a repast fit for his return. But it was all muted for all he could concentrate upon was his father and he knew with a cast-iron certainty that their previous quarrel had been a mere rehearsal, nothing but a practice, for the argument that was to follow now. He found that he was holding his breath.

'God's life!' Fulwar roared, and the very air seemed to go still and then quiver with the resonance of his voice, 'are you a fool, boy? Can I have bred such an utter, unmitigated idiot? It seems well nigh impossible and yet it seems that I have!'

'I—' Simon started to say, but his father was stopping for no man.

'You are married to the most beautiful, loyal, courageous, admirable woman in the entire kingdom, and yet you have the wanton stupidity to throw it all away!' Fulwar's voice, which had moderated a little, now rose to the heights once again. A blackbird flew squawking an alarm call from the nearby oak. 'You want your wife's trust?' Fulwar smashed his fist down on the arm of the bench. 'What else did she do but trust you, there in the woods, when she gave the child into your keeping? Who else did she trust to see the Princess safely back to her father? Who else but you?'

Simon's face set hard. He was not a youth any more to be terrified by his father's blustering. And though a small voice within told him that Fulwar was making a sound point, his anger could not allow him to concede.

'She should have told me sooner,' he said. 'She should have told me that the Princess was hidden away at Grafton. She should never have tried to smuggle the child to safety behind my back.'

'Zounds,' Fulwar said in utter disgust, 'she was fulfilling a sacred trust, one laid upon her by her dying father!'

'Nevertheless, she deceived me.' Simon shut his lips hard.

He was not going to admit to his father that he had hoped Anne had come to love him as he loved her, enough to trust him with the heaviest burden, the greatest secret, the hardest decision. He had hoped for that and his disillusion had torn his soul.

'Your head is full of nonsense,' Fulwar said shortly. He turned abruptly on his son. 'Answer me this, then, and answer it honestly. If Anne had come to you at Grafton, before or after you wed, and told you that she had the Princess Elizabeth in hiding, what then? Would you have sent the child back to the King? Would you?'

Simon paused on the very edge of speech. He wanted to claim hotly that of course he would have done the principled thing and sent Elizabeth to Oxford. He wanted to protest that he, at least, had the honour to do what was right, not what was politically expedient. Yet something, some sliver of doubt, held him back. For the first time he thought about it without the cloudy emotion that Anne's betrayal always roused in him. If she had come to him, not in the heat of danger but in the cold light of day, and told him that within the castle was the King's greatest treasure, a prize far more valuable than mere money, would he have handed the child back? Or would he have decided that this was a matter for his political masters, and sent the Princess to London for Cromwell to decide?

The doubt settled in his mind. He could not be sure. He knew without hesitation that he would never have sought to make personal capital from the child, but it was another matter entirely to go against the express orders of his generals. They would have wanted the Princess in their possession as a bargaining tool to use against her father. There could be no doubt about it. Both Cromwell and Fairfax had been furious with him when they learned that Simon had sent the child back to Oxford of his own accord.

Fulwar was watching him. 'Well?' he said.

'I would have sent her back to the King,' Simon said at last.

'I think you would too,' Fulwar admitted gruffly. 'But you see how difficult it is to be certain. Anne did not have the luxury of taking that risk. She could not afford to do so with a child's life and future at stake. So she made sure that you were spared that decision.'

There was a silence.

'At the very least,' Fulwar said, 'give her the credit for making the most difficult choice of her life. Whether it was right or wrong, she had the courage to take it.'

Still Simon did not reply. He could feel the cold, knotted anger starting to unravel within him and for a moment he was desperately afraid; afraid that once he started to let it go it would hurt more than the deepest wound. But he knew Fulwar would not allow him to retreat cravenly now. He knew he was done for.

Fulwar cleared his throat. 'How do you think Lady Anne would have felt if she had given you that decision to make, and you had decided to send the Princess to Fairfax in London?' he asked.

Simon fixed his gaze on the neat clipped edges of the box parterre. 'I imagine she would never have forgiven me,' he said.

'You are wrong,' Fulwar said. 'She would have forgiven

you because she loves you. But you would have broken her heart.' He brought his hand down with a resounding crash on the chair again and the wood groaned. 'Now I wish to hear no more puling nonsense from you, boy! You have a wife with more courage in her little finger than your entire battalion of men have in their whole bodies. She loves you and she saved your life. And you sit here complaining to me that she does not trust you!' He gave a snort of derision. 'Get you gone to Grafton. And when you are reconciled with your wife, bring her here to me so that I may congratulate her on her bravery and thank her for saving both my sons.' He ran a hand through his thick grey hair. 'A fine state I should be in without her!'

He glared at Simon beneath lowering brows. 'Does she even know that you are here?'

'I sent a despatch,' Simon said.

'A despatch!' Fulwar roared. 'God's bones, boy, you try my patience! Get you home!'

'Very well, sir,' Simon said. He levered himself stiffly to his feet, for the bruises he had sustained at Naseby still troubled him a little. 'I will talk to her.'

'Talk!' Fulwar looked disgusted. 'I wish for an heir for Grafton and Harington and you speak of *talking* to her?'

Simon started to laugh. 'It would be a start, sir.'

For a long moment they stared at one another and all the bitter words and the recriminations and the hostility faded away and the weight of estrangement lifted from Simon's shoulders. He thought in that instant that his father was actually going to embrace him, but then Fulwar cleared his

throat, blinked away some suspicious moisture from his
eyes and said gruffly,

'You will stay with me for dinner. A man cannot travel
on an empty stomach.'

He clapped Simon on the shoulder and Simon knew that
was the closest to approval that he was ever going to get from
his father and he knew that it was enough.

It had been a hot day, but now the shadows were lengthening and the air was cooling and a tiny sliver of new moon
was climbing into the sky above Grafton. Anne had been
sitting in the gardens for most of the day. The warmth of the
sun and the summer brightness of the air made her feel physically well. She had been recovering her strength for days
now, for she was young and healthy and was eating like a
horse. But inside, her spirit was not so resilient. She knew
she would recover; knew that one day she would even be
able to bear Simon's loss because there was no other way,
but she felt beaten and tired and weak.

Now that Gerard Malvoisier was dead and his men
captured, peace had returned to the lands about Grafton.
Under Will Jackson's fast-maturing leadership, the castle
had been peaceful and the villagers were rebuilding their
homes. Muna was preparing for her marriage to Henry
Greville, which was to take place in September at Harington. They had been reconciled during Anne's convalescence,
but she was secretly glad that Henry's duties under
Cromwell kept him from Muna's side at present, for she
knew she could not bear to speak to him of Simon. Living

with her husband's continued absence was like trying to walk on a broken ankle. She hobbled at every step and yet she gritted her teeth and endured the pain.

Anne drew her shawl about her as the shadows edged across the pergola where she was sitting. She could hear the sounds of someone approaching across the gravel of the parterre—Edwina, perhaps, to call her in for supper. Her former nurse had become ridiculously protective ever since Anne had first risen from her sickbed.

The footsteps stopped and Anne looked up, her heart leaping with a mixture of astonishment, fear and exhilaration. Her book of poetry fell unheeded from her lap. She stood up.

'Simon!'

Her headlong rush across the grass took her to within a few feet of him, but then she stopped. He was not smiling. His expression was hard, almost grim. He was dirty and travel stained and he was limping a little. There was a sword cut healing on his cheek.

Anne's heart froze. In her joy at seeing him she had not been wary of showing her feelings, but now she realised there was no answering joy in him. And why should there be? The last time they had spoken had been in Malvoisier's presence, when she had acknowledged the full extent of her betrayal of him. She had had no chance to explain or to beg for understanding, if not forgiveness. Her illness had deprived her of the chance to justify herself to him and then he had been called away to battle, and no doubt time, distance and bloodshed had hardened his heart against her. Her hands, which had been outstretched towards him, fell to her side.

'You are well, madam?'

He was so formal, so cold. The sun was in his dark eyes but there was no warmth in them for her. It was impossible to think of him as the man who had held her in his arms and loved her so tenderly. A lump formed in Anne's throat and she swallowed hard. This, then was how it would end. Not in recrimination but in coldness. They would stay locked in a loveless marriage, becoming ever more distant. God forbid that they would end up hating one another.

'I am much recovered, I thank you, my lord.' Anne's voice quivered slightly. 'And you? I heard you were injured.' She found she was reaching up to touch his face and once again allowed her hand to fall.

He was shaking his head dismissively. 'Merely a scratch. I am sorry if the reports exaggerated it and caused you distress.'

She had been more than distressed.

I have died a thousand deaths thinking you lost to me…

They looked at one another. Suddenly there seemed so little to say and the distance between them was growing all the time.

'Excuse me,' Simon said politely. 'I have ridden hard and would wash the dust of the journey from me.'

He turned away. Anne hesitated. A moment and it would all be lost. A moment and it would be too late…

'Simon, wait!'

He stopped and half-turned towards her, but he did not come back. The chasm between them yawned wider. Anne knew she was the one who would have to try to bridge it. She was the one who had betrayed his trust, after all.

'I need to speak with you,' she said, in a rush. 'Please, Simon…'

Simon ran a hand through his hair. 'Can this not wait, Anne? I have travelled a long way and I am very weary—'

'No,' Anne said. 'It cannot wait.' At least he had called her by her name. At least there was a chance…

'Please hear me out,' she said, 'and then, if you wish, you may walk away from me and never turn back.'

Simon folded his arms. His expression was polite, but no more.

Anne felt wretchedly afraid. She cleared her throat painfully. Her voice felt as strange as when she had first spoken after all those weeks of sickness.

'The Princess Elizabeth…' she said. 'I hear that you sent her to the King.'

'I did.'

A tear slid from the corner of Anne's eyes. She scrubbed it away. She despised the feebleness that made her want to cry.

'Thank you,' she whispered. 'I hope that it did not cause you too much trouble with your commanders?'

Simon looked grimly amused. 'I will survive.'

Still he did not make any move towards her and as Anne struggled to find the right words she could see that he was on the brink of leaving. She knew then that she had to drop all pride and pretence and simply to tell him the truth.

'Simon,' she said, 'I want you to know that the reason that I refused your proposal of marriage from the first was because I knew that one day I would have to betray you.' She stopped. She had his full attention now. He was looking at her with such intensity that she could hardly bear it.

'I knew that when the King asked me to fulfil the duty I owed him, the trust I took on from my father, then I would have to deceive you.' She put out a hand to him and then let it fall as she saw the stoniness of his expression. 'And I thought I could not have borne that had I been your wife.'

'I know.' Simon's voice was very quiet. 'I knew that all along. But it did not help when the moment came for you to betray me.' He sighed. 'You did marry me and then you deliberately kept the secret of the King's daughter from me.'

Anne could hear the grief in his voice now. She opened her mouth to try to explain, but Simon did not give her the chance.

'What I do not understand is why you did not trust me with the truth, Anne,' he said. 'What did you believe?' His voice warmed into anger now. 'That I would imprison an innocent child? That I would use her as Malvoisier tried to use her, to extract a ransom from the King? What sort of monster did you take me for that you kept her presence here secret from me?'

The tears prickled Anne's throat harder now. She had only one chance and she felt unequal to the task. 'I am sorry,' she said. 'When I first knew you, it is true I did not trust you. We were on opposing sides. You were my enemy. How could I tell you the truth?'

'But later—when we married—I thought that you came to believe in me. You said that you respected me.' There was anger and anguish in Simon's voice now. 'I thought, fool that I was, that you had begun to love me.'

'I did.' I *do*. Anne thought of the nights when he had held her so close in his arms and she had felt safe and at peace.

'I did not tell you because I did not want you ever to have to make the choice, my lord.' She rubbed her brow. The sun was making her eyes sting. 'I never believed that you would imprison the Princess.' Her voice rang with anguish. 'I never thought that you would use her to extract a ransom. You are too fine a man for that.' She pressed her hands together. 'But what I could not put from my mind was the thought that you might feel obliged to tell your commanders. I thought that you might hand her to the authorities in London. And that would have changed the course of the whole war. The King would have made peace on any terms and the child would have been a pawn in the politics of men—' She broke off. She could tell that this was doing no good. Simon looked unyielding.

'It comes down to a matter of trust,' he said. 'We were divided by our loyalties. We always have been. And so you only trusted me when it came to a straight choice between Malvoisier and me.' His voice was hard. 'I suppose that I should be grateful for that small mercy.'

Something broke within Anne. She closed her eyes slowly and opened them again. 'There is no need for you to make it appear worse than it already is,' she snapped. 'I may have been slow to trust, but I called to you when I needed your help, Simon Greville. I did not hesitate. At that moment, when I had to make my choice, I called for you and you did not fail me.' She glowered at him. 'You may count that bond between us as nothing if you will, but I shall always remember and be grateful. And I shall remember how you sat beside my bed night after night, so Edwina says, refusing to leave me. So there must be *something* between us, even if it is too late to repair.'

She ran out of breath at last and stood glaring at him whilst he looked steadily back at her. Then, when she was about to burst with frustration over his silence, she saw the glimmer of something in his eyes and caught a painful breath. It had looked like amusement. For a moment it had looked like the Simon she remembered.

'My father says that I am married to the most beautiful, loyal, courageous, admirable woman in the entire kingdom,' he said, 'and yet it seems to me that you are a termagant, madam.'

He came up to her and took her hand in his. Anne started to tremble.

'I fight for what I believe in,' she whispered.

'And you believe in us?' Simon's fingers closed more tightly over hers.

'I do.' Anne took a deep breath. 'But do you?'

Simon was silent for a moment. 'I do believe that we can never be free of one another, Anne. I saved your life. It is forfeit to me.'

Anne shook at his use of the same words he had whispered to her so tenderly in their marriage bed.

'If it comes to that, I saved yours,' she said. She looked him in the eye. 'I took Malvoisier's bullet for you.'

'So you did.' A smile flickered about Simon's mouth. Anne trembled all the more.

'So we are equal,' she whispered.

'Forfeit one to the other.' Now Simon was definitely smiling.

He swooped on her so quickly that she had no time to prepare or protest. His kiss was fierce: passion, forgiveness and benediction all in one. They were both gasping for breath when finally he released her.

'I will never let you go,' he said against her lips.

Anne clung to him, her heart racing. 'Do not,' she whispered. 'I could not bear it.' She rested her cheek against his. 'I am sorry.'

'I understood.' Simon's voice was tender now. 'Even though I was so furious I did understand.'

'I will always support the King's cause,' Anne said. 'It is only fair that I should tell you that now, Simon. No matter what happens, I cannot go against my anointed monarch. But your father was right when he said that alliance and not opposition was the way to forge a future. I want that future to be with you.'

Simon took her hand and drew her down onto the seat beside him. 'The King is in retreat now,' he said. 'I hope that he may come to terms. It is my honest wish that there should be no more bloodshed.'

'There are those who seek his very life,' Anne said.

Simon's arm tightened about her. 'I am not one of those, sweet. I sought only to defend the rights of my fellow men against tyranny. Now I want for nothing more than a settled home and some peace.' He slanted a smile down at her. 'Oh, and an heir for Grafton and Harington. My father commands it.'

Anne snuggled closer. 'Do you think that we may make this marriage of ours work, then, Simon Greville?'

'I think we may—' Simon kissed her hair '—as long as we promise to trust one another.'

'I do trust you,' Anne said. 'I love you.'

Simon kissed her again, gently this time. 'And I love you, Anne Greville. My love for you was what gave you the power to hurt me so deeply.'

Anne pressed her fingers to his lips. 'Do not. I will never forgive myself.'

'You must.' Simon kissed her palm. 'We both have much to forgive ourselves and each other.'

Anne clung closer.

'When I heard about the battle I was so afraid.' Her voice broke. 'I thought that I would never have the chance to see you again and to tell you that I loved you.'

Simon kissed her hair. 'And deep down I knew that I had to survive so that I could come home. I had to give us the chance to love one another.'

'Home,' Anne said. She raised her head from his shoulder and looked at the grey walls of Grafton that encircled them. 'Is this home for you, then, Simon?'

'It is now,' her husband said.

Anne jumped up, grabbed his hand and pulled him to his feet. 'Then you had better come with me.'

She hustled him through the gateway of the walled garden and pulled him towards the house.

'Where are we going?' Simon enquired.

Anne gave him a radiant smile. 'To make an heir for Grafton and Harington. To build an alliance. To make a home.'

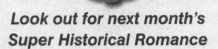

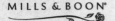

MILLS & BOON®

The *Regency*

LORDS & LADIES
COLLECTION

*Two glittering Regency
love affairs in every book*

6th January 2006	Rosalyn & the Scoundrel *by Anne Herries &* Lady Knightley's Secret *by Anne Ashley*
3rd February 2006	The Veiled Bride *by Elizabeth Bailey &* Lady Jane's Physician *by Anne Ashley*
3rd March 2006	Perdita *by Sylvia Andrew &* Raven's Honour *by Claire Thornton*
7th April 2006	Miranda's Masquerade *by Meg Alexander &* Gifford's Lady *by Claire Thornton*
5th May 2006	Mistress of Madderlea *by Mary Nichols &* The Wolfe's Mate *by Paula Marshall*
2nd June 2006	An Honourable Thief *by Anne Gracie &* Miss Jesmond's Heir *by Paula Marshall*

*Available at WH Smith, Tesco, ASDA, Borders, Eason,
Sainsbury's and all good paperback bookshops*
www.millsandboon.co.uk

REG/L&L/LIST 2

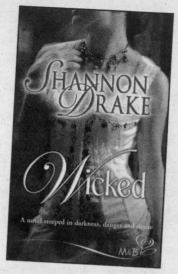

2 FREE

BOOKS AND A SURPRISE GIFT!

We would like to take this opportunity to thank you for reading this Mills & Boon® book by offering you the chance to take TWO more specially selected titles from the Historical Romance™ series absolutely FREE! We're also making this offer to introduce you to the benefits of the Reader Service™—

- ★ **FREE home delivery**
- ★ **FREE gifts and competitions**
- ★ **FREE monthly Newsletter**
- ★ **Exclusive Reader Service offers**
- ★ **Books available before they're in the shops**

Accepting these FREE books and gift places you under no obligation to buy. you may cancel at any time, even after receiving your free shipment. Simply complete your details below and return the entire page to the address below. You don't even need a stamp!

YES! Please send me 2 free Historical Romance books and a surprise gift. I understand that unless you hear from me, I will receive 4 superb new titles every month for just £3.69 each, postage and packing free. I am under no obligation to purchase any books and may cancel my subscription at any time. The free books and gift will be mine to keep in any case.

H6ZED

Ms/Mrs/Miss/Mr ....Initials ....
BLOCK CAPITALS PLEASE

Surname ....

Address ....

....

....Postcode...........................

Send this whole page to:
UK: FREEPOST CN81, Croydon, CR9 3WZ